*"I remember you," she said
a little desperately, because
suddenly it was very important
to her to remember* something.

Images of the rescue flooded her mind. Snow.
Cold. Blinding pain. A vague sense of terror
she couldn't shake even now, as she lay safe
and alive in this unfamiliar bed. But she clearly
remembered this man with the incredible blue
eyes and devil's grin. He'd swooped down out
of the sky and plucked her from the rocks and
snow. As she took in his steady expression and
canny gaze, she remembered vividly how safe
she'd felt in his arms, the solid feel of his body
against hers, the softness of his voice, the
whisper of his breath against her cheek when
he'd murmured gentle words and eased her
terror.

"You saved my life," she said. "Thank you."

* * *

Dear Reader,

There's so much great reading in store for you this month that it's hard to know where to begin, but I'll start with bestselling author and reader favorite Fiona Brand. She's back with another of her irresistible Alpha heroes in *Marrying McCabe*. There's something about those Aussie men that a reader just can't resist—and heroine Roma Lombard is in the same boat when she meets Ben McCabe. He's got trouble—and passion—written all over him.

Our FIRSTBORN SONS continuity continues with *Born To Protect,* by Virginia Kantra. Follow ex-Navy SEAL Jack Dalton to Montana, where his princess (and I mean that literally) awaits. A new book by Ingrid Weaver is always a treat, so save some reading time for *Fugitive Hearts,* a perfect mix of suspense and romance. Round out the month with new novels by Linda Castillo, who offers *A Hero To Hold* (and trust me, you'll definitely want to hold this guy!); Barbara Ankrum, who proves the truth of her title, *This Perfect Stranger;* and Vickie Taylor, with *The Renegade Steals a Lady* (and also, I promise, your heart).

And if that weren't enough excitement for one month, don't forget to enter our Silhouette Makes You a Star contest. Details are in every book.

Enjoy!

Leslie J. Wainger
Executive Senior Editor

Please address questions and book requests to:
Silhouette Reader Service
U.S.: 3010 Walden Ave., P.O. Box 1325, Buffalo, NY 14269
Canadian: P.O. Box 609, Fort Erie, Ont. L2A 5X3

A Hero
To Hold
LINDA
CASTILLO

Silhouette®

INTIMATE MOMENTS™

Published by Silhouette Books

America's Publisher of Contemporary Romance

For Ernest, my hero

 SILHOUETTE BOOKS

ISBN 0-373-27172-7

A HERO TO HOLD

Copyright © 2001 by Linda Castillo

This edition published by arrangement with Harlequin Books S.A.

® and TM are trademarks of Harlequin Books S.A., used under license. Trademarks indicated with ® are registered in the United States Patent and Trademark Office, the Canadian Trade Marks Office and in other countries.

Visit Silhouette at www.eHarlequin.com

Printed in U.S.A.

Books by Linda Castillo

Silhouette Intimate Moments

Remember the Night #1008
Cops and...Lovers? #1085
A Hero To Hold #1102

LINDA CASTILLO

grew up in a small farming community in western Ohio. She knew from a very early age that she wanted to be a writer—and penned her first novel at the age of thirteen during one of those long Ohio winters. Her dream of becoming a published author came true the day Silhouette called and wanted to buy one of her books!

Romance is at the heart of all her stories. She loves the idea of two fallible people falling in love amid danger and against their better judgment—or so they think. She enjoys watching them struggle through their problems, realize their weaknesses and strengths along the way and, ultimately, fall head over heels in love.

She is the winner of numerous writing awards, including the prestigious Maggie Award for Excellence. In 1999, she was a triple Romance Writers of America Golden Heart finalist, and her first Silhouette release, *Remember the Night,* took first place in the romantic suspense division.

Linda spins her tales of love and intrigue from her home in Dallas, Texas, where she lives with her husband and three lovable dogs. You can contact her at P.O. Box 670501, Dallas, Texas 75367-0501.

SILHOUETTE MAKES YOU A STAR!
Feel like a star with Silhouette.
Look for the exciting details of our new contest
inside all of these fabulous Silhouette novels:

Prologue

He was going to kill her this time.

The realization stunned her. Terror and disbelief and an odd sense of incredulity tangled in her chest. She couldn't believe it had come to this, couldn't bear to think everything she'd been through in the last two years had culminated in this single, horrifying moment.

The icy wind buffeted her as she sprinted through the darkness. Rocks and frozen earth cut her bare feet, but she hardly felt the pain. Swirling snow blinded her, but she didn't slow down. Clutching the pistol, she picked up speed and ran blindly, barely negotiating the curve in the road through the darkness and driving snow. Her breaths puffed out in white clouds of vapor as she gave herself over to the flight instinct and pushed her body to the limit.

Headlights sliced through the darkness behind her, the sight bringing a fresh rise of terror. She heard the whine of the engine over the howl of the wind, over the wild beat of her own heart. A scream hovered in her throat, but she knew better than to waste precious energy on something that hopeless. No one would hear her up here in the middle of the night. No one would rescue her. If she was going to get out of this alive, she was going to have to rely on herself.

Too bad she just happened to be fresh out of ideas.

Another turn in the road and the headlights were upon her. A dozen feet away. Too close for escape. Fear and adrenaline twisted inside her as she stumbled to a halt at the side of the road. Cold air burned her lungs as she gasped for breath. Behind her, the vehicle's engine dropped to idle. Vertigo gripped her when she looked down at the jagged rocks of the ravine before her. Heart drumming, she turned and faced her pursuer.

She thought she'd been prepared for this final confrontation, but the sight of him terrified her anew—and made her question whether she had the guts to call his bluff one last time.

She raised the gun, trying in vain to still the quiver in her arms. "Don't come any closer."

"Put the gun down, angel."

"Stay away from me!"

"I can't," he said, starting toward her. "You've left me no choice."

Struggling to remain calm, she stared at his dark form silhouetted against the glare of the headlights, realizing for the first time that if she died tonight no one would ever know the truth.

"Stop!" Her finger curled around the trigger. "I'll do it!"

"You don't have the guts." Never taking his eyes from her, he treaded steadily closer.

She squeezed the trigger. The gun exploded, kicking hard in her hand. The sound of her own scream deafened her.

But he didn't stop. He didn't even flinch. She'd missed,

she realized, just as he'd known she would. He knew her too well, knew she wasn't a killer.

Just as she knew he was.

Heart raging, she gathered the broken pieces of her resolve and turned toward the ravine. There was only one way to save herself, and as surely as she heard him moving ever closer, she knew she didn't have a choice but to do the unthinkable. Pressing her hand to her abdomen, she whispered a prayer and started down the steep incline.

His shout rose over the roar of the wind, but she couldn't make out the words, and she didn't stop. She'd only descended a few feet when the loose rock beneath her crumbled. Reaching out, she tried to break her fall, but there was nothing there except cold air and ice-slicked granite. An instant later the ground rushed up and punched her like a giant fist. She began to tumble, pain stunning her as rock and broken saplings battered her body.

The inevitability of death shouldn't have shocked her; she'd known she wouldn't get out of this mess unscathed. Still, her mind rebelled against the idea of her life ending this way. With so much left undone, so many dreams unfulfilled.

Fragments of her life, the places she'd been and the people she loved flashed in her mind's eye in brilliant hues. But the mountain was relentless, and the steep incline sucked her down, tumbling her like a seashell battered by a frozen, turbulent sea. One by one, her senses shut down until she knew only darkness and the bitter taste of betrayal. As she plummeted deeper into the abyss, the pain slowly relinquished its grip. The darkness embraced her with murky arms and the promise of warmth and truth.

And, at last, she was free.

Chapter 1

"**I**'ve got a visual. Female subject. Two o'clock. She's up and moving."

Search-and-rescue medic John Maitland jerked the strap of his helmet tightly against his chin, stepped over to the chopper's open door and looked down. Sure enough, a woman huddled against an outcropping of rock on the side of the mountain seventy-five feet below.

"What the hell is she doing up here?" he muttered, mostly to himself.

"Waiting for you to harness up and move your butt!" came the pilot's voice from the cockpit.

"Just get me closer, Flyboy," John shouted over the roar of the Bell 412's twin Pratt and Whitney engines and the rush of wind through the door. "Sometime this week, if you don't mind."

"Not in this wind. We're already at forty knots. Gusts to fifty-five." The pilot, Tony "Flyboy" Colorosa, shot him a cocky look. "Don't tell me you can't do an extraction from a measly seventy-five feet up in a little breeze."

John met the other man's expression in kind. "You just fly this sardine can—I'll take care of the tough stuff," he said. Then he added under his breath, "The wind might make it a little more interesting."

"Subject is standing. No visual trauma." Team leader Buzz Malone lowered his binoculars and scowled at John. "Skip the litter," he said, referring to the portable stretcher. "We're going to swoop and scoop. Harness her, and I'll winch her up with you."

"What about spinal movement?" John asked.

"If we don't get her up in the next five minutes, we're going to abort. It will take us too long to reach her on foot. She'll die of hypothermia. Take your pick."

As much as he hated the idea of manipulating a possible trauma patient without the benefit of spinal support, John knew with heavy weather moving in, the situation had boiled down to a quick extraction—and saving her life. There was only so much they could do during an airlift. They'd deal with possible injuries later. "Roger that," he said.

He started toward the door, but Buzz stopped him with a hand on his shoulder. "If it were anyone but you going down there, I'd abort this mission in a New York minute."

"Good thing we're not in New York." Reaching the launch point at the door, John turned to face the other man, his hands moving expertly over his harness as he prepared to drop. "I've never missed an extraction, Buzz. I don't plan to start now."

"Watch those trees." The team leader gave him a thumbs-up. "You get one attempt, then I'm bringing you in."

Giving him a mock salute, John shoved off into space. Cold air slapped him like icy palms. The rat-tat-tat of the chopper's rotor blades deafened him, but both were discomforts he'd come to love despite the dangers of jumping out of a helicopter with nothing more than a cable and his own skill separating him from certain death.

He wasn't worried about missing contact on the first go-round. In the six years he'd been a search-and-rescue medic, he'd never missed an extraction. Besides, high winds or not, there wasn't a man alive who could fly the Bell 412 better than Flyboy. As for aborting the mission, John simply knew better. Buzz Malone might be tough-talking when it came to keeping his crew safe, but John had worked with the older man long enough to know there was no way in hell the team would abort the mission and let that woman die.

Twenty feet down from the chopper, the wind began to twirl him like a yo-yo. Accustomed to the action, John rode with it, maintaining his equilibrium by keeping his eyes on the huddled form below. He wondered how she'd gotten there. Even from a distance of some fifty feet, he could tell from her lack of attire and equipment that she wasn't a hiker who'd lost her way in the storm. She wasn't even wearing a coat, for God's sake. What on earth was a woman clad in little more than street clothes doing at nine thousand feet in the middle of January?

A cross-country skier had reported her stranded on the side of the steep ravine just an hour earlier. The call out to Rocky Mountain Search and Rescue had come in from the Lake County Sheriff's Department twenty minutes ago. The team had been ready to go in less than four minutes.

John didn't know how long she'd been there and had to assume she was hypothermic. If she'd fallen, God only knew what other injuries she'd sustained. For now, the most serious threat was the weather, so he had no choice but to lift her out, then assess her injuries once they got her onboard the chopper.

He scanned the area with a practiced eye. There was no evidence of a vehicle, so he wasn't dealing with motor-vehicle trauma. There was no sign of a wrecked snow-mobile, either. No tent in sight. No sign of other people.

Something bothered him about the entire scenario.

The mystery moved to the back of his mind when the cable jerked with a sudden gust of wind, whipping him perilously close to an outcropping of rock. "You want to keep it steady, Flyboy?" John said into his helmet mike. "If it's not too much trouble, that is."

"Just want to make sure you're awake," came the pilot's voice.

Smiling, enjoying the adrenaline rush that came with the added danger of high winds, John concentrated on the swiftly approaching ground and prepared to touch down. The terrain consisted mostly of jagged rock and ice. Twenty feet away, a stand of spindly pines shivered in the wind from the chopper's blades.

John's feet hit the ground hard, but he was prepared and bent his knees to absorb the impact. In an instant, he jerked the patient's harness from his flight suit and started toward the subject, praying Flyboy could keep the chopper steady enough to prevent him from getting jerked off his feet and slammed into a rock or dragged through tree branches. He could do without a broken arm—or God forbid—a broken neck.

He made eye contact with the woman as he approached her. Dark, frightened eyes, glazed with the effects of hypothermia and wide with terror, met his as she stumbled toward him. Full, colorless lips moved to speak, but she didn't make a sound. He saw the will to live in its rawest form in the depths of her eyes, and an acute sense of urgency overwhelmed him. Hell or high water, he was going to get her out of this.

But it was the beauty of the face staring back at him that nearly stopped him in his tracks. Dark, pretty eyes and a delicate cut of jaw dominated her features. A slash of high cheekbones beneath pale flesh tinged pink from the

cold. Wavy hair the color of an alpine sunset and wild as
a mountain gale tangled over slender shoulders. Even as
dirty and bruised as she was, he could plainly see her body
was lush in all the right places. If it hadn't been for his
medical training and the fact that the chopper was hovering
seventy-five feet overhead in forty-knot winds, he would
have taken a moment just to appreciate the view.

John was accustomed to all sorts of rescues, from the
severe trauma of a mountain motor-vehicle accident, to the
tourist who'd called out the team for nothing more than a
bee sting, to the Boy Scout who'd lost his way during a
hike last summer. But the sight of this particular subject
hit him like the business end of a shovel and went deep.

"Hey, gorgeous." He started toward her, offering up
his best relax-everything's-going-to-be-all-right grin. "I'm
a medic. My name's John. My team and I are going to
airlift you out of here and transport you to the hospital.
Do you understand?"

Her eyes were glassy, her flesh as pale as the snow being
kicked up by the rotor blades. But she was alive. He figured they both had cause to be thankful for that. John had
lost patients before, but he damn well didn't like it. One
thing he'd learned about himself over the years was that he
was a consummate sore loser when it came to the Grim
Reaper coming out ahead. It was the one aspect of his job
he took personally.

He reached her just in time to keep her from sinking to
the frozen earth. Even through his thick gloves, he could
feel her shivering. "Easy," he said. "I've got you. You're
safe."

"Please…no." Surprising him, she twisted in his arms.
"Get…away…from me…bastard."

"Easy—"

The gun came out of nowhere. A big, ugly beast capable
of killing him with a single shot and aimed right at this

face. Releasing her, John lurched back, swearing richly. "What the *hell* do you think you're doing?"

"I'll kill you," she choked. "I swear. I won't let you get away with this."

"Whoa! I'm cool." He raised his hands above his head, aware of the sharp stab of fear in his chest. "Look, my hands are up, Red. Now put the damn gun down before someone gets hurt."

He knew hypothermia could cause mental confusion. One of his Coast Guard buddies had told him about a water extraction off the Alaskan Coast during which the subject had fought so hard, they hadn't been able to get him in the cage. The subject had ended up drowning.

What in God's name was she doing with a gun?

John knew he could handle her if it came down to a physical confrontation. She was small and fatigued and severely hypothermic. All he had to do was get the gun away from her. Considering she could barely hold the damn thing upright told him that wasn't going to be too difficult. But he wasn't a big enough fool not to take the situation seriously.

"Easy, Red. You're hurt and confused. Put the gun down, and let me help you."

She swayed. "Stay away. Just…stay—"

He rushed her. She yelped and swung at him, but was so weakened, John easily dodged the blow. He grabbed for the gun, but before he could get his fingers around it, she lost her grip. He watched it tumble down the ravine and disappear into a stand of juniper twenty feet below.

"What the *hell* were you doing with a gun?" he snapped, giving her a small shake.

She blinked at him as if seeing him for the first time. "I thought—I thought…Richard…"

His concentration wavered as a wave of damp, cinnamon-colored hair washed over his arm. Simultaneously the sweet scent of columbine in spring titillated his senses.

Turning her toward him, he got his first up-close look at her face. Her alabaster skin was as flawless as virgin snow-fall. He winced at the purple bruise above her left temple and the cut on her chin. Even her nose was skinned. But the underlying beauty struck him, and John felt the impact of her all the way through his flight suit and into his bones.

He stared at her, realizing with a stark sense of dismay that she had the most incredible brown eyes he'd ever seen. "What's your name?" he shouted above the roar of wind and engines, watching her carefully to gauge her lucidity.

"I…" Her brows furrowed, then she blinked at him. "I—I'm…"

She was pale and confused; both were symptoms of hypothermia. The condition was assumed in all cold-weather situations. Judging from her state of mind, he suspected she'd been hypothermic for quite some time. Snow-damp jeans and a sweater were no protection against subfreezing temperatures and windchills hovering around zero. Her hair was damp. He looked down at her feet and cursed. She wasn't even wearing shoes. Frostbite would be an issue, as well, he realized, and another wave of urgency surged through him.

"Is anyone with you?" he asked.

Her body jolted, and he saw fresh terror leap into her eyes. "I…I don't know."

"Come on, sweetheart, stay with me." Holding her face between his hands, he made eye contact. "Are you alone?" he pressed. "I need to know if there's anyone else down here. I'll need to get them in the chopper."

"I'm…not sure." She looked over her shoulder uneasily. "I think I'm alone."

"Good girl." Using his left arm to steady her, he quickly secured the patient's harness around her, trying not to notice the way that sweater clung to curves he had no business noticing at a moment like this. "How did you get here?"

"He was...chasing me." Her gaze snapped to his, her eyes widened with what might have been recognition. "Oh, no. Oh, *God!* Richard, please, don't—"

"Calm down," he said firmly. "Just stay calm—"

"I won't let you—"

"Stop it!" An alarm trilled in John's head, and he gave her a little shake. The last thing he needed was for her to go ballistic on him while they dangled seventy-five feet over terrain not fit for a mountain goat. "Look at me."

When her gaze met his, he saw vividly the terror in her eyes and felt the hairs at his nape stand on end. Something—or someone—had this woman spooked in a major way. "My name is John. I'm not going to hurt you. No one's going to hurt you. You're safe. Do you understand?"

Her lids fluttered, her eyes rolling back. Simultaneously her knees buckled. John caught her an instant before she fell.

"Terrific," he muttered. Easing her to arm's length, he drew her harness tight and clipped it to his, so that her limp body was flush against him. "We're going up, sweetheart. Just relax and enjoy the ride."

She stirred. "I can't...feel my hands," she whispered. "They're numb. I can't hold on."

"You don't have to hold on. I've got you." He took her hands in his. Even through his thick gloves, he could feel the tremors wracking her body.

"Don't...let me go," she said.

Setting her palms against his chest, he put his arms around her shoulders. "I'm not going to let you go. I promise."

Dark, shimmering eyes met his. He'd intended to give her a reassuring smile to keep her calm, like he had with a hundred other subjects during a hundred other rescues. But the power behind her gaze stopped him cold. For a split second the flying snow and the roar of the wind faded until his focus narrowed to the feel of her against him, the

smell of her hair and the frightened, striking eyes staring
back at him.

"Come on, Maitland, what are you doing? Picnicking
down there?" Buzz's voice crackled through his helmet
communication gear with all the finesse of a chain saw.
"Get it in gear!"

Shaking off his reaction to the woman, John forced himself to take a mental step back and signaled for the other
man to winch them up. An instant later, the rope drew
taut. She gasped as they were jerked off their feet.

"Damn winch operator has the mentality of a gorilla,"
he grumbled, more to calm her than to complain because
he knew there wasn't a man alive who could operate a
winch better than Buzz Malone.

In only a few seconds, John's thoughts strayed from the
operation at hand to the woman pressed against him—and
how that closeness was affecting his body. He tried to keep
his thoughts on IV fluids, the possibility of frostbite and
the radio call he would be making to Lake County Hospital, but the fact that this beautiful, frightened woman was
pressed flush against him with her head on his chest was
doing a number on his concentration. Her arms were
around his waist, and she clung to him as if he were her
lifeline. Even through the bulk of his flight suit, he was
aware of her body. Small-boned. Soft. Curvy as a mountain back road—and undoubtedly just as dangerous. Her
fragrant hair was loose and blowing in his face.

He shouldn't have acknowledged, even to himself, how
good she felt wrapped around him like that—she was a
trauma patient. He was an in-flight medic. She'd shoved a
gun in his face just two minutes earlier, for crying out
loud! God only knew what kind of a person she was.

All that aside, even under the best of circumstances,
John figured he was the last man on earth who had the
right to indulge in this woman's vulnerability.

Steeling himself against his uncharacteristic reaction to

her and physical sensations he knew better than to acknowledge, he forced his thoughts back to the operation and prepared to board the chopper. The ride up was swift and turbulent. The winds spun them like a top, but the woman didn't make a sound. When a particularly strong gust sent them careening toward the chopper's skid, he swiveled in midair and took the impact in the small of his back, determined to keep her from getting any more bruises.

"About time you showed up." Buzz Malone's voice reached him over the roar of the chopper's engines and rush of wind. "What do we have?"

"Hypothermia. Possible frostbite." Strong hands pulled them into the chopper. John looked down at the woman in his arms and felt a flutter of low-grade lust in his belly. Terrific. "You handled that like a pro," he told her.

Her gaze met his. Despite her earlier terror and the fact that she was seriously hypothermic and shivering uncontrollably, a smile touched the corners of her mouth. The smile reached him as no words could have. For a moment he couldn't look away. Simultaneously something shifted deep in his chest, something new and uncomfortable—and uncharacteristic as hell. He wanted to say something cocky, something to let his teammates know he wasn't the least bit affected by all that red hair and her pretty eyes, but for the first time in his life, his wit failed him. He felt like he'd just been punched right between the eyes. All he could do was stare back at her and pray his team members weren't aware that he'd suddenly lost his power of speech.

"Are you going to stand there all day, or are you going to let me unfasten her, so we can get an IV started?"

John jerked at the tone of Buzz's voice. Realizing belatedly that the woman was no longer supporting herself, that he was just standing there holding her, he unclipped her harness and relinquished her to the two waiting men.

"What the hell, John? Did you get struck by lightning out there, or what?" Buzz asked.

"Must have been that boulder Flyboy slammed me into," John muttered. Not sure why he'd reacted so strongly to her, ready to write it off to his long-neglected male libido, he stepped back, determined to walk away and forget it.

But John couldn't make himself turn away. He damn well couldn't shake the feeling that he'd just stepped out onto thin ice and was about to plunge headlong into something that promised to take a lot more than just his breath.

Her gaze never left him as Buzz and junior medic Pete Scully lifted her on the count of three and eased her onto the litter. Armed or not, she still had the most incredible eyes he'd ever seen. They were soft, expressive pools the color of expensive cognac. Rich with intelligence, they stared back at him with a moving mix of relief and gratitude—and the unmistakable realization that he'd saved her life.

So what if that fed his ego? There wasn't a search-and-rescue professional alive that didn't like having it stoked. So he'd reacted to her. It had been a while since he'd been with a woman. John wasn't any Romeo—not by a long shot. He knew all too well the dangers of getting involved and he wasn't going to go off the deep end over a pair of incredible eyes and handfuls of silky red hair.

Still, his reaction to her disturbed him—almost as much as the fact that she could very well have blown his head off.

"Buzz."

Buzz tore the wrap from an IV needle. "What is it, Maitland?" the older man asked, never looking away from his work.

"Uh…she had a gun."

Buzz swung an incredulous stare at him. *"What?"*

"I said she had a gun—"

"I heard you the first time." Buzz looked down at the woman, his expression incredulous. "Where is it?"

"She dropped it."

"Did she threaten you with it?"

John had debated telling him the part where she'd pointed it at him. But Buzz was an ex-cop. John trusted his judgment. "She was terrified. Confused."

"Holy hell. She did, didn't she?"

"She thought I was someone else," he said, hating it that he felt as if he'd somehow betrayed her. He didn't owe her anything. For all he knew, she could be a criminal.

"Who was she expecting, Jack the Ripper?"

"She was scared out of her mind."

"Scared enough to pull a gun on a man trying to save her life?"

John looked down at the pale woman lying on the litter. "I don't think she planned to use it."

Buzz cursed, his face set and angry. "Open a line for me, Scully," he snapped. "Let's get some fluids into her."

Using the shears from the med kit, Buzz began cutting away her sweater and jeans. He hesitated an instant when the purple bruises on her arms and throat came into view. "Bloody hell."

"Criminy." Scully's jaw tightened, his gaze sweeping from the woman's bruised body up to Buzz.

John stared at the dark bruises marring the flesh of her throat. Bruises that were the perfect imprint of a man's fingers. Outrage burgeoned in his chest. Nausea seesawed in his gut as the memory of another woman taunted him. A woman with fear in her eyes and bruises on her body. The burn of shame sizzled through him followed by the sting of regret so sharp he winced.

"Looks like maybe she was trying to protect herself," Scully offered.

The woman tried to sit up, her eyes glued to the scissors. "Please…don't…."

John knew Buzz had seen too much in his years as a cop and then as a medic to let the sight of her bruises faze him. "Try to relax, honey," the team leader soothed. "We're going to treat you for hypothermia. I've got to get these wet clothes off you. Hold still for me, now, all right?"

Shivering uncontrollably, she lay back on the litter and squeezed her eyes shut. But John could clearly see that she wasn't relaxed. Her hands were clenched into fists, her jaws clamped tight. Her entire body trembled violently. He wondered if it was from the cold—or the terror she'd suffered at the hands of whomever had put those bruises on her. The thought sickened him.

As the beauty of her flesh came into view, John averted his gaze. He'd seen plenty of victims prepped for the emergency room over the years. Most times, that included cutting away the impediment of clothing so the team could assess whatever trauma they'd sustained. In this case, removing her wet clothes was imperative in treating hypothermia. Male or female, in all the years he'd been a medic, the procedure had never bothered him. The fact that it did with this rescue—and this particular woman—left him feeling acutely uneasy. A hell of a reaction for a man who'd devoted his life to the art of never getting involved.

John had one staunch rule that he'd lived by since the day he walked out of the Philadelphia tenement at the age of seventeen and never looked back: Never get involved. Not with the people around him. Not with his patients. And never, ever with women. He'd broken that rule only once in the last thirteen years—and paid a terrible price. He wouldn't do it again. So why was his heart pounding like a drum as he watched the tears well in her eyes and spill down her wind-burned cheeks?

Reaching into the med kit, John withdrew an insulated blanket and snapped it open. Stepping over to the litter, he pulled the blanket up to her chin. "What's with the tears, gorgeous?"

Her eyes latched on to his, heavy-lidded with the effects of hypothermia. "I thought…I was…going to die."

"I forgot to mention this to you, but that wasn't an option," he said easily.

She closed her eyes, but a smile played at the corners of her mouth. "You're…bossy."

"It's an ego thing, actually. I'm a hopeless egomaniac."

"I'm willing to overlook… You saved…my life."

A quick jab of alarm stabbed through John when she slurred the words. Reaching into the cabinet overhead, he broke open a radiant heat pack, gave it a quick twist and pressed it to her abdomen. "I don't know if you realized this, Red, but I'm damn good at what I do."

"Modest…too. I should have…known."

Her voice was so low, John had to lean close to hear her.

Buzz grimaced. "Her respiration is slow. She's stopped shivering. Body temp's at ninety-four. No pupil dilation yet, but I don't want to risk cardial arrhythmia. Let's go to active rewarming. Pete, get some oxygen going, will you?"

Before realizing he was going to touch her, John pressed the backs of his fingers to her cheek to find her flesh cold to the touch. "Stay with me, Red. Come on. Keep your eyes open."

Pete peeled the wrap from another IV needle while Buzz swabbed the top of her hand with alcohol. She didn't so much as wince when the needle slipped into her vein. Realizing both Buzz and Pete had the situation under control, John rose. He knew it was stupid, but he didn't want to leave her.

Shaking off the sentiment, he started for the VHF console to radio the hospital, but the sound of her voice stopped him cold. He turned back to her, found her eyes open and focused on him.

"Thank you…for saving…my life," she whispered.

Feeling the back of his neck heat, he unfastened the top button of his flight suit. "You just hold up your end of the deal, Red."

"What's…my end of the deal?"

"I'll settle for you staying awake until we get to County. Think you can handle that?"

"You gonna sit there and make cow eyes at her all day, Maitland, or call County with our E.T.A.?"

John frowned at his team leader, but for the second time that day, realized he didn't have a comeback, witty or otherwise. He was going to hear about this later, he knew. John the Untouchable, going mush-brained over a female patient with a pretty face, tons of red hair—and trouble written all over her shapely body.

Cursing under his breath, he moved over to the VHF radio, snatched up the mike and summoned Lake County Hospital. "This is RMSAR Eagle two niner. We've got a Jane Doe en route. Approximately twenty-seven years old. Possible closed head wound. Moderate hypothermia. Respiration slow. Body temp at ninety-four. No sign of cardial arrhythmia. Probable extremity frostbite with tissue damage. Numerous superficial injuries. We'll need a CT. E.T.A. twelve minutes."

As dispatch radioed their reply and cleared them for landing, John risked a look at the auburn-haired beauty lying on the litter. He wasn't sure why he was feeling so protective of her. She was going to be all right. Her confusion would ease as soon as they got her body temperature back to normal. Her fingers and toes might be frostbitten, but none of her injuries appeared to be life-threatening. Well, if you didn't count the bruises on her throat.

He'd get over this protective male nonsense by the time they reached the hospital. He looked at his watch. Eleven minutes and counting.

Yeah, he'd be just fine in about eleven minutes.

Chapter 2

Glorious heat wrapped around her as if she'd been immersed in a warm bath. Relaxation spread through her body, rippling through muscle and tendon and radiating all the way to her bones. The lavender haze surrounding her brain cushioned the pain in her head and eased the throbbing ache in her hands and feet.

She'd never floated before, but this wasn't at all unpleasant. She was especially enjoying the dream about the man in the orange flight suit. The man with black, short-cropped hair, electric blue eyes and that devil-be-damned grin. The man who'd swooped down out of the sky and rescued her from…

From what?

Alarm quivered through her. The warmth she'd been feeling fled. In its place, something dark and menacing gripped her. A vague sense of terror crept over her like the shadow of some huge predator about to attack. She felt threatened, pursued, but her mind couldn't seem to pinpoint by what—or whom.

Content to return to the protective warmth of sleep—
and her dream about the man with those vivid blue eyes—
she sank back into the darkness and let the tide send her
adrift.

"Rise and shine, honey. You've got a visitor."

The jazzy female voice turned her peaceful netherworld
on its ear. She opened her eyes. Light stabbed into her
brain like a hot laser, bringing a wave of pain so powerful,
her vision blurred. Withholding a groan, she raised her
hand to shield her eyes, only to find her fingers encased
in bandages. Blinking in confusion, she lowered her hand
and tried to focus on the two blurred figures standing a
few feet from her bed.

"Where am I?" Her throat felt as if it had been through
a cheese grater. Twice.

"Lake County Hospital," came the female voice. "You
were brought in yesterday morning. How are you feeling?"

She blinked to clear the fog from her brain. A silver-
haired woman with kind eyes and chocolate-colored skin
came into focus and smiled down at her. "I'm Cora, your
nurse. Let me get your pulse while you're awake."

A nurse, she thought. A look at the monitor beside her
bed confirmed that she was in a hospital. A vague sense
of confusion swirled in her head. She was in a hospital. A
hospital?

What the hell was she doing in a hospital?

Before she could voice the question, the nurse took her
hand and set her finger against her wrist. Only then did
she remember her other visitor. She turned her head and
squinted at the man standing just inside the door. The man
she'd been dreaming about stared back at her, his gaze
riveted to hers, his chiseled mouth pulled into a cocky grin.

"Hi, Red. How's tricks this morning?"

Red? It took her befuddled mind a moment to realize
he was talking to her. When she tried to answer, her voice

grated like bad brakes. She cleared her throat and tried again. "The only thing doing tricks this morning is my brain." She didn't have the energy to mention her stomach was doing tricks, too—every time the smell of hospital bacon and eggs wafted into the room.

"Sorry to hear that. You're looking good."

"If how I feel is any indication as to how I look, I'd say you're probably lying."

Even with her head pounding and her vision blurred, she couldn't help but notice the power behind his smile. He'd traded the jumpsuit for a pair of faded jeans that hugged lean hips and muscular thighs. A flannel shirt opened to a black T-shirt with the word Medic emblazoned in white and stretched tightly over a wide, muscled chest. Laced-up hiking boots lent him the appearance of an outdoorsman. But it was his eyes that drew her gaze and held it so that she couldn't look away. She'd never seen bluer eyes. They were high-altitude blue with a touch of ice, a trace of winter dusk—and a lot of male attitude. His short black hair was spiked military-style, but he didn't look clean-cut. Not with the five o'clock shadow darkening his jaw or that dangerous grin and sculpted mouth. Even in her dazed state, it took her all of two seconds to realize he was every woman's fantasy incarnate.

Good grief, he was something to look at. Too bad the best she could hope for was to get through this without throwing up on his shoes.

"How do you feel?" he asked.

"Headache." She tried to swallow, but her mouth felt as if someone had filled it with gravel while she slept. "The freight train variety."

The nurse released her hand, then gave it a maternal pat. "A headache is normal with a concussion. I can give you some acetaminophen if you like."

Confusion closed in on her. Concussion? Well, that certainly explained the headache and the nausea twisting her stomach into knots. But how on earth had she gotten a concussion? She raised her hands and squinted at the bandages. Why were her fingers bandaged? What was she doing in the hospital in the first place? And who in the world was the handsome outdoorsman standing over her, looking at her as if he was waiting for her to tell *him* the answer to questions she had absolutely no idea how to answer herself?

"What's your name, honey?" the nurse asked.

The question threw her. Only for an instant, though. Of course she knew her name. It must be the concussion clouding her mind and making her feel so confused. Her name. Sure. It would come to her in a minute. All she had to do was close her eyes and relax a little so her brain could settle down and think.

"My name?" Fear coiled in her chest as it slowly dawned on her that she didn't have a clue what her own name was. Her heart began to pound, keeping perfect time with the throbbing in her head. The ensuing panic sent her to a sitting position. A thunderbolt of pain behind her left temple sent her back down.

The nurse and the man moved closer simultaneously.

She tried to push herself back up, but the pain in her fingers stopped her, and for the first time she wondered how serious her injuries were. Good Lord, had she been in some kind of terrible accident?

"Easy, honey. It's just the concussion fuzzing things up for you," the nurse said. "Try to relax. Dr. Morgan is making rounds. She should be in shortly to talk with you."

That wasn't what she wanted to hear. That wasn't what she *needed* to hear. The first order of the day was for her to remember her name. How could anyone forget their own name, for Pete's sake?

"I don't know my name." Her own words turned the fear lurking inside her into a reality more frightening than the vague nightmare that still lingered in the back of her mind. "My God, I don't remember my own name." She looked from the nurse to the man and back to the nurse. "How can that be?"

They exchanged looks comprised of equal parts sympathy and concern that did little to quell her growing sense of panic. Propping her elbows on the pillow behind her, she struggled to a sitting position. "How did I get here? What happened?" Remembering the bandages, she raised her left hand and studied it, half-afraid to ask why it was bandaged.

Her gaze swept to the man. He returned her look levelly. Even though he hadn't answered her questions, she found herself thankful he could at least meet her gaze without looking away. If she was facing bad news, she could tell by the character in his eyes that at least he'd have the guts to give it to her straight.

"I'll go find Dr. Morgan." The nurse patted her knee through the blanket. "Sit tight, honey. I'll be right back."

She watched the woman leave, trying in vain to ignore the grip of panic that had her breaths coming shallow and fast.

"Easy, Red, your blood pressure's up a tad this morning."

Her gaze snapped to the man. The sensation of the automatic blood pressure cuff tightening around her left biceps slowly registered, and for the first time she realized how close she was to all-out panic. "Yeah, well, I think my blood pressure is the least of my worries at the moment," she muttered.

"Why don't you sit back and take a couple of deep breaths?"

"I don't think that's going to solve anything."

"It won't solve anything, but it might help you deal with it." He winked. "On the count of three. Deep breath. Ready?"

Resisting the urge to roll her eyes at the futility of deep

breathing exercises when her entire life was nothing more than a black hole, she drew a shuddering breath. He did the same, and they exhaled simultaneously.

"Well, at least now we know my lungs work." But even as she made the remark, she realized the panic had released its vise grip on her chest.

"Better?"

"Yeah. Unfortunately it didn't do a thing for my memory'." Another wave of panic threatened, but she forced air into her lungs and fought it back. "I don't believe this is happening."

"You've got a concussion. Disorientation isn't unusual. Your memory will come back."

She wasn't so sure, but decided not to argue against something she wanted desperately to believe. "I remember *you*," she said abruptly, a little desperately, because suddenly it was very important to her to remember *something*.

Images of the rescue flooded her mind. Snow. Cold. Blinding pain. A vague sense of terror she couldn't shake even now as she lay safe and alive in this unfamiliar bed. But she clearly remembered this man with the incredible blue eyes and devil's grin. He'd swooped down out of the sky and plucked her from the rocks and snow. As she took in his steady expression and canny gaze, she remembered vividly how safe she'd felt in his arms, the solid feel of his body against hers, the softness of his voice, the whisper of his breath against her cheek when he'd murmured gentle words and eased her terror.

"You saved my life," she said. "Thank you."

"I had a little help from the rest of the team." He extended his hand. "Just a little. I'm John Maitland."

She attempted to take his hand, but the bandages hindered her. Despite the anxiety clenching her chest, a helpless laugh squeezed from her throat. "I don't think I'm going to be shaking hands anytime soon."

Unfazed, he took her hand gently between his. "I'm a

medic with Rocky Mountain Search and Rescue. You gave us quite a scare.''

His accent was distinctly northeastern—deep, clipped, with a hint of the streets etched into it. "I remember you. Of course I do. But I don't seem to remember...anything else. Can you tell me what happened?''

"We got the call out yesterday morning and picked you up on Elk Ridge at about nine thousand feet. You were hypothermic.'' He looked down at the bandages on her hands. "Frostbitten. We airlifted you here to Lake County Hospital.''

She remembered the rescue. But as the memory materialized, something dark and disturbing stirred in the back of her mind like the remnants of a nightmare. An acute feeling of unease. A sense of being pursued. The unmistakable aftertaste of terror.

"Where's Elk Ridge?'' she asked.

"Not far from Fairplay, about sixty miles west of Denver.''

She swallowed, realizing with a stark sense of dismay she hadn't even known what state she was in. Oh, dear God, what had happened to her?

"What else can you tell me?'' she asked, trying in vain to keep the desperation out of her voice.

His smile tightened into a grimace, and she got the distinct impression he was about to give her some bad news. But he didn't. Instead he reached into the pocket of his jeans and pulled out a tattered piece of paper. "I thought this might be important. Buzz Malone, my team leader, found it in the pocket of the jeans you were wearing.''

An uncomfortable sense of vulnerability encompassed her when she remembered her clothes being cut away. She knew the men who'd saved her hadn't had a choice; they were professionals and did that sort of thing on a daily basis. Still, the fact that she'd been so exposed left her disconcerted.

Hoping whatever was on the scrap of paper would help unscramble her memory, she reached for it, but the bandages on her hands stopped her.

"Sorry." Unfolding the paper, John held it up for her.
Hannah, meet me at the shop at noon.

She stared at the words, waiting for a lightning bolt of memory, a flashback, anything that would tell her who she was.

"Ring a bell?" he asked.

"No." The jab of disappointment cut her with the precision of a straight razor. Oh, how she wanted to remember. She *needed* to remember. She stared at the words in desperation, hoping against hope for a flare of recognition. Anything but the abyss of nothing her memory had become. "Do you think that's my name? Hannah?"

"Could be."

"Did I have identification when you found me?"

He shook his head. "No wallet. Not even a driver's license. Just the clothes on your back, which were ruined— sorry—and that note in your pocket."

Leaning forward, she pulled her knees to her chest. "This is nuts. I don't remember...anything. How I got up on the mountain. Why I was there. Where I live. My entire life is just...blank."

Her mind raced in circles, like a rat trapped in a maze with no destination, no way out. Swallowing the knot in her throat, she looked at John, wishing desperately he could tell her something, anything that would help her remember. "How can someone just forget their entire life?"

"It isn't unheard of for head trauma to cause temporary memory loss."

The word *temporary* took her panic down a notch. She clung to it with the desperation of a rock climber to a safety line. "How temporary?"

He shrugged. "I'm not an expert, but I've heard of cases where a head injury has caused amnesia."

"Amnesia?" The sound that erupted from her throat was half laugh, half groan. "That sounds like something from a soap opera."

"Last year we picked up a snowmobiler who'd gotten up close and personal with a blue spruce. He suffered a closed head injury. Took him two days to remember he was from Iowa. Missed his flight home and everything."

"Two days?" she echoed hopefully.

"Look, Lake County may be a small hospital, but I did my training here. Doc Morgan is good. She'll do what needs to be done to get you back on track, even if it means referring you to a specialist. But I'll bet the farm your memory will return before you're even released."

It made sense, of course. Unfortunately not even cold, hard logic could make the situation less frightening. Sighing, she looked down at her hands. "What's with the bandages?"

"You had some frostbite on your fingers and toes. There was some tissue damage, blisters mostly, but nothing severe. You've got some healing to do, but you won't have permanent scarring." Pulling the chair next to the bed, he straddled it and rested his chin on the back.

The scent of his aftershave drifted lazily through her brain, conjuring notions of piney forests and mountain air. Her sudden awareness of him caused a ripple of pleasure strong enough to make her stomach flutter.

"Was—was I in some sort of accident?" she managed after a moment.

"We didn't find a vehicle. Not a car. Not a snowmobile. You weren't dressed for skiing or hiking."

"So what was I doing up on Elk Ridge?"

For the first time, he looked uncomfortable. She got the distinct impression there was something he wasn't telling her. Simultaneously, something dark and frightening jumped in the back of her mind, like a predator lunging out of the shadows, claws extended, fangs bared. The ensuing flash of terror sent a violent shudder through her.

"You're not telling me something," she said.

"Easy, Red—"

"I see it in your face. You know something, but you don't want to tell me."

"Don't go jumping to conclusions on me."

"Keeping secrets from someone who can't even remember their own name is cruel."

He arched a brow. "Look, you're getting yourself worked up over—"

"Yeah, well, I tend to get a little worked up when I can't remember my own *name*."

She flinched when he leaned forward and put his hand on her forearm. Her first instinct was to pull away, but the gentleness of his touch stopped her. She looked down where his hand rested on her forearm. His fingers were thick and dark against her pale flesh. The man had fascinating hands, a doctor's hands made rugged by the elements. Warmth radiated from him into her and spread throughout her body like a slow-moving current.

"You're shaking," he said. "You okay?"

Swallowing hard, she risked a look at him. The power behind his eyes jolted her all the way down to her toes—and made her remember what it had felt like to be wrapped within his embrace in the harrowing minutes they'd dangled from the helicopter.

"I'm just…scared," she said after a moment.

"Everything's going to be all right."

Looking into the startling blue of his eyes, she almost believed him. She wasn't sure why, but this man made her feel safe. Yet even with the warmth of his touch searing her, she couldn't shake the sense of danger pressing down on her. A feeling that told her she wasn't safe no matter how badly she wanted to believe it.

"I think something terrible happened to me up on the mountain," she whispered.

"How do you know that?"

"I don't know…exactly. I mean, I don't remember details. It's like a dream. Or a nightmare—" An image flashed in her mind, cutting her words short. The ensuing grip of terror was so powerful, she flinched. Images played in her mind's eye, like clips from a horror movie. She remembered snow. The silhouette of a man against the glare of headlights. The feel of cold steel in her hand. The blast of a gunshot.

Suddenly she knew why she'd been up on Elk Ridge— at least part of the reason. The realization settled over her as horribly as a handful of earth tossed over a lowered coffin.

"I remember…" Her voice was thin and breathless. She wasn't sure what she was trying to say. She *didn't* actually remember. But as she fought to keep her voice steady, her hands from shaking, she knew someone had been pursuing her. Someone who'd wanted to hurt her. Someone who wanted to…

John's hand tightened on her arm. "What is it?"

Raising her gaze to his, she fought back another rise of fear and let out a shuddery breath. "I think someone was trying to kill me."

Chapter 3

John had known better than to come to the hospital. In the six years he'd been a search-and-rescue medic, he'd never crossed the line between professional duty and personal involvement. He'd sure as hell never visited a patient. Well, except for the time he and his team transported a woman who'd gone into premature labor during a camping trip and delivered a preemie while en route to the emergency room. Even then, he hadn't actually talked to the woman, just checked with the nursing staff to make sure the five-pound baby girl was all right.

So why hadn't he been able to stay away this time?

He told himself he'd only stopped by to deliver the note they'd found in the pocket of her jeans. After all, *someone* from the team had to do it. Why not him? It wasn't like he was going to stick around. Or get involved. Just because he didn't like the bruises on her neck or the possibilities behind the dark mystery surrounding her rescue didn't mean he was going to get caught up in her plight or, God forbid, fall into the soft depths of those incredible eyes.

He should just wish her luck, bid her farewell and walk away. It wouldn't be the first time he'd taken the easy way out. John Maitland had walking out down to a fine art. He was good at it. Almost as good as he was at not getting involved. He'd learned a long time ago the cost of personal involvement, and it had always been a price he wasn't willing to pay.

He just wished the nagging little voice in the back of his mind would stop telling him this time was going to be different.

Who was he trying to fool anyway? He was a lot more interested in this woman than he wanted to admit. A hell of a lot more than was wise. He understood the dynamics of high adrenaline and danger. Like so many other men like him, he lived for the high. Rescues could be simultaneously emotional and exhilarating and hair-raising. In the past he'd never felt anything more than the need to decompress afterward. A couple of beers with his team-mates or a workout at the gym usually sufficed. But this time was different. He couldn't explain it, but something had happened between him and this woman up on the mountain. Something that didn't have anything to do with adrenaline or ego or even the fact that she appealed to him on a physical level. Somehow, and as unlikely as it seemed, he'd connected with her in a way that went against everything he'd ever believed about himself. The realization that he might be vulnerable to that curvy body and those bottomless brown eyes disturbed him almost as much as the words she'd just uttered.

As he gazed down at her, he realized he hadn't driven all the way from Conifer to Lake County Hospital in six inches of snow just to check on her physical condition.

"Why would someone want to kill you?" In the back of his mind he thought about the pistol she'd shoved in his face and wondered if he remembered *that* little detail. Or if it had anything to do with what had happened to her.

"I'm not sure," she said. "I mean, I don't really have a clear memory of it. Just sort of vague...impressions."

"What else do you remember?"

"I remember being afraid," she said. "I remember running. Snow and darkness and cold. I think someone was chasing me."

"Look, Red, I'm not discounting what you're telling me, but I've seen a lot of concussions, and even more cases of hypothermia over the years. Both can cause mental confusion—"

"I'm not wrong about this."

"Even moderate hypothermia has been known to cause hallucinations," he said.

"I wasn't hallucinating."

"Were you hallucinating when you shoved that pistol in my face?"

Her gaze snapped to his, her expression stricken.

"I see you remember that part just fine," he said dryly. "You could have taken my head off."

"Oh my God." Raising her bandaged hand, she pressed it to her mouth. "I wouldn't have...hurt you."

"You sure had me fooled. That .38 you were packing looked pretty deadly."

"I'm sorry," she said.

"Whose gun was it?"

"I don't know."

"Why did you have it?"

"I...don't...remember."

John studied her, annoyed with her because he couldn't tell if she was lying, annoyed with himself because all he seemed to be noticing about her was the way that sexless hospital gown fell over curves that were anything but sexless. Curves he had absolutely no business noticing as a medical professional, even less as a man with his history. If he had an ounce of common sense, he'd get the hell out of there. But John knew his interest in her had moved beyond logic and into an area that was as foreign to him as the phenomenon of amnesia.

"Am I in trouble?" she asked. "I mean, with the police?"

Lowering his head, he pinched the bridge of his nose and sighed. "If my team leader had his way, you'd be on your way to a jail cell right now."

A shiver rippled the length of her. "Why aren't I?"

"Hopefully it's not because I'm a fool." John couldn't tell her the truth, of course. He couldn't tell her that even after they'd dropped her off at the hospital, he hadn't been able to get her out of his mind. That he hadn't been able to stop thinking about the way he'd responded when her body had been pressed against his and all that red hair had spread over his chest like an ocean of fragrant silk. For hours afterward, her scent had clung to him, as sweet and tantalizing as a first kiss.

Shoving the memory aside, he blew out a sigh. "Buzz filed a police report but he didn't mention the gun." He shot her a hard look. "I convinced him not to."

John saw the question in her eyes. She wanted to know why they'd covered for her, but she didn't voice it. He found himself relieved because he wasn't sure he had an answer.

"You don't think I'm some kind of...criminal, do you?" she asked.

"I think you've got some explaining to do."

"I'm not sure how I can explain something I don't remember."

"That's why we're going to give the sheriff's office a call."

The color leached from her cheeks so quickly, he thought she would faint. "No police," she whispered.

Suspicion fluttered like a big, gangly bird in the pit of his stomach. He hadn't wanted to believe it, but she was obviously hiding something. Disappointed, he scrubbed a hand over his jaw. *Terrific.* His instincts were telling him one thing, his gut another—and the part of him that was a man didn't necessarily give a damn about either.

"Why not?" he asked.

"I don't know. I just…need some time to sort things out first. Please."

John sighed again. He wasn't sure how he was going to handle this. He wasn't sure how he was going to handle *her.* Or what he was going to do about the way he was reacting to her.

"What else do you remember?" he pressed.

"Not much more than I've already told you. I remember running. Being…terrified. I remember…cold and snow. It was dark, and I couldn't see…" Her gaze dropped to her bandaged hands. When she held them out, they trembled. "How is it that I can't remember, yet I'm terrified? I don't even know what I'm afraid of. I don't even know my own *name,* for God's sake. This is nuts."

"The name thing bothers you a lot, doesn't it?"

A humorless laugh escaped her. "I know this sounds strange, but not knowing my own name, not knowing who I am makes me feel like…I never existed."

"What about the name on the note?"

"Hannah? What about it?"

"I like it a hell of a lot better than Jane Doe."

"Hannah." A tentative smile touched the corners of her mouth. "Yeah, I like it. I mean, temporarily."

"Even if it's not your name, chances are it was at least familiar to you."

"Maybe if I hear it often enough, it will shake loose a memory and help me remember."

"There you go."

Something went liquid and warm in John's chest at her smile. It was an unfamiliar sensation he normally would have shied away from, but didn't this time. As long as he stayed in control of the situation, he'd be all right, he assured himself. If the balance shifted, he'd know when to walk away. John had a sixth sense when it came to knowing when to walk away. It had never failed him; it wouldn't now.

But the knowledge gave him little solace, considering those incredible eyes of hers knocked him for a loop every time he looked at her.

"I know this must sound crazy, but I can't shake the feeling that I was in trouble up on that mountain," she said. "I'm not wrong about this. Someone was trying to...hurt me."

He didn't like the sound of that. Not about her memory loss. He sure as hell didn't like the possibility that someone might have been trying to hurt her. But it would explain the gun. And the bruises on her arms and throat. The rest of her body had been so battered in the fall, they hadn't been able to tell if the other bruises were suspicious or not.

John tried to stomp the outrage that rolled slowly through him at the thought of a man hurting her. Nothing gave a man the right to hurt a woman. He knew all too well the devastation that kind of violence wreaked on someone's life. He'd walked away from it thirteen years ago, only to realize a man couldn't ever outrun his roots.

So why the hell was he sitting here trying to help her remember when he had absolutely no intention of getting involved?

As if reading his thoughts, her gaze sharpened on his. "There's something else, isn't there?"

John gazed back at her, telling himself it wasn't his responsibility to tell her about the bruises—or the very real possibility that someone had, indeed, tried to hurt her.

"I'll go see what's keeping the doc," he said, rising.

"Look, whatever it is you're not telling me, I can handle it. It's not like I'm going to fall apart or something. I deserve to know what happened to me."

The edge in her voice stopped him. Trying not to look

at the bruises on her throat, trying not to let his outrage show, he met her gaze levelly. "You've got some suspicious bruising."

"What do you mean by suspicious?"

"Bruises probably not sustained in the fall. Around your neck area. Your arms."

"You mean like someone…" Her words trailed off. What little color she had left in her cheeks fled. She stared at him, her eyes dark and frightened within the pale frame of her face.

Even through the bandages John could see that her hands were shaking. He should have known she wouldn't let him walk out of there without asking the question he had no desire to answer. He didn't want to be the one to tell her she may have been battered, or that she may have been the victim of a crime. He might be adept at walking away, but John had never been one to hedge the truth, no matter how ugly. Judging by the way she was looking at him—and the way he was responding—he wasn't going to start now.

"I didn't mean to upset you," he offered. "I thought you should know."

Shoving a lock of hair away from her face, she looked at him squarely. "It's okay. I needed to know. I can handle it."

She didn't look like she could handle anything at the moment. She looked pale and troubled and so vulnerable, it took most of his discipline not to go to her just to let her know she wasn't alone. John might be good at dangling from a cable a hundred feet above the ground, but when it came to the more delicate side of medical care, he figured there were times when he could use a little more tact. Times like now when he should have kept his mouth shut and let the doctors deal with her questions.

Turning away, she looked out the window. An alarm clanged in his head when she blinked rapidly. The alarm burgeoned to an all-out wail when he saw the first tear slip down her cheek. He'd never known how to deal with female tears; he'd spent most of his life avoiding those kinds of situations. He didn't want to have to deal with them now. Not on top of those bottomless brown eyes and all that flowing red hair. The combination was doing funny things to his resolve to walk out the door. Hard telling what it would do to his resolve not to touch her.

John spotted the pitcher of water next to the bed and poured a glass for her. "Here."

Wiping the tears from her cheeks with the bandages, she sipped, then relaxed back in the pillows. "Thanks."

A spike of heat hit him low in the gut when her hair fanned out beneath her, framing her face like a pool of glossy silk. For a crazy instant, John was tempted to lean forward and take it between his fingers, just to see if it felt as soft as it looked.

"You're good at that, you know," she said.

"At what?"

She looked at him from beneath her lashes. "A few minutes ago my heart was pounding, and I was an inch away from losing it. Thanks for calming me down."

The thought that it might be interesting to get her heart rate up in a different way fluttered in the back of his mind, but he quickly stomped the notion, knowing that was the one line he'd never cross no matter how sexy she was. "Well, Red, I'm not sure if I've told you this, but I'm pretty damn good at what I do."

"I think you've mentioned that. Twice, actually."

John's IQ slipped another notch when she smiled. He should have known it would be dazzling. He tried not to notice the dimple in her left cheek or the way her eyes tilted at the corners; he knew better than to let himself be charmed. But he'd fought enough personal battles over the years to know he was losing this one.

"Do you flirt with all your patients?" she asked.

"Shamelessly." He couldn't help but grin. "For a head trauma patient you're not doing such a bad job yourself."

Color rushed back into her cheeks. John liked the dimple, he decided, even though he'd never been taken in by "cute" when it came to women. He figured as long as he didn't let his interest in her go any further than harmless flirting, they'd both be just fine.

Movement at the door caught his attention, and he turned to see Dr. Anna Morgan enter the room and head directly for her patient. She was a petite woman with salt-and-pepper hair and rhinestone-studded bifocals that sat on the end of her nose like fancy little marquees. "Are you flirting with my patient, Maitland?" she asked, picking up the chart and making a notation with the sweep of her hand.

John was acquainted with most of the staff at Lake County. Over the years, he'd transported dozens of patients to the emergency room. He'd trained under the expertise of Dr. Anna Morgan when she'd headed up the E.R. Though she was old enough to be his mother, they'd developed a relationship that teetered comfortably between professional regard and personal friendship.

Rising, he approached her and extended his hand. "I just needed an excuse to see you, Doc."

The doctor humphed good-naturedly as she shook his hand, then looked at the woman lying in the bed and rolled her eyes. "Don't let this man charm you. It's lethal, and I've yet to come up with an antidote."

John had intended for the banter to alleviate Hannah's anxiety, but one look at her told him all the humor in the world wasn't going to help. He couldn't blame her. He'd had to rebuild his life once. As many times as he'd wished he could rewrite his past, he didn't envy the chore ahead of her.

Hannah's gaze swept to Dr. Morgan. "I don't remember anything that happened before the rescue," she blurted. "I don't remember how I got up on the mountain. Or how I fell. I don't remember…anything.''

The doctor's brows creased as she regarded the younger woman. ''The CT scan shows you received a concussion, more than likely during a fall.'' Easing the bandage away from Hannah's temple, she assessed the stitches beneath.

John winced at the size of the cut. The sight of the injury itself didn't bother him—he'd long ago grown accustomed to that aspect of his job—but that this particular woman had been purposefully hurt put a hot ball of outrage squarely in his gut.

''A concussion is caused by head trauma,'' the doctor explained. ''In your case, there was no bleeding around the brain. However, some minor swelling occurred. That's not unusual, but it can affect short-term memory and mental clarity.''

''I wouldn't be quite so worried if it was just a little mental clarity I was lacking, but my entire life is just…gone.''

''Actually, you remember more than you realize,'' the doctor said. ''I treated a young man last winter who sustained a severe head injury in a ski accident. He had to relearn how to walk, how to feed himself and even how to speak.'' She replaced the bandage, then stepped back and crossed her arms. ''Memory loss, or amnesia if you will, is extremely rare but certainly not unheard-of when it comes to head trauma.''

''How long will it be before I start remembering?''

Dr. Morgan shrugged. ''I'm not an expert, but from what I've read about amnesia, most head-trauma patients begin remembering within minutes or hours after the initial injury. You could remember everything all at once. Or you might remember bits and pieces over a period of time. You could wake up tomorrow and recover your memory fully. Or it could take days or weeks or even months, I'm afraid.''

Hannah didn't look happy about the situation. John couldn't blame her. He didn't like the helplessness he felt with not being able to help her. He was a rescuer by nature. He fixed things. And he liked being in control—something he'd never had while growing up. But without a single clue to go on, there wasn't much he could do.

Dr. Morgan lifted the penlight from her smock and checked each of Hannah's eyes. "Your pupils respond nicely." Reaching for the chart at the foot of the bed, she made another notation. "How are you feeling physically?"

"Sort of like I fell into a ravine and didn't miss a single rock on the way down."

Dr. Morgan smiled. "Headache?"

"Like there's a guy with a jackhammer behind my right eye."

"I'll order up some acetaminophen. You'll need it for the next couple of days. You're pretty bruised." The doctor smoothed the sheet with her left hand. "Any nausea?"

"A little. Is that from the concussion, too?"

John didn't miss the minute tightening of the doctor's jaw. "Do you have any idea why you were up on the mountain?" she asked casually. "Or who you were with?"

"No." He could tell by the way Hannah shifted beneath the sheets that she knew it wasn't a casual question.

"Were you alone?" the doctor asked.

The younger woman's gaze swept to John. He looked from Hannah to Dr. Morgan, and realized belatedly the doctor hadn't missed the silent communication that passed between them. "Could you step out of the room for a minute, John?" she asked.

An alarm went off in the back of his head. Remembering the bruises—the undeniable marks left by a man's fingers—he rose, trying not to think about how they might have gotten there.

Taking a mental step back, he reminded himself he didn't have anything at stake. After all, he didn't get in-

volved. Hell, he hadn't even gotten too close to his team-
mates at Rocky Mountain Search and Rescue. So why was
he finding it so difficult to walk out that door?

"I've got to get back to headquarters," he said.

"I'd like you to stay," Hannah said abruptly. "Please.
I mean…if you…don't mind."

Surprise rippled through him and landed with a thud in
the pit of his stomach. He glanced over at the woman lying
in the bed, felt the familiar tightening in his chest at the
sight of all that red hair. He knew he should do the right
thing and walk away. She didn't need him. Of all the people in the world, John figured he was the last kind of man
she needed.

But he didn't have the heart to leave her, not when she'd
asked him to stay—and was now looking at him like he
was her only friend in the world. Even John Maitland the
Untouchable had his limits.

Shoving his hands into his pockets, he shot her a grin,
hoping it didn't look as uneasy as it felt. "Sure thing,
Red."

Hannah hadn't intended to ask him to stay, but she was
feeling scared and alone and the words had tumbled out
before she had a chance to think them through. She knew
it was unreasonable for her to ask such a thing. He was a
complete stranger; he may not even *want* to stay. But unreasonable or not, the thought of him walking out that
door, the thought of never seeing him again, filled her with
a loneliness so deep it brought tears to her eyes.

Her heart pounded as she watched Dr. Morgan move to
the window and raise the blinds. Gray light slanted in from
the overcast day beyond. Lowering her clipboard, she
looked down at Hannah. "I'm sure you know those bruises
on your neck and arms weren't caused in the fall."

Tension snapped through Hannah's body. Even though

she'd expected to hear those very same words, the meaning behind them hit her hard.

"Do you remember having an argument with someone?" the doctor asked gently. "Or someone hurting you in the past?"

She reached deep for the memories, but even with desperation clenching her like a giant talon, her past remained a blank. "I don't remember," she said after a moment.

"I know the chief of staff of the psychiatric department of Lutheran Hospital in Denver," Dr. Morgan said. "Dr. Wu has done several studies on amnesia. I'll give him a call if you like."

Amnesia. There was that word again. It rang inside Hannah's head like the retort of a killing shot. "I'd like to see him as soon as possible. I need to know who I am, Dr. Morgan. I need to know what happened to me."

"I'll brief him on your case." The woman paused, then gazed at her over the tops of her bifocals. "There's one more thing."

The tone of the doctor's voice snapped Hannah's head up. Next to her, John went very still. One look at the other woman's face and Hannah knew this revelation was going to be a doozy. Like she needed one more heaped on top of all the others she'd gotten in the last hour.

"I had some blood work sent down the lab when you were brought in," Dr. Morgan said.

"Blood work?" Hannah took a deep breath and braced herself, a thousand scenarios thundering through her brain. "Go ahead, Doc. Give it to me straight. I can handle it. What do I have? Cancer? A brain tumor?"

"Nothing like that." Dr. Morgan chuckled. "You're pregnant."

Chapter 4

*P*regnant.

The word reverberated in her head like the echo of a thunder clap. Hannah stared at the doctor, shock and disbelief punching her, stealing what little equanimity she'd managed to scrape together in the last hours.

She was going to have a baby.

She couldn't believe it.

How on earth could she be pregnant and not know how she got that way? Who had she loved enough to create a child? How could she be carrying a baby and not remember, for God's sake?

"Easy does it, Red."

Tearing her gaze from Dr. Morgan, Hannah risked a look at John. His guarded expression told her he was nearly as surprised as she. He shot her a smile, but for the first time since she'd known him, it didn't look genuine.

"It's going to be all right," he said.

Swallowing the lump that had risen in her throat, she

turned her attention back to the doctor. "I can't be pregnant," she blurted. "I'd remember something like that."

Dr. Morgan tapped her pen against her clipboard. "There's no room for error. I checked the results myself. You're definitely pregnant."

She stared at the doctor, torn between laughing herself into hysterics and crying herself dry. Stupidly she looked down at her abdomen. She didn't *feel* pregnant. "Are you sure?" she asked.

"I know news like this can be a shock—"

"I wouldn't call having a ten-ton boulder dropped on your head a shock exactly."

John cleared his throat. "In light of the hypothermia and the concussion, is the baby okay?"

A jab of concern sent Hannah's hand to her abdomen.

"The baby is fine," Dr. Morgan said.

"But I fell…"

"The body is amazingly resilient. You're a strong woman."

Relief swirled through her, and Hannah found herself thankful she was lying down. Things were moving way too fast; she felt as if she were on an out-of-control roller coaster that was about to derail. She'd only been awake a few hours and already her life was in chaos.

A hundred questions converged on her brain simultaneously, like a swarm of bees, crawling over a honey-laden hive. "How far along am I?"

"About three months."

"I'm healthy?"

"As a horse."

Another shock wave rocked through her as the reality of the situation sank in a little deeper. How in the world was she going to handle having a baby in six months when she didn't even know her own name?

"Aside from your memory loss, you've got a clean bill

of health," the doctor said. "That's why I'm going to release you."

Fear quivered in her gut at the thought of leaving the protective walls the hospital. "Release me?"

"A friend of mine runs a women's shelter in Denver. Angela Pearl is a gem. She'll set you up for a few days, until your memory returns. I'll give her a call. They've got an old van and can pick you up out front."

Hannah was still trying to absorb the fact that she was going to be released when the realization of where she would be going struck her. A homeless shelter. Good Lord, she was homeless and battered and pregnant. She had no money, no job skills that she knew of and not a friend in the world to call upon for help. Well, at least none that she remembered.

Setting her hand protectively over her abdomen, Hannah tried not to wonder if her situation could get any worse.

The acetaminophen wasn't helping. Not with the headache. Or the nausea. Or with the aches that had crept steadily into her bones since she'd wakened. It certainly wasn't helping to ease the shock of learning she was three months pregnant.

Stepping out of the shower, Hannah quickly toweled her body and tried in vain not to worry about what the coming hours would bring. Venturing out into that great big world out there scared the bejeebers out of her. For the second time in the last hour, her hand dropped protectively to her ever-so-slightly rounded tummy. The gesture surprised her—and brought an unbidden smile to her face. "Everything's going to be okay," she whispered. "Mommy just needs to get used to the idea of you being in there."

As she stared down at the place where a tiny life grew inside her, a profound sense of warmth enveloped her. A sense of rightness and calm and sweet inevitability all but vanquished the anxiety plaguing her. In that moment, somehow, she knew everything would be all right.

Clinging to the thought, she slipped into the faded scrubs and fluffy blue sweatshirt that wielded the hospital's insignia. Because of the frostbite on her feet, she couldn't yet wear regular shoes, but the E.R. respiratory therapist had donated a pair of clunky, open-toed sandals big enough to accommodate her bandaged feet. Hannah wasn't going to win any fashion awards anytime soon, but she was warm and comfortable and figured for a woman who'd gambled with the Grim Reaper and won just twenty-four hours earlier, she couldn't ask for much more.

She was alive. Her injuries were minor—well, aside from her memory loss—which continued to drive her to slow insanity. But the prognosis was good, she reminded herself. Even if it took a visit to the psychiatrist Dr. Morgan had recommended, Hannah swore she wouldn't rest until she knew her identity.

Pushing open the door, she stepped out of the bathroom. A smile curved her mouth when she saw Cora, her nurse, bent over the bed packing an overnight bag that had definitely seen better days. "I could have packed that myself," Hannah said.

Turning, Cora held out two packages of Girl Scout cookies. "Do you like peanut butter or chocolate?"

"Chocolate...I think."

"A woman of my own heart." The older woman turned back to her packing and laid both boxes of cookies inside. "At least you remember what you like to eat."

"I see you're all packed."

Hannah's heart stuttered at the sound of the deep male voice. She spun to see John Maitland standing in the doorway. His short-cropped hair might have looked conservative on another man, but the day's growth of beard and that careless grin conjured anything but conservative images. He looked good enough to make even the most cautious woman long for recklessness. And as much as Hannah wanted to believe she was immune to his blue eyes and chiseled mouth, the sudden quiver low in her belly told her she wasn't.

His gaze swept down the front of her. "Nice duds."

"The nurses took up a collection and donated the sweatshirt, scrubs and even a pair of jeans...." Her voice trailed as he crossed to her and stopped just short of invading her space.

"You look really good in scrubs, Red."

The towel she'd been holding slipped from her hands and fell to the floor. "I thought you had to get back to headquarters."

"Just doing a little follow-up care."

"I didn't realize medics did that sort of thing."

"I do, but just for the pretty redheads."

She blinked, charmed and flustered at once, and felt her cheeks heat. "You're flirting with me again."

"Bad habit of mine." He shoved his hands in his pockets.

Not quite sure how to react, she forced a laugh. *Okay, brain, you can start working now,* a desperate little voice whispered.

"How's the head?" he asked.

Spinning, she thought dully, then gave herself a quick mental shake. She knew better than to let his presence affect her, but her heart was doing tricks in her chest, refusing to pump enough blood to her brain. The lack of oxygen was making her dizzy.

"Better," she said, but her voice was breathless and high. His proximity wasn't helping matters, but then neither was his size. The man was at least six-four. His shoulders were nearly as wide as the door and just as solid looking. Hannah judged her own height to be about five-six. Not short by any means, but standing next to John Maitland, she felt dwarfed.

Her cognitive powers ground to a halt the instant the piney woods scent of his aftershave curled around her brain. She couldn't bring herself to smile or say anything even remotely intelligent. If her heart beat any faster, the damn thing was going to explode. Then she'd *really* be in trouble. Well, at least she was in the right place if they needed to rush her down to the emergency room.

Why did the man have to complicate matters by being so damned attractive, anyway? She shouldn't even be noticing such a thing, considering she was carrying another man's child.

"Any luck with your memory?" he asked.

"The biggest revelation I've had is that I prefer chocolate over peanut butter."

"Ah, there's some headway." His grin was quick and lethal. "At least you've got your priorities straight."

Okay, heart, you can slow down now. Hoping for a second in which to regain her composure, she knelt to pick up the towel she'd dropped. John must have gotten the same idea at precisely the same moment, because he stooped and reached for the towel.

"I've got it," she said, but her mind fumbled the instant his gaze met hers. All she saw was blue. Electric blue that reminded her of dusk on the mountain, bracing and clear and so vivid, she wanted to step forward and free-fall into its depths—and worry about the consequences later.

His grin widened. "I've got it."

She gave the towel a small tug.

He tugged back.

Not quite sure how to deal with him, she looked away, found herself staring at her sock-and-sandal-clad feet. Embarrassment washed over her. Oh, terrific. Not only did she have a brain that seemed to be working at twenty-five percent capacity, but she also had a scrape the size of Pikes Peak on her nose, a bruise on her cheek that looked like an overripe eggplant and shoes that would make even the most practical woman dive under the bed and not come out until Mr. Gorgeous left the room.

"Don't worry about the shoes," he said. "They look great."

Hannah choked out a helpless laugh and relinquished the towel. "The nurses of Lake County Hospital know how to pull together when they have a tough case on their hands."

Setting his hand gently against her biceps, he rose, easing her up with him. "I brought you something."

"A few pounds of ginkgo biloba?" she muttered under her breath.

He smiled and held out a shopping bag. "Better."

She looked down at the label on the bag and her heart did a weird little roll in her chest. "That wasn't necessary."

"Routine follow-up," he said deadpan.

Not knowing what else to do, she reached for the bag and looked inside. Her throat tightened at the sight of the coat.

"It's down-filled," he offered. "With a hood to keep you warm."

"Thank you." Her voice broke unexpectedly as she ran her fingers over the silky material. "It's beautiful...and practical. I mean, I hadn't even thought about needing one."

"It's hovering around zero outside." Reaching into the bag, he pulled out the coat.

Cora shuffled over and looked at it with a mother's critical eye. "Oh, yeah, honey, this will keep you plenty warm. The blue looks good with all that red hair of yours, too." Taking the coat from John, she held it out for Hannah to try on. "Well, John Maitland, I always wondered if your mama raised a gentleman. I reckon she did."

He winked at the nurse. "A scoundrel in gentleman's clothes."

Cora rolled her eyes. "Don't I know it."

As Hannah slipped her arms into the sleeves, a jab of uncertainty assailed her. She didn't have a way to pay for any of the things that had been given to her, she realized suddenly. Not her medical bill. Not the overnight bag or the clothes in it. Not even the coat.

"Perfect fit," Cora said. "Looks nice and warm, too."

Hannah glanced up to see John's gaze sweep down the front of her. An uncomfortable awareness crept over her, and she resisted the urge to shiver. Not because she was cold, but because the man's assessing gaze did funny things to her nerve endings. All two million of them.

"I don't have any way to pay for this," she blurted. "I mean, I don't have any—"

"The coat is a gift," John interjected.

Cora huffed. "I don't want to hear any talk about paybacks, honey. You just concentrate on getting settled into that shelter and getting your memory back."

Hannah tried not to show how much the thought of leaving the hospital scared her. She couldn't afford to be scared. Now was not the time to act like a frightened twelve-year-old. She wanted her life back. All of it, including her past—even if that meant remembering something unpleasant. She needed to know who she was. Where she lived. Who'd fathered the child growing inside her.

Who'd tried to kill her.

The thought brought gooseflesh to her arms.

Hannah jumped when the intercom next to the bed sounded. Cora made a rude gesture at it, then smiled. "I've gotta run, honey. Mr. Bowerfind down the hall needs me. You take care of yourself, you hear?"

On impulse, Hannah reached for the other woman and hugged her. "Thank you," she whispered. "For everything."

Cora hugged her back fiercely, then set her at arm's

length. "I'll expect a call when you get settled in at Angela Pearl's."

"I'll call. Thanks."

Sniffing once, Cora patted John's arm, then left the room.

Hannah stared after her, acutely aware of the press of silence—and the solid presence of the man standing next to her. "I'd better get going," she said.

He looked down at the solitary bag sitting open on the bed. "Need some help with that?"

"No, I've got it. Thanks."

He didn't move away, and the moment turned awkward. Okay, so he'd been nice enough to bring her the coat. That didn't mean she was going to hug him the way she'd hugged Cora. The man might have saved her life, but Hannah didn't need her memory to know he was dangerous. He was far too attractive, and she just happened to be three months pregnant. That meant there was another man in her life. A man with whom she obviously had a serious relationship. A man whose name she couldn't even remember.

John Maitland unsettled her; she couldn't afford to be unsettled. She might have lost her memory, but she hadn't lost her mind.

Rattled by her awareness of him, the stark reality of her situation and an uncomfortable sense of vulnerability, she drew a breath and turned to him, a smile pasted to her face despite the fact that her eyes had warmed with unshed tears. "Cora is worse than an old mother hen. Girl Scout cookies, for goodness' sakes."

The tone of her voice didn't ring true even to Hannah, and she winced with every overly cheerful word. She wasn't sure why she felt the need to prove that none of this had gotten to her. Not the amnesia. Not her injuries, or the mysterious bruises that marred her throat and arms. All she knew was that it was suddenly very important to her for this man to know she was strong and capable and in control.

Without looking at him, she eased the coat from her shoulders and turned away to drape it over the bag. "I appreciate you stopping by, but I have to check out now."

"Hannah…"

"My discharge papers haven't even been signed yet. I've got a million things to—"

"Hannah."

She jolted when a pair of strong hands closed gently around her upper arms. She wasn't sure why, but she didn't want to look at him, didn't want him to see her like this. Not with a bruised face and tears in her eyes and no place in the world to go or call her own. Not with her emotions scraped raw and fear slithering like a reptile inside her. She didn't even know this man, but she couldn't bear the thought of him feeling sorry for her because all she had were the clothes on her back and the promise of a bed at a women's shelter full of strangers.

Slowly he turned her to face him. "What's with the cheerleader act?"

Hannah looked everywhere but into his discerning gaze. "I don't know what you mean."

"I know this isn't easy for you. You don't have to—"

"I'm fine, and for the record you can stop looking at me like I'm going to cry." It was a stupid statement, since the blasted tears had already spilled over and proceeded to run down her cheeks, betraying her bravado and taking the last of her dignity with them. Determined to keep a handle on her emotions, she raised her hand and swiped at the tears with the back of her bandaged hand. The last thing she wanted to do was let her emotions spiral out of control when this man was standing so close. If that happened, she might do something stupid like step into his embrace and let him wrap those strong arms around her one more time.

In a small corner of her mind, she wondered how the father of her unborn child would feel about that.

The thought jolted her, sent her back a step to a safer distance. "Don't you have a rescue or something to go to?"

A thick, black brow arched. "Look, I didn't mean anything by bringing the coat. I just thought—"

"It's not the coat. I appreciate it very much. I just want you to know I've got the situation under control."

"Sure you do."

"I don't need…you know, rescuing or anything."

"I'm not here to rescue you."

"As long as you understand that. I don't want you to get the wrong idea about me."

"Wouldn't dream of it."

"I'm handling this just fine."

"That's obvious." He pulled a handkerchief from his jeans pocket and handed it to her. "Here."

Taking the handkerchief, Hannah scrubbed the tears from her cheeks. Okay, so she was losing it a little. Pregnant women were supposed to be overly emotional, weren't they? She wasn't even sure why the damn tears kept coming. Just that she was frightened and alone and so lost, she felt it all the way down to the pit of her stomach.

Putting his fingertips beneath her chin, he forced her gaze to his. "It's all right to be scared."

Her first impulse was to deny it. She didn't know why, but something inside her equated fear with weakness. A sudden jolt of insight told her that her need to stand on her own two feet, to be strong and in control sprang from something that had happened in the past. Some profound event that had changed her forever and left a permanent mark deep in her psyche.

Easing away from him, she forced a smile and met

his gaze. "I'm not scared," she said. "Just a little…unsettled."

"Unsettled?" He had the gall to look amused. "I'd be pretty damn terrified if I were in your shoes."

Hannah looked down at her ugly shoes, and felt a helpless laugh bubble up. "You're just saying that to make me feel better."

"I never say anything I don't mean, Red."

She didn't doubt it. The man was direct, not to mention intense. At some point, he'd invaded her space again. Her heart was beating way too fast. She needed to swallow, but wasn't sure her throat could manage it, so she didn't. Instead, she gazed into his alpine-blue eyes, starkly aware of his size, the intensity of his gaze, and the clean, masculine scent of his aftershave.

"I have to go arrange for a van," she whispered, stepping back. "Thanks again for the coat."

He shot a glance toward the window. "There's snow moving in. Knowing Angela Pearl, she probably doesn't have tire chains on her van or any other vehicle she owns."

"You know her?"

"I was a paramedic in Denver a couple of years before I started with Rocky Mountain Search and Rescue. Angela and I go way back. You'll like her. She runs a decent shelter." He contemplated her with thoughtful scrutiny. "What do you say we skip the van and I'll drive you?"

John hadn't always been such a sucker. He figured he would probably live to regret offering Hannah a ride. But as he'd stared into the depths of her soft eyes, taking in the mix of uncertainty and courage and another emotion he couldn't quite put his finger on, he knew he wasn't going to walk away—even if his instincts were screaming for him to do just that.

He'd looked the other way too many times in his life

when it came to women in trouble. As a boy, he hadn't been able to do anything about it. As a man, he knew all too well what he was capable of. He wondered how Hannah would react if she knew what had happened the last time he'd decided to get involved.

John knew what he was. Just as he knew why he felt the constant need to atone for it. And whether being a rescuer was his saving grace—or his fatal flaw—he knew himself far too well not to realize he didn't have a choice but to help her.

His mission should have been clear: take her to the shelter and forget about her. But he was quickly realizing that nothing was clear when it came to the feelings this woman evoked. Her plight touched a sore spot on his heart. Her vulnerability made it impossible for him to turn the other cheek. Ever since he'd dropped down out of the chopper he hadn't been able to get her off his mind. Not a good situation for a man who prided himself on his ability to walk away. He told himself once he got her safely to Angela Pearl's shelter, the savvy ex-hooker would make sure whomever had put those bruises on Hannah didn't come back to finish the job. But John knew there were no guarantees. And for the first time in his life, he wasn't so sure walking away was going to be the easy way out.

Logic told him he didn't have to get involved to help her. He could walk away from the situation any time he felt the need. He was in control, after all. John Maitland was always in control. He'd learned the importance of control the day he'd walked away from that Philadelphia tenement thirteen years ago. An education that had cost him a piece of his humanity—and taken a chunk out of his soul that could never be replaced. But he'd walked away wiser nonetheless—particularly when it came to matters of the heart.

The brutal wind slapped at his face as they crossed the hospital parking lot toward his Jeep. Intermittent snow whipped down from a brooding afternoon sky. Beside him, Hannah huddled in her new coat, her hair tangling in the wind like strands of fine Oriental silk. Even from two feet away, he could smell her. A titillating mix of wildflowers infused with the mysterious essence of woman. A scent that had simmered in the backwaters of his brain since the moment he'd clipped his harness to hers and taken her into his arms to save her life. It was a scent that had been with him every waking hour since, haunting his dreams in the dark hours of night, disturbing his intellect by the light of day.

He wasn't exactly sure how it had happened—he sure as hell didn't want to define what "it" was—but with nothing more than a look and a silent communiqué, this woman had somehow broken through a wall he'd spent years fortifying. The realization that he might be vulnerable to her disturbed him more than he wanted to admit. He couldn't help but wonder where this breach of his personal code would lead—or if he'd be sorry for it in the end.

They reached his four-wheel-drive Jeep a moment later. John opened the door for Hannah, making sure—without touching her—that she could make the climb into the cab with her injured hands and feet. After stowing her bag in the rear, he slid behind the wheel and started the engine.

Hannah broke the silence the instant his door was closed. "I appreciate the ride."

"No problem."

"I was wondering…um, why you're doing this for me."

John had spent a good bit of the morning pondering the very same question himself. He couldn't deny that initially his sudden sense of goodwill had been based on nothing more than good old-fashioned attraction. Faded scrubs or not, the woman could definitely turn a man's head—even his. But John could handle his needs. He'd proven it to himself a hundred times over since he'd been in Colorado.

He'd lived by the code of control for a long time, and not even a sexy, vulnerable female in trouble up to her eyebrows was going to make him break it. That she was three months pregnant would undoubtedly help. The last thing he needed in his life was to get tangled up with a pregnant woman who just happened to belong to another man.

So what the hell was he doing driving her to the shelter, for God's sake?

"You mean aside from the fact that I'm a great guy?" he asked after a moment.

She cut him a look. "I mean in light of the fact that I...you know...pointed that gun at you."

"Oh, that."

"I probably would have taken that personally."

He shrugged. "I'll admit that's not the reception I'm used to getting when I pick up a hypothermic patient clinging to the side of a mountain."

"I'm sorry I did that to you. I can't stop thinking about what might have happened—"

"Nothing happened. Don't worry about it."

"I'm worried because I don't know what kind of person I am."

"I consider myself a pretty good judge of character, Red. Unless that amnesia has turned you into a Jekyll and Hyde, you're good as gold."

A smile touched the corners of her mouth, and John's heart stuttered. Man, if she could do that to him with a little half smile, just imagine what would happen if she laughed. Not wanting to ponder the possibility too deeply, he put the Jeep in gear.

"What was I doing with a gun?" she asked. "Why did I point it at you?"

"Maybe you thought I was someone else, and you were trying to protect yourself." John's gaze dropped to her abdomen. "Or your unborn child."

Pressing her hand to her stomach, she shivered.

"Cold?" he asked.

"No, just...worried."

"Who's Richard?"

Her body gave a minute jerk. "I'm not...exactly sure. The name... It's...familiar."

"You called me Richard right after you pulled the gun."

"Maybe that means I know the man who...did this to me."

"It's a scenario we should probably consider."

Leaning forward, she put her face in her hands. "This just keeps getting worse."

John glanced over from his driving, hating that she'd gone pale again. "You need to get the police involved, Hannah."

Taking a deep breath, she relaxed back into the seat and sighed. "I know."

"We can't ignore those bruises."

Worry crept into her gaze like a storm cloud darkening the ground beneath it. He hated to be the one to put it there, but when it came to the kind of trouble he was referring to, he knew firsthand that ignorance was never bliss.

"You need to talk to the police and make sure they have a description of you and know the circumstances of how you were found. If a missing-persons report is out and you fit the description, they'll be able to make the match."

"What if they run my prints and it turns out I'm an escaped convict or something?"

She was serious, he realized, and had to stifle a smile. "Take my word for it, Red, you're not an escaped convict."

"I could have killed you, John."

"You didn't."

"That's not the point."

Even though he was pretty sure she wouldn't have used that gun, the possibilities of why she'd had it in the first place left a rank taste at the back of his throat. "Buzz Malone is an ex-cop. I'll check with him and see if he has any ideas as far as getting you identified. He might be able to cut through some of the red tape and speed up the process."

"I appreciate that." She fiddled with the bandages on her fingers. "I probably have...family looking for me, anyway."

John looked down at her naked ring finger and felt an odd sensation he refused to identify sweep through him. "Probably."

"It's been twenty-four hours. There's probably a missing-persons report out this very minute," she reasserted.

John nodded, realizing belatedly how alone she must feel, and that she was putting up a valiant front. He wondered if she realized her hands were shaking. "I'll call the *Rocky Mountain News.* I know a reporter there. I'll fill him in on your story, and see if I can get him interested. If the newspaper runs an article, someone might recognize you."

"Good idea." She brightened. "Maybe we could even get one of the local TV stations to run my picture."

John risked a look at her. Huddling deeper into her coat, she leaned back in the seat and closed her eyes. He tried not to notice the fullness of her mouth or the way her hair curled wildly around her shoulders. He'd never been drawn by a woman's hair before. He wasn't even unduly attracted to redheads, though now he couldn't imagine why. What was it about her that had him bucking his better judgment every time he looked at her?

He was so caught up in his thoughts, he didn't notice the sport utility vehicle until it was alongside his Jeep. Damn impatient drivers annoyed the hell out of him. He couldn't count the number of accidents caused by Mr. Type-A personality trying to pass a slower-moving Mr. Type-B.

"Come on, Speed Racer," he muttered.

Abruptly the SUV veered toward the Jeep. Adrenaline punched through him when the vehicle crossed the yellow line into his lane. He jerked the wheel to the right, but the SUV kept coming.

"What the *hell?*" He barely had time to shout a warning before the SUV slammed into the side of his Jeep. "Hang on!"

The Jeep fishtailed on impact. John fought the wheel, looked up in time to see the SUV loom large and menacing inches from his window. He hit the brakes only to realize the tires had already relinquished their grip.

The screech of rubber against asphalt filled the air. Hannah's scream rang out over the roar of the engine. Fighting the wheel for control, he steered into the skid. A curse flitted through his brain when the Jeep began a slow, sickening spin. As if in slow motion, he saw the guardrail approach at a stunning speed. As the Jeep careened toward it, he tried not to think about the woman and her unborn child whose lives now rested in his hands—or the two-hundred-foot drop on the other side of the rail.

Chapter 5

John's Jeep impacted solidly with the guardrail. The momentum threw him against his shoulder harness with such force that he nearly lost his grip on the steering wheel. His left temple knocked against the window, the sound of cracking glass sputtering through his brain.

Abruptly everything went deathly still.

Blinking against the stars exploding behind his eyes, he shook his head to clear it, then glanced over at Hannah, concern for her jumping through him. "Are you all right?"

"I'm okay…I think."

He looked toward the road in time to see the taillights of the SUV disappear ahead. "Damn crazy driver."

Shoving her hair out of her face with shaking hands, she raised her gaze to his. "What about you? Are you okay?"

"I'm fine." He wasn't so sure—his head hurt like the dickens—but at the moment he was more concerned about her. Her face was pale in the dim light from the dash. But even with his adrenaline pumping and his temper riding a fast second, he couldn't help but notice how pretty she looked with her eyes wide, her hair tumbling about her face. That was a hell of a thing for him to notice when he should be more concerned by the fact that he'd only managed to get a partial license plate number of the maniac who had nearly sent them to their deaths.

"Stay put." He reached for the door handle. "I'm going to come around to check you out, all right?"

"I'm really okay."

"You're also three months pregnant." Releasing his safety belt, he tried to open his door, only to realize it was stuck. Muttering a curse, he shouldered it and the door opened with a creak. John stepped into the bracing wind only to realize his knees were weak. Damn, that hadn't ever happened before. Bending at the waist, he put his hands on his knees and sucked in a couple of breaths. His heart was still racing, pumping adrenaline to his muscles and anger to his brain.

That crazy son of a bitch had just about killed them.

Dusk had fallen, and it was so quiet he could hear the wind coming through the pines on the north side of the road. There was no sign of the SUV. No traffic for miles. The fact that they were alone on a desolate stretch of highway sent an acute sense of uneasiness creeping over him.

Working a kink out of his neck, he crossed in front of the Jeep, all too aware that Hannah hadn't so much as moved. Dammit, the last thing she needed was any more physical or emotional trauma. Even though they hadn't been moving fast enough to cause serious injury, it didn't take much force to bring on a case of whiplash.

He yanked open the passenger side door to find her leaning against the seat back watching him from dark, cautious eyes. "I told you I'm all right," she said.

"So you said. Turn toward me." Using both hands, he reached out and cupped her face, then slid his hands down her neck, to her shoulders, her arms, briefly touching her hips and ending on her thighs.

Hannah shivered.

"Cold?"

"Uh, no."

"Any pain? Any dizziness? Nausea? Cramping?"

"I'm terrific, John, just a little…shaken up."

"That's what all my patients say."

She rolled her eyes. "I'm not your patient any longer."

"I'm a medic, Red. Humor me, okay?" He grinned to put her at ease, but it felt plastic on his face. He was still shaking inside. Maybe *he* was the one who needed to relax. His patient seemed to be taking all this in stride. "Can you move your arms and legs?"

She wiggled her fingers, then did a little tap dance against the floorboard with her feet. "All I need is a little music."

"Stop being a smart-aleck and slide out for me, okay?"

She smiled. "We weren't going that fast."

"Fast enough. Come on. Up and at 'em."

She slid out of the Jeep. Before he could stop her, she glanced over the guardrail into the ravine below. "Oh, my God."

The last vestiges of color leached from her cheeks so fast, for a moment, John thought she was going to pass out. Quickly he leaned her against the Jeep. "That's what I thought you'd say."

"Good Lord, if you hadn't gotten the Jeep stopped, we would have…we could have—"

"Shhh. Don't go there." John was a toucher. He touched people on daily basis. He slapped his friends on the back. Held his patients' hands to ease their fears. He squeezed worried family members' shoulders to comfort. The urge to touch Hannah now was unusually strong. Normally he wouldn't have thought twice about reaching out to comfort her, but some inner warning told him to use caution.

Letting out a pent-up sigh, he looked up and down the

highway, still trying to convince himself this hadn't been as premeditated as it seemed. "Dammit, that was close."

"Too close."

He looked at her and knew she was thinking the same thing he was. The driver had purposefully tried to run them off the road at a place in the highway where death would have been imminent.

"Do you think he's gone?" she asked.

John looked over his shoulder, felt the hairs at his nape prickle. "Yeah. Not that I was hoping he would stop and render aid." Reaching up, he touched the sore spot at his temple, and felt a lump the size of a hen's egg. Wonderful. He looked at his fingers, relieved when they came away dry.

"You're the one who's hurt," she said.

He knew better than to let her concern warm him, but it did. "Careful, Red. I like it when women worry about me."

"I'll bet." She looked as if she might touch him, but stuck her hands in her pockets instead. "That's quite a bump."

"I've got a really hard head."

She didn't quite smile, but he saw the play of amusement behind her eyes and felt another wave of warmth settle in his chest. "You're probably going to think I'm being paranoid," she said, "but the SUV...I mean, it seemed...deliberate."

"He could have been a drunk driver." He said the words, but knew neither of them were buying it.

A gust of wind whispered through the treetops. Standing next to him, unprotected from the cold and wind, Hannah's teeth began to chatter.

"Get in the Jeep." Leaning forward, John plucked his cell phone from the floor where it had slid off the seat, then gave her plenty of room to climb back into the vehicle. "Your teeth are chattering. You shouldn't be out in this cold."

"Says the man with a bump the size of a Volkswagen on his temple."

"I'm not the one recovering from hypothermia." John punched numbers into the phone. "Get inside. I'm going to call the Lake County Sheriff's Department." He cursed when a recording told him the party he'd called was out of range. "Damn."

"What's wrong?" she asked.

"I'm not getting through. It happens along this stretch of highway. The mountains block the signal."

"What are we going to do?"

"RMSAR Headquarters is only a couple of miles from here. If I can get the Jeep started, we'll call from there."

John slammed the passenger side door. As much as he disliked the thought of taking Hannah to headquarters where he would undoubtedly face questions about his association with her, he figured this was probably a good time to let Buzz Malone in on what had just happened because he was pretty sure someone had tried to kill them.

Despite the blast of hot air from the Jeep's heater, Hannah was still shivering when they reached Rocky Mountain Search and Rescue Headquarters a few minutes later. Only, she wasn't sure if the shakes were from the cold—or because John hadn't taken his eyes off the rearview mirror since the maniac in the SUV had nearly driven them off the road.

She wanted to think the incident had been a random act of road rage or even a drunk driver. But no matter how hard she tried to convince herself of that, Hannah couldn't shake the feeling that the incident had been deliberate. The only question that remained was why. Why had someone tried to run John off the road? Or maybe John wasn't their target at all. Maybe it was *her* they'd tried to send over the side of the cliff.

He turned the Jeep into a narrow gravel drive and parked next to a pickup truck with giant tires and a Rocky Mountain Search and Rescue emblem emblazoned on the door in black-and-gold lettering. "We're in luck," he said. "Buzz is still here."

"Is he the one who used to be a police officer?" she asked.

"He got shot a couple of years back and had to retire, but he still keeps in touch with the guys on the force. We'll file a report with the Lake County sheriff about the SUV driver. Then Buzz might be able to come up with some ideas as far as getting you identified." He shot her a steady gaze. "Ready?"

Nodding, she opened the door and got out of the Jeep. The night met her with icy fingers and wind that cut like icicles. Full darkness had fallen, but a sodium vapor street lamp illuminated a rustic building and several small outbuildings. A snowplow sat like a sleeping dinosaur to her left. Twenty yards away, tucked into the interior of a lighted hangar, a helicopter shone like a new car fresh off the showroom floor.

"So this is Rocky Mountain Search and Rescue," she said, crossing in front of the Jeep.

"We have one full-time pilot, four medics and half a dozen volunteers. Mostly police officers and firefighters and a few guys who just like to help out and get in on the action. We also have an equine unit headed up by Jake Madigan. Then there's that pretty Bell 412 I saw you admiring." He grinned at her. "She's nice looking, isn't she?"

She wished he wouldn't smile at her like that. Every time he did, she felt a funny flutter in the pit of her stomach she knew didn't have anything to do with her pregnancy.

''We can be geared up and in the chopper in less than four minutes.'' He reached the door first, swung it open and stepped back for her to enter. ''The rest of the team are...rowdy, but harmless, so don't let it get to you.''

''Considering they saved my life, I'll cut them some slack.''

''They're good guys, just a little...''

''Boisterous?''

''I was going to say obnoxious.''

''I know how to handle myself.''

''I don't doubt it.'' He grinned. ''But they love a challenge.''

''So do I.''

Squaring her shoulders she passed through the door. The first thing she noticed was the music. Rock and roll colored the air with a piercing serenade of steel guitar and a lilting male voice. The smell of stale coffee and burning pine mingled with the subtler scents of aftershave and man. Ahead and to her left, a sliding window opened and a young man not long out of college stuck his head out and grinned at John. ''I thought this was your day off, Maitland. What's the matter, can't you find anything better to do with your private—?'' He fell silent the moment he spotted Hannah. ''Oh, uh, didn't see you there.'' His eyes flicked from her to John then back to her. ''Hi, I'm Aaron.'' He stuck his hand through the window. ''But everyone calls me Dispatch.''

''Glad to meet you, Dispatch.'' She offered her bandaged hand, and he shook it thoroughly. ''I'm Hannah.''

His eyes narrowed. ''Aren't you the...''

''Yes, I'm the...'' Uncertain how to finish the sentence, she fumbled for the word.

''The Jane Doe we scooped up on Elk Ridge,'' John finished.

''I remember the red hair.'' Aaron's smile widened.

"Well, I'm damn glad to meet you, Hannah. I like that name a lot better than Jane Doe."

She laughed. "Me, too."

"How are you feeling?"

She liked this young man, she decided, and returned his smile. "I'm feeling really good." *I just don't have the slightest idea who I am.* "Thanks."

"Where's Buzz?" John asked.

Releasing her hand, Aaron motioned down the hall toward the back. "He's in the office ranting about the budget. What's up?"

"Damn, I forgot about the budget." John scrubbed a hand over his jaw. "Some maniac ran us off the road a few minutes ago. I couldn't raise Lake County on my cell, so I thought I'd file a report from here."

Movement at the end of the hall drew Hannah's attention. She looked up to see a man with whisky brown eyes, hair the color of midnight and an expression designed by the devil himself standing at the end of the hall looking from John to her as if they'd just beamed down from another planet. "Damn, Maitland, you're keeping better company these days."

John started toward the other man. "Flyboy. How's tricks?"

"They just got a hell of a lot better." The other man's gaze never left Hannah, curiosity and mischief glinting in his expression. "Did I hear you mention Lake County?" he asked John.

"I need to file a report."

"They just got slammed with a multiple injury on Highway 285," the other man said.

John stopped. Hannah actually felt the tension snap through the air. "Did we get the call out?" he asked.

The other man looked at John for the first time. "Boulder took it. We're on standby." His gaze swept back to Hannah, and his mouth curved into a smile that was much

A Hero To Hold

too sensuous for a male. "Aren't you going to introduce us, Maitland?"

"Nope. I need to see Malone."

"He's in the back, making out with the budget." Never taking his eyes from Hannah, the man sauntered past John. "Maitland, you've got the manners of a damn armadillo." Grinning, he extended his hand to Hannah. "I'm Tony Colorosa."

She remembered his face from the hazy minutes she'd been onboard the helicopter. Smiling, she stepped forward with her hand out. "I'm Hannah. Pleased to meet you."

"The pleasure's all mine."

"You're the helicopter pilot."

"And a damn good one."

"I wanted to thank you for…getting me off the mountain the other day."

"Hey, no problem."

An unexpected jab of emotion tightened her throat. Great, here she was surrounded by a kiloton of testosterone and about to break down and cry. Talk about a fast way to clear a room.

"No, I mean it," she said. "You guys saved my life. I won't forget that."

Surprise rippled through her when Tony raised her hand and brushed a kiss across her bandaged knuckles. Even without her memory to draw upon, Hannah knew when she was being charmed. This man put out the charm the way the sun put out light—by the megawatt. Feeling her cheeks warm, she eased her hand from his.

"Who has the manners of an armadillo?" A third man with green eyes and a small goatee shuffled into the hall and stopped cold on spotting Hannah, his gaze doing a quick sweep of her.

John frowned. "This is Pete Scully, our junior medic."

The young man with the goatee grinned. "Don't believe

anything John told you about me because it's probably not true.''

Hannah smiled. ''Nice to meet you.''

Standing next to Scully, an even taller man with a lean build and gunmetal eyes stepped forward to have a look at her. He wore a calf-length duster, well-worn cowboy boots and a belt buckle as big as his palm. She guessed him to be in his mid-thirties, but he had a weathered look about him that told her he spent a good bit of time outdoors.

''Jake Madigan is a deputy sheriff down in Chaffee County.'' John continued the introductions. ''He's a volunteer with RMSAR and heads up the equine division. He's the one who found our lost Boy Scout last year.''

''Ma'am.'' Jake removed his black Stetson.

''Can we help you with something?'' Scully asked.

Feeling the need to explain her presence to the curious men, Hannah stepped closer to Scully and Jake only to feel John's hand encircle her arm. ''She's with me, Scully,'' John said. ''We're here to see Buzz.''

Her heart fluttered against her ribs when he eased her closer to him. She told herself it wasn't a possessive move. John hadn't laid claim to her in any way. He hadn't given her any reason to believe he was interested in anything other than getting her to the women's shelter and asking his ex-cop friend to give her a hand with whatever the local law enforcement might be able to do as far as helping her find her identity.

So why was her pulse jumping around like a toad on a hot plate?

Not wanting to deal with the implications of that line of thinking, Hannah smiled at John's teammates, trying in vain to ignore the heat where his fingers burned through her coat.

Scully winked at her, then his face creased into a grin.

"Well, damn, Maitland, you must be having a good day off."

"I am." Maintaining a gentle grip on her arm, John started down the hall. "If we get the call out, I'm in."

Hannah looked over her shoulder toward the men as John guided her down the hall. The young man called Dispatch was leaning out of the window, staring after them with unconcealed curiosity. Jake Madigan had put his hat back on, shadowing his eyes, but she could feel his gaze on her. Tony Colorosa stood in the center of the hall, grinning like a naughty kid. Scully had made eye contact with John and was moving his eyebrows up and down like Groucho Marx.

"Idiots," John muttered.

"Men," Hannah said quietly.

He looked over at her, and they grinned at each other. "Yeah," he agreed.

At the end of the hall, John guided her to a small kitchen where the smell of coffee was strong. Beyond, Hannah could see yellow light pouring out of an open office door. John went directly to the coffeemaker, pulled out a foam cup and poured from a green carafe. "It's decaf. Tastes like burned rubber, but it's hot." When she hesitated, he added, "You're shivering. It'll warm you up some."

Hannah wasn't sure if she was shivering because of the cold outside or the remnants of fear from the SUV incident, but she took the cup anyway. "Thanks."

"Coat warm enough?"

"Plenty."

"Considering you were hypothermic just over twenty-four hours ago, you don't want to get chilled." One side of his mouth quirked. "Medic's orders."

Staring into the endless blue of his gaze, she felt anything but chilled. In fact, she was starting to feel downright warm, especially when he looked at her like that. The man didn't have a problem with eye contact, that was for sure.

Unsettled by the warmth radiating through her, Hannah let her gaze slip to his mouth. Oh, my. She'd dreamed about that mouth, she realized, had traced every chiseled contour with her fingertips, remembered the feel of his breath against her cheek, stirring her blood. He was standing less than a foot away, so close she could smell his aftershave, feel the heat of his gaze. He shouldn't be looking at her mouth like that. She shouldn't be allowing it, either. But the pull was too strong to resist. The moment stretched, the promise of something sweet yet elusive filling the small space between them....

"I should warn you that RMSAR is not responsible for injuries sustained while drinking that stuff loosely referred to as coffee."

Hannah started so abruptly at the sound of the gruff, male voice that she spilled her coffee. She turned to see an older man watching them from the doorway of the kitchen. Hardened eyes the color of a winter sky swept from John to Hannah and back to John.

"What brings you to headquarters on your day off, Maitland?"

"We ran into a problem out on the highway and need to contact Lake County," John said.

"Is that how you got that hen's egg on your head?"

"Yeah, well..." John touched the bump in question. "We needed some advice, anyway, and decided to stop by."

The other man nodded, his gaze moving to Hannah. "I'm Buzz Malone."

Hannah told herself she and John hadn't been doing anything improper but that didn't keep the blush from warming her cheeks. Struggling to maintain her composure, she stepped forward and extended her hand. "I'm Hannah."

If he wondered why she didn't offer her last name, he didn't show it. "How are you feeling?" His grip was firm, his eye contact unwavering and a little too intense for comfort.

"Better." She looked down at her bandaged fingers, not sure how to explain the amnesia without sounding like a loon. "Just a little frostbite and a…concussion."

"I'm glad to hear it. It could have been a lot worse." Buzz motioned toward his office. "Come in and have a seat."

Hannah wasn't sure why, but the instant she walked into the man's office, a vague sensation of unease moved over her, like the shadow of a thunderhead promising a violent storm. She knew it was crazy to feel…threatened when neither man posed any danger. But no matter how hard she tried, she couldn't shake it. Attributing the response to the SUV incident, she settled into one of the chairs in front of the desk.

"Why do you need to file a report with Lake County?" Buzz asked John after they were all seated.

John took off his parka and draped it over the back of his chair. Hannah tried not to notice his wide chest or the way those snug-fitting jeans hugged his hips. But, mercy, the man was a heartbreaker.

Her response elicited a quick jab of guilt. Here she was pregnant and more than likely involved with another man—maybe even married—and she was taking note of attributes she had absolutely no business noticing.

"We got run off the road by some maniac in an SUV on the way from the hospital to the Denver shelter," John said.

Snatching up the phone, the older man punched a number on the speed dial pad and handed it to John. "Drunk driver?"

"Maybe." John leaned forward to take the phone. "But I don't think so. It seemed deliberate."

"Did you get a plate number?"

"Colorado plates." John set the phone to his ear. "The first three letters are HBS."

Hannah hadn't even thought about getting the plate number. She'd been too busy being scared out of her wits.

Buzz wrote the letters down. "Well, that narrows it down to a few thousand," he said dryly. "What about the make—"

Raising his hand for silence, John spoke into the phone, relaying the incident and describing the vehicle right down to the fancy wheels. All the while Buzz scratched notes on his legal pad.

Hannah looked around the small office as John filed the report, trying without success to quell the uneasiness that had been pressing down on her since she'd entered the room. What was making her so uneasy? Not John. As much as she didn't want to admit it, he'd become a source of comfort in the last hours. She didn't think Buzz Malone was the source of her uneasiness, either. He hadn't given her any reason to mistrust him. Still, she couldn't deny that her heart rate was up. Resisting the urge to wipe her wet palms on her scrub pants, she studied the plaques and framed certificates on the wall behind the desk. A photograph of a young boy in a cowboy hat warmed her. A framed commendation certificate from the Denver Police Department told her Buzz had been successful during his tenure in law enforcement. On the bookcase near the window, a photo of several uniformed police officers drew her gaze.

Out of nowhere, a burst of memory exploded in her mind's eye with the violence of a grenade. Stark black-and-white images. A man in a blue uniform. Sandy hair and hazel eyes. A familiar smile. Before she could make sense of it, another image burst forth. The same man— only, he wasn't smiling now. Fear spiked through her. Fear that was familiar and bitter and ugly. He was angry. Threatening her. Touching her. Hurting her. A tangle of emotions jumbled in her mind. Emotions that ran the gamut from love to hate and every gray area in between. She remembered pain, both physical and emotional and so deep, she felt it all the way to her soul.

The images hit her like a series of blows. Her heart beat out of control beneath her breast. Perspiration spread like ice down her back. Vaguely she heard John speaking—his voice soothing her, bringing her back. His hand rested on her arm, comforting her.

"Hannah?" He patted her arm. "Hey, are you all right?"

She tore her gaze from the photograph. As abruptly as they'd come to her, the images stopped. Gasping for air, choking back tears, she focused on the strong face before her and realized John was kneeling in front of her, his every feature etched with concern. "What is it?" he asked. "What's wrong?"

"I—I'm okay," she whispered. "I just…"

Buzz had risen and stood behind his desk staring at her with an odd mix of concern and suspicion in his eyes.

"My God, you're shaking," John said. "Are you in pain?"

Embarrassment washed over her, drowning the remnants of fear and the lingering sense of danger that had threatened to consume her seconds earlier. "I'm…all right."

"Are you dizzy?" he pressed. "Headache?"

"No. Nothing like that. I just…felt really strange for a second." She looked down, not sure how to explain, only to realize she'd dropped her coffee at some point and the cup now lay at her feet in a puddle. "I'm sorry about the coffee—"

"Don't worry, the floor's coffeeproof." Catching her gaze, John flashed her an uneasy grin. "Even Buzz's coffee."

The older man came around the desk. "Head injury?"

"Concussion. CT was fine. No bleeding."

"She's pale." Buzz started toward the door. "I'll get some water."

Raising her fingers to her forehead, Hannah rubbed the sore spot between her eyes where a headache had broken through. "I didn't mean to make a scene."

"You didn't. You just sort of zoned out for a second. I thought you were going to pass out." Putting his finger under her chin, he forced her gaze to his. "What happened?"

What *had* happened? One minute she'd been taking in the aspects of Buzz's office, the next, her mind had taken her to a place that had left her trembling with fear. A terrible place she prayed wasn't the life she couldn't remember. "I think I had some sort of…flashback."

Buzz came through the door, a paper cup in hand, his eyes sharp on Hannah. "Drink this," he said, handing her the cup.

Needing to do something with her hands to keep them from shaking, Hannah reached for the cup and drank deeply, using that moment to gather her thoughts—and her composure.

"I heard you use the word *flashback*," Buzz said. "What do you mean by that?"

Hannah looked up to find the older man standing behind his desk, his hands on his hips, waiting for an explanation she had no desire to give. "We haven't had a chance to explain yet, but one of the reasons we're here is because I'm suffering from what appears to be…some form of…amnesia."

"Amnesia?" Thinly concealed skepticism laced the older man's voice. "As in memory loss?" His gaze swept to John. "Are you serious?"

His tone elicited a sharp look from the younger man. "She suffered a concussion, Buzz, and has some memory loss." Scrubbing a hand over his jaw, he looked over at Hannah. "She doesn't even remember her name."

Something inside Hannah winced when she saw doubt on the other man's face. She wasn't sure why, but his opinion was important to her. Maybe because she knew it was important to John.

"Let me get this straight." Buzz's gaze cut from Hannah to John, then back to Hannah. "You woke up in the hospital without your memory, and you don't even remember your own name?"

Steeling herself against the disbelief in his voice, she jerked her head once.

"What about where you work? Or where you live?"

"I know it sounds...unlikely," she said, hating the uncertainty in her own voice, "but it's true. And it's been very frightening."

Incredulity shone clearly on Buzz's face. He didn't say the words, but Hannah didn't need to hear them to know he didn't believe her. She told herself she should have expected skepticism. Amnesia was as far out as it got when it came to medical conditions. If she wasn't experiencing it firsthand, she, too, might have been a skeptic. Even so, it hurt that Buzz doubted her.

"John told me you used to be a police officer," she began. "We thought you might be able to help me find my identity through fingerprinting or know of some other avenue we could pursue. Maybe help us with missing persons reports."

"Or warrants," Buzz said.

John's gaze narrowed on his team leader. "That's enough."

The other man's gaze didn't falter from hers, and he didn't bother to look chagrined. "I didn't appreciate having a gun pointed at one of my medics," he said. "You're lucky you're not in a jail cell right now."

Hannah felt herself recoil, starkly aware of her heart beating wildly in her chest. She wished she could deny having that gun, but she couldn't because she remembered the deadly weight of it in her hand, her resolve to use it pounding at the back of her brain. ''I'm sorry...I wouldn't have...''

''Shot the man who was trying to save your life?'' Buzz snapped.

''I don't even know why I had it or where it came from.''

''That's convenient.''

''I'm not a criminal,'' she said.

''I thought you didn't remember *who* you are or aren't,'' Buzz returned evenly.

Cursing under his breath, John shot him a dark look. ''Dammit, Buzz, that's enough.''

The older man arched a brow. ''I can't believe you're buying this.''

''I believe her.'' John's gaze didn't falter.

''Oh, for crying out loud!''

''She doesn't need this right now, Buzz—''

''I can speak for myself,'' Hannah cut in.

Both men ignored her. ''When do you suggest we ask the hard questions, John?''

''We're working on that.''

''That must have been what you were doing when I walked into the kitchen.''

John raked a hand over his five o'clock shadow. ''She's pregnant.''

The older man lowered his head and pinched the bridge of his nose, then looked at John over his knuckles. ''I'd like a word with you.'' Lowering his hand, he glanced at Hannah. ''Alone.''

Hurt that he hadn't given her the benefit of a doubt, angry that she couldn't disprove his suspicions, Hannah rose abruptly. She told herself it didn't matter what Buzz Malone thought of her. It didn't matter what John thought of her, either. But she knew she was only lying to herself.

Squaring her shoulders, she raised her chin and looked Buzz in the eye. ''You're wrong about me.''

''I hope so,'' he said quietly.

Without waiting for a reply, she turned on her heel and left the room.

Chapter 6

"Well, that was subtle as hell," John said angrily.

"About as subtle as someone shoving a gun in your face." Leaning back in his chair, Buzz scowled at him. "You've got too good a head on your shoulders to be spending time with a woman who pulled a gun on you."

"Maybe she thought she didn't have a choice."

"Maybe she sees the way you look at her and knows a sucker when she sees one."

Curbing the nasty retort on his tongue, John rose and stalked across the room, trying in vain to reel in his temper. He'd known bringing Hannah here wasn't the best idea he'd ever had. An ex-cop, Buzz was suspicious by nature and a stickler for procedure. He also had strict rules about fraternization and appearances when it came to the team. They hadn't exactly followed the rules when it came to Hannah's rescue. If it hadn't been for her injuries—and the bruises—he knew Buzz would have turned her over to the police.

John blew out a sigh of frustration and faced Buzz. "I

told you, she was confused and hallucinating. She thought I was someone else."

"Oh, so since she was hallucinating, it's okay for her to stick a gun in your face—"

"Dammit, you saw those bruises on her. Maybe she was protecting herself."

"And maybe you're a hell of a lot more involved than you should be. For God's sake, John, I thought you of all people had better judgment than to fall for this kind of cockamamie story."

"My judgment is just fine—"

"Except when it comes to women. I don't need to remind you that you've had your fair share of problems."

The words rankled him, but John didn't bother to deny it. He *was* more involved than he should be. And he'd definitely had more than his fair share of problems with women. Buzz knew about Rhonda. It had been five years ago, but John still carried the scars. Not the physical variety, but the kind that marked a man's soul for the rest of his life.

Buzz also knew about what had happened back in Philly. What he didn't know was that John had made not getting involved his life ambition. John might like the way Hannah looked. He might like her smile and her scent and the way all that red hair tumbled over her shoulders. But he was still in control of the situation. When the time came, he'd have no qualms about walking away. As much the other man's words ticked him off, he just didn't see fit to explain.

"I should have turned her over to Lake County the second you told me about the gun," Buzz growled.

"We both know why you didn't."

The older man scowled.

"You saw those bruises, Buzz. You saw what someone did to her. Dammit, she's three months pregnant. What kind of monster does that to a pregnant woman, for God's sake?''

"Bruises don't warrant taking up arms even if she is pregnant. Dammit, this is not our problem. *She's* not our problem. I wish like hell I'd put that in my report and let the sheriff's department handle it.'' He shot John a sage look. "Especially now that I see you're getting cozy with her.''

John stared at his team leader and felt a sinking sensation in the pit of his stomach. "I'm not getting cozy with her.''

"Sure looked that way when I walked into the kitchen and saw you making cow eyes at each other. You don't want to get in the middle of this, John.''

"I'm not involved.''

"As far as you know, she's got a husband—''

"She's not wearing a ring—''

"Like that makes a damn bit of difference.''

"It would to her.''

Buzz's brows shot up. He laughed but there was no humor in it. "Oh, holy hell.''

"I'm not involved with her, dammit.'' John rubbed the back of his neck. "She's in trouble, Buzz. She doesn't have anywhere to go. No one to help her. She doesn't even remember her own name.''

"That woman is trouble, John. I have radar when it comes to women and trouble, and believe me, she has it written all over her.''

"Look, Buzz, I don't mean to make this personal, but just because Kelly burned you—''

"This isn't about Kelly,'' he growled. "It's about a vulnerable woman with a pretty face and an unlikely as hell story.'' His jaw flexed. "Is she staying with you?''

John's temper unfurled. "Oh, for crying out loud!''

Unfazed by the younger man's wrath, Buzz frowned and waited for an answer.

"I'm taking her to a shelter in Denver. Not that it's any of your damn business."

"What happened five years ago makes it my business."

John tried not to wince, but he did. And he knew Buzz saw it. "Regret your decision?"

"Hell, no I don't. I just want to make sure you remember how expensive mistakes can be."

Turning away, John shoved his hands into his pockets. No matter how hard he tried, he would never forget. Those events had left a permanent mark on his life, a wound on his heart that would never fully heal.

"Do yourself a favor and take her to the shelter, then wash your hands of it. You've done your part. I'll call the police department and have someone standing by to take her prints and run them through the database. I'll give Missing Persons a call."

"That's all I'm asking."

"You sure about that?" Buzz asked pointedly.

John glared at him.

"If the media gets a hold of this story, I don't want RMSAR involved. They'll turn it into a circus."

John's temper spiked another notch. "Are you finished?"

"Look, John, I don't know what's going on between you two—"

"Nothing's going on."

"She might have the face of an angel, but you don't know who you're dealing with. She could have killed you. You don't know if she's stable. Or if she's got a record. Or if she's lying about the amnesia."

"I'm a big boy, Buzz."

"Yeah, and hopefully Bruno, her husband, isn't the jealous type."

The thought annoyed the hell out of him, but John refused to let Buzz see it. He didn't have a reason to be annoyed, after all, since he had no intention of getting involved with her. "Yeah, well, maybe he's the one who put those bruises on her."

Buzz stared hard at him across the desk. "Do us both a favor and stay away from her, at least until I can find out who she is. Can you do that for me?"

John didn't like being told what to do. He could handle Hannah and whatever it was he felt for her. He had the situation under control. Damn Buzz for doubting him. Grinding his teeth in anger, he turned, grabbed his parka from the chair and strode to the door. "Let me know if you hear anything on that SUV."

Buzz's voice stopped him. "I could have traced that gun, you know. It's pretty convenient that she dropped it."

He turned, gazed levelly at the other man. "Maybe I'll rappel down and get it just to prove you wrong."

"Watch your back."

"I always do," he said, and walked out.

"I guess it's safe to say Mr. Malone doesn't trust me."

"Buzz doesn't trust anyone."

"He doesn't believe me about the amnesia, either, does he?"

John stopped the Jeep at a traffic light, then turned left toward the shelter. "Buzz is an ex-cop. Law enforcement has warped his mind."

A humorless laugh squeezed from Hannah's throat. "To be perfectly honest, I can't blame him," she said. "This amnesia thing is pretty…wild."

He didn't like the hopelessness in her voice. He wished he could dispute her words, but he couldn't and that rankled him, too. Damn Buzz and his uncompromising attitude.

"He thinks I'm some kind of criminal," she said.

"He probably frisks his own mother before Sunday dinner, for crying out loud."

Sighing, she shot him a troubled look. "He shouldn't have doubted you."

John didn't have a reply for that one. Maybe because he wasn't all that sure he agreed with her. Hannah didn't know about Philly; she didn't know about Rhonda. Buzz knew about both fiascos and had taken him on anyway.

He pulled curbside in front of the shelter and put the Jeep in park. "Buzz's wife, Kelly, divorced him a few months back. He won't talk about it, but I think it hurt him a lot. He's pretty down on…you know, women."

"Oh." That bit of information seemed to hold water with her. "Do you think he'll help me?"

"He's going to set up fingerprinting and expedite running them through the national database. He's also going to check with Missing Persons."

"I guess I should start hoping I don't have warrants out for my arrest."

"That's not funny, Red."

"Who's joking? As far as I know, I could be a…a serial killer."

If the situation hadn't been so serious, he might have laughed. "I consider myself a pretty good judge of character. Believe me, you're no serial killer."

"That coming from a man I nearly shot."

"A man who knows sometimes things aren't always as they appear."

She seemed to consider his words for a moment, then smiled at him from beneath her lashes. "Personal experience?"

"Skeletons in my closet. Lots of them."

"Oh."

He looked over at her and grinned. "Just kidding. I only have a few."

Her smile dazzled him. He stared at her, suddenly acutely aware of her proximity, the tangle of hair, the sweetness of her scent, the power of her presence. Shaken by the rush of feelings he had absolutely no desire to explore, he put his hands on the steering wheel and looked at the old house beyond the window.

He knew making eye contact with her now would be a mistake, but he did it anyway, and he felt the impact of her gaze all the way down to his bones. A sweet, sensuous ache that lodged just behind his breastbone and left him feeling pleasantly buzzed and more unsettled than he'd felt in a long, long time.

She stared back at him, surprise reflecting in her eyes. ''I've got to go.''

''I know.'' He'd told himself it wasn't going to be difficult leaving her at the shelter. She would be safe here. She'd be close to the hospital where Dr. Morgan had arranged for her to speak with the psychiatrist. She would be within walking distance of the police department where Buzz would arrange for her to be fingerprinted and check in with Missing Persons.

John's responsibility for her had ended. A clean break, just like he'd wanted. He should have been relieved, but the tightness he felt in his chest wasn't relief. He told himself this was the right thing to do. That it was only natural for him to walk away like he'd done a dozen other times from a dozen other women in the last five years. Women he could have loved, but didn't.

He told himself Hannah wasn't any different. He didn't have feelings for her. Well, aside from a healthy dose of lust that seemed to tie him up in knots every time he looked at her. But John could handle his lust, just as he could handle that hollow feeling in the pit of his stomach as he shut down the engine and looked across the snow-covered lawn toward the rambling old Victorian known as Angela Pearl's Shelter for Battered Women.

What he couldn't handle was the forlorn look in her eyes every time she forced that smile they both knew wasn't real. Dammit, she was afraid and alone and trying like hell to be tough about this. It would have been easier for him if she'd cried. He admired courage, knew what it took to smile when the fear was clamping down like a steel trap.

"Well, I guess this is it." Holding on to her smile, she stuck out her hand. "Thanks for everything."

John stared dumbly at her hand a moment before taking it. Without looking at him, she pumped it a couple of times, then released him. "Take care of yourself, will you, John?"

"You do the same." So, if this was the right thing to do, why did he feel like such a jerk? "I'll get your bag."

In an instant, she had the door open and had stepped out into the cold. "No, I'll get it."

Giving himself a firm shake, John opened his door and stepped into the brutal wind. Thankful for the distraction the cold offered, he walked around to the rear of the Jeep and opened the door. Hannah stood next to him with her arms wrapped around herself, shivering.

Tugging the single canvas bag from the rear compartment, he put it over his shoulder. "I'll carry it in for you."

"No. I've got it."

"Your hands—"

"I need to do this on my own, John. I don't want you to feel…you know, responsible for me. I may be a little down on my luck at the moment, but I'm capable of handling this."

"Look, Red, it's not like I expect you to be indebted to me for the rest of your life just because I was doing my job. That went out about the same time mummification did."

She didn't relent.

Clenching his jaw, he handed her the bag, watched her loop the strap over her shoulder. He wanted to carry it for her, dammit, but reminded himself this was not his concern. He was outta there. Back to his cabin. Alone. Where he was in control and didn't have to worry about feeling something that would disrupt the balance he'd struggled so hard to achieve for so many years.

Reaching into his pocket, he pulled out one of his cards. "Take this."

When she only shook her head, he took her hand in his and pressed the card to her bandaged palm. "If you have any problems in the coming days, call me. Anytime. Day or night. I'll come no matter what. You got that, Red?"

He wasn't sure why, but she looked stunned, like the young female cougar he'd seen up on Elk Ridge last winter, all restless and frightened and a tad too curious for her own good. John's heart beat a hard staccato against his ribs as he absorbed the impact of her. The simple beauty of her face. The vulnerability etched into her features. The layers of mystery he longed to peel away. All of it veiled by a thin veneer of bravado that moved him more than anything else could have.

"Th-thank you for…everything you've done. I mean that. You saved my life. You bought me the coat." Her hand was small and soft and warm within his. She tried to tug her hand away, but he didn't release her. The fact that he didn't want to unsettled him. He knew better than to indulge in a moment like this. She was vulnerable—not to mention pregnant with another man's child and more than likely blissfully wed. But her scent was doing funny things to his common sense, and his body had taken note. Blood pooled in places he didn't want to acknowledge. If he wasn't careful, he was going to do something really stupid like kiss her.

The thought sent a wave of heat slicing right through his middle.

The wind in her hair made her look wild and inviting. He glanced down at her mouth and wondered if she would taste as sweet as she smelled. If her eyes would glaze with pleasure or if an impulsive kiss would panic her and make her pull away.

His brain told him to release her. He was John Maitland the Untouchable, after all. The one who never got involved. The man who didn't need anyone. The man who was better at being alone than he was at being with a woman.

His body wasn't listening to the rhetoric.

Throwing logic to the wind, he put his hands on her shoulders and gently backed her against the Jeep.

"Wh-what are you doing?" she whispered.

"I'm going to kiss you goodbye, if that's all right."

"Well, um…I…" She might not be able to get the words out, but he saw the answer clearly in her eyes. That was all he needed.

He eased the canvas bag from her shoulder and let it drop to the snow. Her eyes widened when he cupped her face with his hands. A small sound escaped her as he lowered his mouth to hers. And with the first sweet brush of her lips against his, John felt the thin ice upon which he'd been treading shatter beneath his feet.

Hannah didn't need her memory to know the man knew how to kiss. She would even go so far as to call him an expert. The instant his mouth touched hers, every pleasure center in her body jolted as if it had been hit with a thousand volts of electricity. Her brain shorted out, and she promptly forgot all the reasons she shouldn't be letting him kiss her, including the fact that she was pregnant with another man's child and more than likely involved in a serious relationship.

But his breath was incredibly warm and sweet against her cheek. The scent of his aftershave curled around her brain like drugging smoke. His clever mouth coaxed hers into compliance with gentle efficiency. She didn't have a choice but to open to him. When she did, the ground beneath her feet simply crumbled.

With a low growl, John took her acquiescence to heart

and moved against her. The hardness of his body shocked her almost as much as the pleasure it evoked. The ensuing rush of heat made her feel feverish and dizzy and more than a little out of control. Need coiled and sprang free inside her. His hands skimmed through her hair, then roamed over her shoulders and back. When they stopped at the small of her back and pulled her closer, her body went liquid, and she knew the battle was lost.

John's breath quickened. He deepened the kiss, but Hannah was too involved to think about caution. Instead, she marveled at the silky feel of his mouth, the taste of mint spiked with a hint of male lust. The combination thrilled her, shocked her, pleasured her until she was breathless and shaking and hungry for more.

His hands grew restless, skimming over the curve of her backside, brushing her breasts through the coat. Then he was touching her face, her throat, tangling his fingers in her hair. Angling her head for better access to her mouth, he plundered. When her legs went weak, she wrapped her arms around his neck and held on for dear life.

Thoughts tumbled drunkenly through her mind. The shelter, her memory loss, the uncertainty of her future, even the cold wind cutting through her coat melted away as his mouth worked magic against hers. She didn't need her memory to know she'd never been kissed like this before. Amnesia or not, a woman didn't forget something like that. And Hannah knew she would never, ever forget this moment.

But no matter how good John Maitland kissed her, she knew it wasn't going to help her situation. In fact, falling for that devil-be-damned grin and those vivid blue eyes of his promised to complicate her life in ways she was far from equipped to handle.

It took every ounce of discipline she possessed to pull away. John let her go easily, but reached out to steady her when she leaned against the Jeep for balance. Mercy, the man's kisses were potent. She felt the effect all the way down to her toes.

"You might not remember your name, but you sure as hell didn't forget how to kiss," he said huskily.

Hannah would have laughed if her heart hadn't been in her throat. She ordered her pulse to slow, her head to stop spinning. If she could just get some oxygen into her lungs, she might be able to say something halfway intelligent. Something that would let him know the kiss hadn't affected her ability to speak or think or even stand upright without assistance.

"I—I have to go," she said at last.

His eyes were dark as midnight in the dim light from the street lamp. He studied her as if she were a puzzle he'd just realized wasn't going to get solved anytime soon. "I didn't mean for that to get out of hand."

"It didn't. I mean, it did, but…it was just a goodbye kiss."

"Yeah, and Everest is just a mountain."

She choked out a helpless laugh. "I have to go."

For a moment, he looked like he wanted to argue, but he didn't. His jaw flexed. "Take care of yourself, okay?"

"You, too." She didn't want to step away from him, but she did. The effort cost her, but she didn't let it show. "Put some ice on that bump."

She wanted him to smile for her one last time, but he didn't. He just stood there, watching her, his jaw set.

Aware that her heart was still beating out of control, that her emotions were spinning just as wildly, she picked up her bag and set the strap on her shoulder. "Goodbye, John Maitland."

Before he could respond, she turned and started toward the shelter at a brisk clip. She told herself it was for the best that she walk away now, while the walking was still good. Another kiss like that one and she might just be willing to stand out on the sidewalk in the cold and let him kiss her until she was mindless—or they both got a bad case of hypothermia.

John Maitland was a dangerous man to a woman in her predicament. She wasn't a free woman and knew it wasn't in her makeup to betray the man who loved her. It was just as well that she was walking away from John. After that kiss, it was obvious neither of them would settle for friendship. Hannah didn't want anything more complex. She needed to concentrate on finding out who she was, not fall for a man with to-die-for eyes, a cocky grin and kisses good enough to make a woman weep for more.

Behind her, she heard the door of the Jeep slam shut. Her heart pinged hard against her ribs, but she didn't stop walking. If she stopped now, she wasn't going to make it all the way to that front door. Dammit, she didn't need John Maitland complicating her already complicated life.

The Jeep's engine turned over. The realization that she would never see him again hit her hard. The thought was almost too much to bear. Still, she forced one foot in front of the other. She was halfway to the house. He would be gone soon. And the temptation to turn and run to him and fling herself into his arms would disappear as well.

Ice crunched beneath the Jeep's tires as he pulled onto the street. Hannah stopped walking, felt her throat contract. Only then did she feel the sting of tears on her cheeks. Surprised and more than a little annoyed with herself, she brushed them away with the back of her bandaged hand. Like crying was going to help, she thought with dismay. If her emotions hadn't been so close to spiraling out of control, she might have laughed at the absurdity of it.

Oh, why had she let him kiss her like that? Why hadn't she just walked away from him and been done with it?

Determined to get through this with her emotions in check, Hannah hefted the bag. She was going to be fine, she assured herself as she started for the house. She would settle in for the night and get acquainted with Angela Pearl.

Tomorrow she'd get her fingerprints taken at the police department. If she didn't have her memory back by then, she'd make an appointment with the psychiatrist Dr. Morgan had recommended. She'd find out who she was and where she lived. She'd find the man she loved, the man who'd fathered her unborn child, the man who was probably out of his mind with worry and searching for her this very moment.

The sound of an approaching vehicle halted her in midstride. Despite her resolve to forget about John and that blasted kiss, joy burst through the cloak of despair. Dropping her bag in the snow, smiling like a fool, Hannah spun. She'd already taken several steps toward the street when she realized the vehicle wasn't a Jeep, but a large SUV with dark windows and fancy wheels—and a huge dent in the passenger side door.

The kiss wasn't going to change anything, John assured himself as he drove toward the highway that ran west toward his cabin. So what if it was the most mind-numbing kiss he'd ever experienced? Just because he could still feel the low ache of arousal in his groin didn't mean he was going to forget everything he knew about the costs of caring for a woman. Just because his chest hurt at the thought of her spending the night alone and amongst strangers didn't mean he was going to do something stupid like turn around and go back to her, did it?

Hell, no, it didn't.

Walking away from emotional entanglements was what John Maitland did. He was good at it, he reminded himself. He knew what the alternative held, and he'd vowed a long time ago to never take the same path as his father. Even if he had inherited Dirk Maitland's temper, John would never become the same kind of man. As a boy he'd witnessed the thin line between love and hate too many times to partake in such a vicious cycle. And he'd sworn a thousand times he would never breach that line.

His short but disastrous relationship with Rhonda had reaffirmed what he'd always known to be true. She'd burned him badly, and he felt the scald to this day. The logical side of his brain told him Hannah wasn't anything like Rhonda. But the caution ran wide and deep, the scars even deeper, and John simply refused to lay himself open ever again.

But Hannah's wildflower scent lingered, and it wasn't doing much for his resolve. It made him remember that damn kiss—and what it had been like to hold her. It made him remember the shock in her eyes when she'd realized he was going to kiss her, and how that shock had transformed into pleasure when he had. He'd watched her eyes glaze, felt her body turn to liquid heat. Then she'd sighed and opened to him, giving him the sweetness of her mouth and the most erotically charged kiss he'd ever experienced.

He cursed in the silence of the Jeep.

That blasted kiss had changed everything.

But John knew his limits. His attraction to her pushed those limits and made warning bells clang in his head. The fact that she was pregnant with another man's child should have him running away like a racehorse from the chute. He was insane to be thinking of her in intimate terms when he knew she was probably involved with somebody else. Still, he couldn't deny there was a small part of him that didn't care. A part of him that wanted to take her away from the man who'd put that child inside her, the man who hadn't been able to keep her safe. And he couldn't help but wonder if the man she was involved with was the same man who'd put those bruises on her throat and left her up on that mountain to die.

The thought sent the slow burn of fury through him.

Even if she wasn't attached—she wasn't wearing a wedding ring, after all—Hannah wasn't the kind of woman he took home for a one-night stand. Not only was she vulnerable because of the amnesia, but she was warm and real and kind with a heart as big as the Continental Divide. A heart he wanted absolutely nothing to do with.

So why couldn't he stop thinking about her?

"Because you're a damn hypocrite," he muttered.

Rapping his palm hard against the steering wheel, he cursed and whipped the Jeep into a U-turn so fast, the wheels skidded.

John Maitland the Untouchable had been touched. The realization thoroughly shocked him. For the first time in his life, he didn't want to walk away. Couldn't walk away no matter how staunch his belief that it was the right thing to do.

As long as he didn't relinquish control, he assured himself. As long as he didn't let his emotions get involved, he would be able to walk away when the time was right. And John knew as surely as he'd ever known anything in his life that the time to walk away always came sooner or later.

Holding that thought, he sped toward Angela Pearl's.

Chapter 7

Hannah stared at the SUV, frozen, telling herself it wasn't the same vehicle that had driven her and John off the road just a few hours earlier. But she knew it was—she remembered the fancy wheels—and knew as surely as she saw the exhaust spewing into the cold air, as surely as she heard the rumble of the engine over the pounding of her own heart that she was in danger. She sensed it, felt it in the air like the zing of ozone a second before a deadly lightning strike.

A dozen yards separated her from the front door of the shelter. The urge to run was strong, but she resisted, not wanting to draw attention to herself in case the driver hadn't yet spotted her. She stood frozen as the SUV idled up to the curb. The burn of adrenaline ripped through her when the passenger side window eased down. Fear transformed into horror when the black muzzle of a gun emerged, like a deadly snake slithering from its hole.

Terror and disbelief tangled in her brain. Realizing there was no place to hide, she sprinted toward the house. She'd only gone a few feet when two shots snapped through the air. Something whizzed past her head so close, she felt the puff of hot air. Another wave of disbelief sliced her when she realized it was a bullet.

Someone was shooting at her!

Another shot rang out. Simultaneously she heard the metallic whisper of the bullet, felt a tug on the sleeve of her coat like a menacing ghost. On instinct, she ran in a zigzag pattern, but lost her footing on a patch of ice and went down on her hands and knees.

"Help me!" Scrambling to her feet, she stumbled up the porch steps. Next to her, a window exploded. Glass tinkled onto the wood planks of the porch. "Please! Someone, *help me!*"

The groan of a revved engine drew her attention. A dozen emotions jammed her throat when she saw John's Jeep ram the SUV hard enough to send the other vehicle over the curb and into the yard. The sound of crunching metal followed by the blare of his horn split the air.

He'd come back for her!

The SUV's engine had died, and the driver worked frantically to restart it. Gears ground when the Jeep reversed as if in preparation to ram the SUV again.

Hannah never took her eyes from the two vehicles as she streaked across the porch. Arms outstretched, she hit the front door and slapped her palms against the wood surface. "Help me!"

Behind her, the SUV's engine whined. Snow spewed high into the air as it spun out of the yard and into the street. Hannah's heart hammered out of control in her chest as the Jeep jumped the curb and slid to a stop a few yards away. John had the door open before the vehicle had even come to a stop, and sprinted toward her. "Hannah!"

She took a step toward him on quaking legs. "John. Oh my God."

"Are you hurt?"

"I'm okay." Her pulse skittered wildly with the remnants of shock and terror as he took the porch steps two at a time. If it hadn't been for her adrenaline, she felt sure she would have fainted on the spot. "Wh-what are you doing here?"

"Are you hurt? Did that bastard—" His curse burned the air. Raw fury darkened his face. Intensity shone bright and hot in his eyes as his gaze raked her. "I need to know, honey. Are you hurt?"

"I'm all right," she heard herself say.

He crossed the distance between them in two resolute strides. "I need to see for myself."

Not waiting for her consent, he reached out and touched her shoulders, a curse slipping from his lips. Hannah glanced down at her right shoulder, found herself looking at an untidy hole in the fabric. Slowly it dawned on her that she hadn't torn her coat at all, that the damage was the handiwork of a bullet. The realization that she'd come within inches of being shot sent a wave of nausea rolling over her.

"Hell." Wrapping one arm around her shoulders, he drew her against him and used his free hand to pound on the door. "Open up!"

"I'm okay, John. I'm not—"

"Take off your coat." Pushing her to arm's length, he proceeded to unzip it with shaking hands. "Let me get this off you. I want to look at you."

"Okay, but I'm—"

"That son of a bitch."

"John. Easy. Calm down."

As if realizing he was overreacting, he stepped back and blinked at her, took a deep breath. "That was too damn close," he said.

A near-hysterical laugh broke free. "Have I complimented you on your timing?"

"Not recently."

"Another minute and I would have—"

"Be quiet, Red." His jaws clamped tight as he eased the coat from her shoulders. Her nerves jumped when his hands brushed down her arms. Her waist. Her hips and thighs. "Okay?"

She nodded.

Taking her hands in his, he squeezed them, then brought his own hands to her face. An interesting mix of emotions shone like blue diamonds in his eyes. "Are you sure you're all right? You weren't hit? Sometimes it takes a while—"

"I'm okay." The gentle touch of his fingers against her face had her heart rolling into an uneven staccato that made it hard to breathe.

"Your knees are bleeding."

"Oh." She looked down at her knees. "I must have skinned them when I fell." A laugh choked out of her tight throat. "In the scope of things, I figured my knees aren't very important."

His jaw flexed, and he tossed a look over his shoulder at the empty street. "I hit 911 on my cell when I saw the SUV, but I didn't get a chance to finish the call."

The porch light flicked on. Both Hannah and John turned toward the door as security chains rattled. An instant later the door swung open. A large African-American woman wielding a baseball bat in one hand, a cordless phone in the other glared at John. "Holy Moses! John Maitland, you've got some explaining to do," she snapped. "Scaring the bejeepers out of me like that!"

"Hi, gorgeous. I'll answer your questions later. Right now I need to get her inside and call the police."

The woman clucked her mouth impatiently. "Don't 'gorgeous' me." Her gaze swung to Hannah. "Are you okay, honey?"

Without waiting to be invited inside, John stepped forward and kissed the woman's plump cheek. "It's good to see you, too, Angela. You got the cops on the line?"

"They're on the way."

"Good girl." He reached for Hannah's hand and tugged her inside. "This is Hannah," he said.

Angela's sharp gaze landed on Hannah and promptly softened. "You're Dr. Morgan's patient," she said.

"Yes." Hannah looked over her shoulder. "Sorry about the window."

"Windows can be replaced." The woman stuck out her hand. "Welcome to Angela Pearl's Shelter for Battered Women."

No matter how hard she tried, Hannah couldn't stop shaking. Her entire body quaked as Angela Pearl led her to the kitchen and eased her onto a chair. She was still trying to digest what had happened, and get a handle on her emotions, when the other woman shoved a cup of hot tea into her hands.

"That's chamomile with raspberry and mint to calm your nerves. I think there's some kava in there, too." The large black woman crossed the kitchen and set her bat against the stove. "I've drank a fair share myself last couple of years."

"Thank you." Hannah took the cup with both hands and sipped.

"We haven't had this much excitement around here since Lisa Price's husband set her car on fire last year."

Hannah nearly choked on her tea. "Her *husband?* Why did he do that?"

Angela Pearl humphed. "Because she fixed pork chops for dinner and that man don't like pork."

"That doesn't make any sense."

"It never does." John entered the kitchen after checking the front door for the fourth time in the last two minutes, his face pulled into a scowl. "You got anything more efficient than that bat to protect yourself with, Angela?"

"John Maitland, you know I don't keep guns around here," she scolded.

"Just checking."

Touching Hannah's shoulder lightly, Angela Pearl sighed. "I'm going to go turn on the porch light for the police."

John started to go with her, but Angela stopped him by raising her hand. "Stay with Hannah, tough guy."

"Angela—"

"I'll be fine." Waving off his concern, she left the room.

He stared after her for a moment, then turned and began to pace the room. Hannah's gaze followed him to the rear door, where he peered out the window, tried the knob, then spun to face her. That was when she noticed she wasn't the only one who was shaking. John was every bit shaken as she.

He paced the length of the kitchen twice, working off his parka as he went. It was an odd time for her to notice how well he wore those button-down jeans, but she couldn't deny it. The man was definitely in-your-face handsome. She told herself her attraction to him stemmed from the fact that he'd just saved her life for the second time in as many days. She might have believed it if her pulse didn't give her away every time he looked at her.

"How are the knees, Red?"

She started at the sound of John's voice and looked up to find him standing a couple of feet away, staring down at her intently. "Uh, they're…fine."

"I guess that's why they're bleeding."

She looked down at the torn, bloodstained fabric. "Oh."

"I need to have a look at them, all right?"

"Later, okay?" A sudden gust of wind rattled the screen door, and she jumped.

"Easy." He took a step closer, and knelt in front of her. "He's gone."

She laughed self-consciously. "I'm jumpy, I guess."

"Yeah, me, too."

Since every time she looked at him, all she could think of was the kiss, she studied her cup. "What about you, John? You hit that SUV pretty hard."

"If our shooter wasn't wearing his seat belt, I suspect he's hurting a hell of a lot more than me."

"What about the Jeep? Is the damage bad?"

"I've got a push bar on front. It took the brunt of the impact."

His eyes were dark blue and fringed with lashes that were far too long for a male. She needed to look away from his gaze, just until she got a handle on her pulse, but the power behind his eyes held her captive. She told herself the reaction was nothing more than the aftereffects of high adrenaline, but she knew it wasn't quite that simple.

"You're getting into the habit of saving my life," she said after a moment. "That's the second time in two days."

"Maybe I just have good timing when it comes to you."

"No, it's more than timing. If you hadn't come by when you did, I would have—"

"Don't go there, Red. You don't want to go down that road."

He was right. Just the thought of what might have happened if he hadn't shown up when he did made her hands shake. "In any case, thank you. Again."

"I'm no hero." An emotion she couldn't quite decipher flicked in the depths of his gaze. "You'd be wise to remember that."

Hannah was about to argue when Angela Pearl breezed into the kitchen. Her canny gaze swept from John to Hannah and a smile curved the corners of her mouth. "I didn't realize you two were friends."

"We aren't," Hannah said, then thought better of it. "I mean—"

"I just drove her into town from Lake County," John finished.

"Uh-huh." Angela Pearl chuckled. "Whatever the case, John Maitland, I'm certainly glad you were here to help out." Taking the head off an alligator cookie jar in the center of the table, Angela started arranging cookies on a green plate. "Officers Rodriguez and Miller love my gingersnaps. Sometimes I think that's the only reason they get here so quick when I call."

If she wasn't seeing it for herself, Hannah wouldn't have believed the woman could be so nonchalant about getting her front window shot out. "You make it sound like you call the police often."

"Unfortunately, honey, I do. Running a shelter for battered women has its days—"

"Angela?"

Hannah looked up to see a thin woman standing just outside the kitchen door, her pale hand on the jamb, her face in the shadows. She wore a ratty green robe and pink slippers. Her thin blond hair cascaded over one side of her face. Only when she raised her hand and shoved it aside did Hannah see the black eye and swollen cheekbone.

"Hi, Lori." Smiling, Angela excused herself from the table, then rose and approached the woman. "Sorry about the noise outside, but we had some trouble. How are you feeling?"

"Better." Her eyes flashed to John and Hannah, then she stepped back into the shadows of the hall. "I thought maybe Kerry had...you know, come back," she said in a low voice.

"No, child, he won't be back. He and I had a nice talk earlier, and he promised to abide by the restraining order.

I'll walk you back upstairs. The doctor said you should rest.''

Hannah couldn't keep her chest from tightening at the haunted look in the woman's eyes, the lines of pain etched into her face or the evidence of the physical abuse she'd suffered at the hands a man she knew well enough to call by his first name.

Sadness welled like a giant tear and spilled over, clinging to her like a slick of oil on water. The emotion was so powerful that for a moment, she had to blink back tears. She risked a look at John. The smile and cocky attitude had vanished. His face had gone as hard and pale as granite. When he raised his hand to rub his temple, his hand shook. Hannah had never seen him look so unsettled. Not John Maitland with his ready grin and quicksilver wit.

"Are you all right?" she asked.

He jolted. "I hate seeing that," he said.

"Me, too. It's sad."

"It ticks me off," he growled.

Hannah held his gaze. He must have seen the question in her eyes, because he added, "I was a medic for a few years in Denver. Quite a few of my calls were domestic disputes. I saw a lot in those years, but it never gets any easier to look at."

For a moment, the only sound came from the drip of water from the faucet in the sink. Hannah wanted to ask him why his hands were shaking, why he'd gone pale, his eyes cold as ice, but she didn't. Whatever demons had assailed him when he'd set eyes on that woman's battered face, he obviously didn't want to share them.

"Why do the women stay?" she asked after a moment.

"I asked a woman that once." He looked down at his boots for so long, Hannah thought he wouldn't finish. When he finally looked at her, his eyes were so tortured, she knew instinctively he wasn't just a medic relaying a war story, but a man remembering an event that had forever changed his life. "She was a pretty thirty-five-year-old who'd once been a cheerleader. A woman with two kids and dreams of becoming an interior designer. On her tenth wedding anniversary, her husband gave her a broken jaw and a fractured wrist."

"My God." The ugly words twisted Hannah's heart like a tourniquet. "Why did she stay with him?"

"She said she couldn't leave him because she loved him. This man who shared her bed and hit her so hard he'd broken her bones."

"That isn't love."

"Maybe not. But whatever the reason, nine times out of ten, the women stay." John shook his head. "Some of them don't have anywhere else to go. The lucky ones break the cycle. The unlucky ones end up in the hospital—or worse."

Hannah wasn't sure why, but his words disturbed her deeply, made her think of her own life. She thought of her own bruises and wondered for the hundredth time if she'd suffered the same fate.

Simultaneously something hovered at the edge of her consciousness. Something dark and menacing that pressed down on her like thunderhead in the moments before a cloudburst.

An instant later her senses faltered and the world around her faded. Darkness closed in like a cloak, transporting her to another place, another time. She saw snow and darkness and the glare of headlights. She felt the slap of cold, the ache of bruises, the sickening realization of violence and the bitter taste of betrayal.

The glint of memory shocked her. Terror gripped her chest like a white-knuckled fist. Dread twisted inside her so violently, a sob bubbled up from her throat. She reached for the memory, clawed toward it, but the darkness refused to relinquish its grip.

"Easy, Red. Easy..."

Vaguely she was aware of John's voice, edged with concern, reaching out to her through the swirling mist of confusion. Her breath coming shallow and fast. The warmth of his fingers against her biceps. The press of fear all around her.

"I'm all right," she heard herself say. But she wasn't all right. It was as if her senses had shut down the present and transported her back to a place she didn't want to be, showing her just enough to terrify her, but never enough for her to understand.

"What is it? Hannah? Are you with me? Talk to me."

The mist thinned. Slowly her confusion subsided, and the world around her materialized. Hannah rose abruptly, her chair grating against the tile. Breathing hard, her heart rapping against her ribs, she blinked and focused, only to find John's gaze drilling into her, his expression perplexed and concerned.

"You zoned out again," he said. "Are you all right?"

"Yeah…I'm…okay." Shaking off the fear, she eased away from him and walked unsteadily to the back door. Embarrassment and a terrible sense of vulnerability pressed down on her as she looked out the window at the snowy landscape beyond.

"You don't look okay," John said.

"I don't have a choice but to be okay."

She started when she felt his hand on her shoulder. "You're shaking. Come here and sit down."

"I need to just stand here for a moment." Hannah needed a moment to pull herself together. She didn't want to face him when she was falling apart. Not when his strong arms were so inviting—and the comfort they promised far too powerful to resist.

"Did you…have another flashback?" he asked.

"It was more like a moment of déjà vu." Realizing that didn't make much sense, she made a sound of frustration. "It's like I'm seeing something I've done before." Slowly she turned to face him, met his gaze. "I think my memory is trying to come back, only it's coming in bits and pieces."

"Doc Morgan said it might happen that way." He continued to study her. "When you...flashed back, what did you see?"

"Just like before, when we were in Buzz's office. I'm running through snow. It's cold and dark. Someone is behind me. I'm terrified of him, but I don't know why. The only thing that's clear is that he wants to hurt me." Saying the words aloud made the nightmare real and ugly and frightening. A shiver wracked her body. "Does that sound totally crazy?"

She'd asked the question lightly in an attempt to break the tension that had descended, but he didn't smile. "It sounds as if maybe this wasn't the first time he hurt you."

She closed her eyes, sickened by the thought, praying it wasn't true. "I could be wrong."

"It's something we've got to consider. Domestic violence is at epidemic proportions in our society. It doesn't discriminate between race or income bracket or social status. It's an equal-opportunity evil, and it almost always escalates unless someone gets help."

The thought twisted her heart with unexpected cruelty. Domestic violence. Sadness flowed like tears inside her. She thought of her unborn child, and outrage made her clench her fists. "I can't stand this not knowing, John. I need to find out what happened to me. I've got to know who I am. I need to find out who..." She struggled to finish the sentence, but her voice box had climbed into her throat.

"Who's trying to kill you?" John stood less than a foot away, his gaze intense and searching and so blue, she could almost step into it and find the clouds.

"Yes," she whispered.

"What else did this flashback tell you?"

She swallowed, determined not to let his previous question shake her. "I'm pretty sure I know the person who…did this to me."

A dark emotion she couldn't readily identify flicked like hot silver in his eyes. "The man in the SUV?"

"Maybe. I'm not sure. But I have a…"

"Gut feeling?" he offered.

She smiled. "Yeah."

"Do you know his name?"

The low, dangerous tone of his voice surprised her, made her wonder just how personally he was taking all this. "No. I mean, I do, but I don't remember. I'm pretty sure he's not a stranger to me. I think he's someone I know or have known in the past."

"Someone you've…had a relationship with?"

The word jolted her. Not because it surprised her, but because it hurt unexpectedly. She didn't want to believe someone she'd cared for could breach the sanctity of love with that kind of violence. That perhaps the same man who'd fathered her child was the person who'd left her to die up on the mountain. "Maybe. I don't know."

"This is the second time in just a few hours he's tried to get to you."

She tried to suppress a shiver, but it rippled through her hard enough to make her shoulders shake. "We don't know that for sure, John. I could be wrong."

"Or you could be right."

Silence thickened the air around her as she considered his words. She hated being afraid almost as much as she hated not knowing who she was.

"If you're right, and you know this person, he obviously knows you're here." He cut her a hard look. "You can't stay here."

I don't have anywhere else to go. The unspoken words hung in the air between them like an unpleasant smell. But Hannah couldn't bring herself to utter them. She didn't like the sense of vulnerability they induced. "How did he know I was here?"

"Maybe he followed us from the hospital." Grimacing, John muttered a curse. "I thought the incident up on the highway was suspicious, but I didn't think he'd follow us here."

"John, there are other shelters—"

"Women's shelters aren't exactly high security."

Angela Pearl came through the door. Having evidently caught the last couple of sentences, she humphed. "I don't turn my ladies out on the street just because of a little trouble, John Maitland. You know me better than that."

Hannah looked up to see the other woman cross to the stove where she put a kettle on to boil.

John scowled at her. "A drive-by shooting is more than a little trouble, Angela."

"Angela Pearl takes care of her own."

"She's also wise enough to know when to close her doors to keep the other women safe."

Hannah hadn't considered the possibility that her staying here could put the other women at the shelter in danger. Squaring her shoulders, determined to do the right thing, she stepped forward. "He's right, Angela. I won't endanger—"

"And I won't put you out on the street." Putting her hand on a generous hip, Angela Pearl challenged John with a raised brow. "Unless our superhero here has a better idea."

John's gaze didn't falter. "She can stay with me."

The words rolled over Hannah with all the finesse of a Sherman tank. "I don't think that's a very good idea."

"Why not?"

Out of the corner of her eye, she saw Angela Pearl cock her head in interest.

"Because it would be…inappropriate," Hannah said.

"I'm not asking you to move in with me, Red. Until

we figure out what's going on, you can sleep in my guest room,'' he said. ''I'll take you to the police department first thing in the morning. We'll get your prints taken and check with Missing Persons.''

Angela Pearl folded her arms across her generous bosom. ''If you're worried about spending the night with a strange man, honey, I can vouch for John Maitland. I've known him for several years, and he's a pure gentleman.'' She winked at John. ''Even though he doesn't act like it most times.''

The offer tempted her. She was exhausted and emotionally wrought and a hell of a lot more afraid than she wanted to admit. She knew the man in the SUV was a threat and could return at any time. The last thing she wanted to do was endanger Angela Pearl or the other women. Logic told her to accept his offer. But another part of her brain that wasn't thinking quite so logically told her she would be opening herself up to another danger that wasn't so cut-and-dried.

''You're dead on your feet,'' John said. ''You'll feel better in the morning after you've gotten some rest. You might even have your memory back by then. What do you say?''

Hannah looked at Angela Pearl. The other woman gave her a minute nod, the meaning of which didn't elude her. She could trust John, the silent message said.

Of course, trusting him wasn't the biggest issue she was wrestling with. It was that blasted kiss that was troubling her. That unforgettable, mind-bending, totally inappropriate kiss that had her wanting to run in the opposite direction—or else throw herself into his arms. She'd rather sleep out on the frozen curb than admit she was attracted to John. How could she stay with John when her heart could belong to the father of her child?

As long as she didn't let him kiss her again, she decided, she'd be just fine. If she took John up on his offer, she'd have to set some ground rules. Let him know she wasn't interested in anything more than a safe place to spend the night until she found an alternate shelter.

"Maybe for just one night," she heard herself say.

Angela Pearl smiled. "I'll put some of my raspberry tea and gingersnaps in a container for you."

John's eyes never left hers. Hannah wasn't sure, but she thought she saw victory in the depths of his gaze. "I'd better get started patching up that front window," he said.

She can stay with me.

John figured he was going to regret those words. They rang in his head like the beginning of a migraine. The feeling had solidified and augmented throughout the evening as two of Denver's finest made their report and consumed a dozen or so of Angela Pearl's gingersnaps. By the time the police had gathered the information they needed and had headed out the front door, John had known his offer to let Hannah stay with him was a downright bad idea. As he turned the Jeep onto Highway 285 and headed west, he felt the sentiment all the way to his bones.

What the hell had he been thinking?

That was the problem, he realized. He hadn't been thinking at all. Offering up his cabin to a woman he couldn't seem to keep his hands off wasn't the smartest thing he'd ever done. Here it was, past midnight, and he found himself faced with the prospect of spending the night with a curvaceous redhead who'd just hours earlier knocked the world out from under him with a kiss so hot he'd burned. Yeah, real smart move, Maitland.

"We need to discuss…what happened," she said.

John glanced over at the woman in question. He tried not to be annoyed when he noticed she was hugging the passenger door. "You mean the guy in the SUV?"

"I mean the…you know, the…"

"The kiss," he finished.

''Well, if you can even call it that.''

He studied her in the dim light from the dash, taking in the stubborn set of her mouth, the tons of red hair, and felt a flare of lust hit him low and hard. Well, this was a hell of a time for him to realize he was partial to redheads. Especially one that was off-limits for too many reasons to count.

Soft, determined eyes met his and held them. Her full mouth was pulled into a frown that shouldn't have been sexy considering it was aimed right at him. But her mouth *was* sexy. Too damn sexy. Not to mention talented when it came to kissing a man senseless. A few wisps of red hair had fallen in her eyes. He wondered what it would be like to reach around and unleash the rest and let it tumble over her shoulders.

''There's no question about it, Red. That was definitely a kiss.''

''Yeah, well, call it what you will, but it was definitely inappropriate,'' she said.

''High adrenaline,'' he said simply.

''High adrenaline?''

''That's right. High adrenaline.''

''I'm not following you.''

''The aftereffects of highly stressful situations. Emotions are charged. Adrenaline is pumping. Blood pressure is elevated. Senses are heightened. It's a scientific fact that people tend to react…strongly during those kinds of situations.'' It was as good a rationalization he could come up with so he was sticking to it.

''I thought you'd be accustomed to that sort of thing,'' she said.

''Well, usually I'm with a bunch of guys. Being with you… Well, let's just say it's not the same.''

She laughed, a throaty sound that was far too sexy in the confines of the vehicle. Damn, just about everything about her was turning out to be sexy.

John grinned at her, felt something warm jump in his chest when she smiled back. She had one of the most dazzling smiles he'd ever seen. And that dimple... Oh, boy, this was not looking good at all.

"I just thought if we're going to be spending time together, I think we should set some...ground rules," she said.

"Look, Red, I didn't mean for that to happen any more than you did."

"I know. It's just that—"

"It's just that it was pretty damn good, and we'd both be lying if we claimed we hadn't enjoyed it."

She opened her mouth to speak, but nothing came out. John looked away, staring sightlessly at the road, wishing he'd kept his mouth shut.

Turning slightly in her seat, Hannah looked at him from beneath her lashes. "I think we both know I could be seriously involved with someone." Absently she rested her hand against her abdomen. "I mean, I could even be married—"

"I know," he snapped, realizing with a stark sense of dismay that he was annoyed.

"It can't happen again," she said.

He blew out a sigh. "Yeah."

"And I think it would probably be a good idea if we didn't...you know...touch each other."

He studied her a moment, taking in the serious set of her mouth, the way she seemed to look everywhere but into his eyes. She was right, of course. Touching wasn't such a good idea, either. One innocent touch, and all he wanted to do was touch her more—in ways that were anything but innocent. "All right," he said. "I can abide by that."

"I think it will make things easier for both of us."

"If it's any consolation, Red, I hadn't planned on kissing you. What happened back there was a spontaneous reaction to high adrenaline. Things like that happen when two people experience an intense situation together.''

"I'm sure that's all it was."

He wondered if she really believed that. He sure as hell didn't. That was what worried him about the whole situation.

Releasing a pent-up sigh, she shot him a challenging look. "I want to make certain you're okay with this. I don't want you to feel like you have to feel responsible for me in any way," she said. "I have some options."

"Give me a little credit, will you?" he growled. That she believed he would turn her away and leave her with no place to stay rankled him almost as much as the damn rules she was laying down. "Like I would put you out on the street."

"I didn't say that."

"Well, be advised that I wouldn't do that, all right?"

"I didn't mean to annoy you." Folding her arms, she turned her attention to the window.

He raised his hand to touch her, belatedly remembered rule number two and let his arm drop to his side.

Damn, it was going to be a long night.

Chapter 8

Hannah knew she'd annoyed him with her ground rules. But the way she saw it, she hadn't exactly had a choice—especially after that kiss back at Angela Pearl's. She was vulnerable to him not only because of her amnesia and the fact that someone had declared open season on her, but because of her insane attraction to him. With her life in turmoil—and apparently in danger—she couldn't afford that kind of distraction.

John Maitland definitely distracted her.

Since the moment he'd swooped down from the helicopter and taken her into his arms, she hadn't been able to get him out of her mind. Even in the face of danger, he made her feel safe—though she knew another kind of danger may very well lie within the man himself. Falling for those arctic-blue eyes and daredevil grin would be a fatal mistake. No matter how stressful the circumstance—or how intense the attraction—the fact remained that she carried another man's child within her womb.

She was insane to be thinking of John in terms of the

way he'd kissed her when she was obviously involved with someone else. Just because she couldn't remember her lover's name didn't mean she wasn't in love with him.

"Home sweet home."

Hannah was so caught up in her thoughts, she didn't notice the Jeep had slowed. She looked up in time to see a narrow lane, the headlights playing over hundred-year-old pines and aspen the color of old bone.

"Nice neighborhood," she commented.

"So long as the neighbors stay out of the garbage."

She cut him her best what's-that-supposed-to-mean look.

He grinned. "Bears."

"Oh. Friendly bears, I hope."

"They make pretty good neighbors, actually. They hardly ever complain about the music."

Hannah rolled her eyes. "Or borrow tools and forget to return them."

"Right." He parked in front of a detached garage and shut down the engine. "The place needed a lot of work when I bought it, but the location and view were too good to pass up."

Ahead and to her left she could make out the shape of a small cabin nestled in a shadowed forest. The moon wasn't full, but enough light reflected off the snow for her to make out the wraparound front porch and river-rock chimney.

She started when John opened his door. "I guess we're both a little jumpy tonight," he said.

"All that talk about bears."

"Stay put," he said. "The walkway is slick. I haven't shoveled the snow yet."

Hannah opened her door, but before she could get out, he'd walked around the Jeep and reached for her. His hands slipped beneath her arms, and he gently lowered her to the ground.

"Thank you."

The night was bracingly cold and so quiet, she could hear the wind whispering through the treetops.

"It's so...quiet," she said.

"The wildlife is pretty incredible, too. Mule deer. Raccoons. I saw a small herd of elk last weekend."

Ice crunched beneath their feet as they tromped through the snow toward the front door. Hannah wasn't sure why she felt so apprehensive. She told herself it was a combination of her amnesia and the shooting back at Angela Pearl's, but she knew the tingle of nerves as John opened the door had little to do with either of those things—and everything to do with the way she was reacting to him.

The door swung open. The first thing she noticed was the tang of burning pine from an earlier fire, the remnants of this morning's coffee and the faint scent of aftershave and man. John flipped a switch next to the door, and light from a single lamp illuminated a small living room. Rough-hewn beams and dark paneling bestowed a rustic ambience. A brown leather sofa draped with an Indian-print afghan lined the wall to her left. A mismatched chair and a braided rug lent an air of masculine comfort. A river-rock hearth dominated the center of the room and swept up to the rafters like a stone waterfall. One look at the mismatched pillows piled on the floor in front of it, and the hardback thriller lying facedown, told Hannah it was used often and enjoyed.

"Nice place." Her voice sounded high and tight in the silence of the room.

"It suits me." He took off his coat and hung it on the rack behind the door. "I can hang your coat if you like."

"I've got it." She slipped the coat from her shoulders and hung it on the rack.

"Hungry?" He started toward the kitchen.

"No thanks."

She knew better than to watch him cross the room, but

her eyes took on a life of their own and played over the
length of him. The man knew how to fill out a pair of
jeans, that was for sure. He didn't do too bad in the area
of filling out that flannel shirt, either. In fact, he seemed
to do a pretty good job of filling the entire room.

"I'll just get you something to drink, then. I've got milk
or juice. Hot chocolate if you prefer."

Thinking of the baby growing inside her, Hannah was
about to opt for milk when movement in the kitchen sent
her heart to her throat. Something large and dark lumbered
toward them. Good Lord, a grizzly bear? In the cabin?
Weren't they supposed to be hibernating this time of year?

The scream died in her throat when she realized the bear
wasn't a bear at all, but a monstrous dog with a thick black
coat, massive head and a lolling, pink tongue.

The dog galloped from the kitchen toward John.

"Whoa! Down!" John raised his hands, but the dog
paid no heed. Two huge paws crashed against his chest.
Hannah heard a grunt, and then John reeled backward and
landed on the floor with the giant beast standing proudly
on his chest.

"Get off me, you big mutt!"

Realizing they were no longer in grave danger, Hannah
put her hand to her chest and laughed. "I think he missed
you."

John turned his head to avoid the dog's overzealous
tongue. "I forgot to warn you about my watchdog."

"What does he do, lick prowlers to death?"

"Uh, he's still in training, actually. Midlife career
change."

"That's tough."

The dog sat, his tail thumping hard against the pine
floor. John struggled to his feet, wiping his cheek with the
sleeve of his shirt. "He didn't get his walk today."

"No wonder he decked you." She looked down at the

dog, charmed by the sagging eyes and jowls. "What *is* he?"

"Newfoundland Retriever."

"What's his name?"

"Honeybear." He shot Hannah a sheepish grin. "I didn't name him."

The denial freed the laugh from her throat. "Of course not." She ran her hand over the animal's head. "He's beautiful. Where did you get him?"

"He was a search-and-rescue dog for an outfit up in Vail. He got hurt during a mission—broke his hip—and couldn't work anymore. No one on the team could take him at the time. My buddy asked me." He scratched the dog's head with shoddily concealed affection. "One look at those eyes, and I couldn't walk away."

Hannah caught herself grinning back, not sure if she was more charmed by the dog or the man. "He's lucky."

The look he gave her went on way too long. "I'll just put him outside. Make yourself at home. The guest bedroom is down the hall. I'll get your bag when I come back." His eyes skimmed down her legs. "I'll have a look at those skinned knees, too."

Without waiting for a reply, he snagged the dog's collar. Honeybear proceeded to drag him toward the kitchen where Hannah assumed the back door was.

The cabin was exactly how she'd pictured it from the outside. Practical. Comfortable. A hint of male clutter without being messy. Clean, but not immaculate by any means. She looked around the living room for pictures or photographs or mementos, but found nothing. Either John didn't have a family, or he chose not to be reminded of them.

Grabbing her bag, she made her way down the hall toward the bedroom. A navy towel lay on the floor in the bathroom. In the room across the hall, a set of weights cluttered the floor next to a desk and leather chair. The larger bedroom was masculine, as well, with dark paneling, a geometric bedspread in hues of navy and cream, and a bookcase loaded with everything from the latest thriller to search-and-rescue emergency field medicine guides.

"The first-aid kit is in the kitchen."

Hannah spun at the sound of his voice. John stood in the doorway, his arm braced against the jamb, watching her.

The sight of him made her feel breathless. The thought of him getting close enough to look at her knees, of him putting his hands on her legs made her dizzy. Abruptly the room seemed too small for the both of them. "That's not necessary."

He pointed in the general direction of her knees. "I hate to point this out to you, Red, but your knees are probably scraped."

She looked down at her knees in question, realized she'd been so distracted she'd forgotten about the fall. "Oh."

"I can't stand to see unattended wounds." Not waiting for a response, John turned and headed toward the kitchen. "Come on. I'll fix you up."

Taking a deep breath, Hannah followed.

The kitchen was as no-nonsense as the rest of the cabin. Pine cabinets lined the walls. A plate and a single mug drained neatly in the sink. The butcher-block counter held a set of knives. A navy dish towel was tossed haphazardly on the counter. A fifty-pound bag of high-quality dog food sat in the corner.

John opened the cabinet above the sink and removed a first-aid kit. Setting the kit on the kitchen table, he pulled out a chair. "Have a seat."

"This really isn't necessary."

"I'm a medic. It's what I do. Humor me, okay?"

She didn't have a comeback for that, so she sank into the chair.

"That glass of milk is for you," he said.

"Oh." She picked up the glass, sipped. "Thanks."

He knelt in front of her and slipped her foot out of the too-large sandal. "We'll need to get you some decent shoes in a couple of days."

"I tried some sneakers at the hospital, but my feet were swollen from the frostbite."

"The inflammation should go down in a day or two. Maybe even tomorrow."

Hannah knew she should say something, but the power of speech deserted her when he set her foot on his thigh and began to roll the hem of the scrub toward her knee. "H-how long have you been a medic?" she asked, trying to keep herself from noticing the gentle brush of his knuckles against her calf.

"I've been with Rocky Mountain Search and Rescue for six years."

"Do you like that sort of work? I mean, jumping out of helicopters must be…stressful."

He shot her a cocky grin. "I'm an adrenaline freak, so it's not stressful at all. I love it. But it's not all exciting work, either. We get called out for bee stings. Lost dogs. Last summer we geared up and flew to a site only to realize a hiker had fallen and broken his pinkie finger."

"Oops."

"Buzz wanted to break the other one for good measure, but we talked him out of it."

"Is your boss always so surly?"

"Ever since his divorce, the man's had the personality of a rabid wolverine."

Hannah knew firsthand just how cutting the older man could be. "Is search-and-rescue work what you've always wanted to do?"

"Well, when I was a kid, I wanted to be a cop," he said.

"What made you decide not to?"

The shadow crossed John's expression so quickly, she

wasn't sure she'd seen it at all. But she didn't miss the tremor in his hand as he peeled the hem of her scrub pants over her knee.

"I didn't mean to upset you," she said.

"You didn't." Glancing up at her, he grimaced, then turned his attention back to her knee. "Hurt?"

"Not too much."

"Liar. You've got a deep abrasion and a hell of a bruise. Those hurt."

"I guess that'll teach me to dive onto somebody's icy lawn the next time bullets start flying."

"Let's just count our blessings that it wasn't worse." His jaw flexed. "I'll clean it and apply some antibiotic. You'll be good as new in a day or two."

She watched as he removed a cotton ball from the kit and saturated it with antiseptic. Then with those doctor's hands, he held her calf and pressed the cotton to the wound. The sting was sharp and instantaneous.

"Yow."

"Sorry."

She bit her lip against the sting. "So what did you do before you started with the search-and-rescue outfit?"

"I was a paramedic in Denver."

"That's how you met Angela Pearl?"

"Yep. She was my first transport."

"What happened?"

After removing the cotton ball, John opened a tube of ointment. "My partner and I were called out to a domestic. She was in bad shape when we got there. Broken nose. A couple of broken ribs."

"Her husband?"

"Yeah. He cried like a baby the whole time the cops were arresting him. The spineless worm."

"That's very sad."

"I don't have any sympathy for men who hit women. The cops had been called out to their apartment a dozen times. The warning signs were there. But no one did anything." Something dark and angry flashed in the cool blue depths of his eyes. "We thought we were going to lose her that first night."

The words put a lump in Hannah's throat. "Things worked out for Angela."

"She was smart—and very lucky. We kept in touch. She became somewhat of an advocate after that. I'd see her every so often at the hospital. She took some social work courses at the community college. Got a license from the city. Then she opened her shelter."

"She's making a difference."

"She's found her calling. She's incredibly committed. I admire her." He shot Hannah a canny look. "It takes guts to walk away from something like that."

The statement made her think of her own bruises and the dark mystery surrounding them. She didn't relish the thought of being trapped in an abusive relationship. She couldn't believe she would do that to herself. Certainly not while carrying an innocent unborn child.

After applying the ointment with a cotton swab, John withdrew a gauze bandage from the first-aid kit and set it against the abrasion.

Hannah watched his hands move expertly over her skin, mesmerized by the smooth efficiency with which he worked.

"You never answered my question," she said after a moment.

"Yeah?" He looked up from his work. "What question is that?"

"You mentioned you wanted to be a police officer. I think you would have been good at it. What made you decide not to?"

John's hand quivered slightly as he pressed the first-aid tape to the gauze. It had been a long time since he'd thought of why he wasn't a cop, even longer since he'd discussed it with anyone. The topic still had the power to eat a hole in his gut. "Let's just say I make a better medic than police officer and leave it at that," he said.

"Raw area?"

"Off-limits."

"Oh." She made a show of brushing at a smudge on her scrubs. "Sorry."

He saw the question in her eyes, but he wasn't going to elaborate. The biggest failure of his life wasn't a topic he liked to discuss. He wasn't going to lie about it, but he sure as hell didn't want to analyze it over milk and cookies, either. The last thing he wanted to discuss with this woman were the secrets he'd left back in Philly—and the one that had brought it all rushing back to him five years ago right here in Colorado.

Shoving thoughts of the past aside, he secured the last strip of tape and put it back in the first-aid kit. He'd been so intent on the bandaging—and dodging her much-too-perceptive questions—he'd barely noticed the softness of her flesh beneath his fingertips. When he finally looked down and saw her calf cradled in his hand, he swallowed hard.

Her skin was soft against his palm, the muscle rounded and firm. He wasn't sure why he'd noticed something like that at a moment like this. He'd bandaged hundreds of arms and legs over the years. But as he felt the blood pool in an area he didn't want to think about, he couldn't deny this particular patient had the most incredible legs he'd ever laid eyes on.

"That should keep it from getting infected. Bandage can come off tomorrow." Clearing the cobwebs out of his throat, he unrolled her hem then eased her leg aside, praying she didn't notice the state she'd left him in. Oh, yeah, it was going to be a long night.

When he straightened, she was looking right at him with

those striking eyes. The power of her gaze stopped his brain cold. The space between them seemed to shrink. Awareness of her close proximity, of her scent washed over him. He knew he should step away, give himself some breathing room, but his legs refused to obey the command.

"I was wondering," she began, "why did you come back tonight? I mean, after you left the shelter?"

The truth hovered on the tip of his tongue, but John swallowed it, knowing it wouldn't do either of them any good for him to acknowledge what he could no longer deny. That something had clicked between them up on the mountain, that he hadn't been able to get her out of his head, that she was in danger and he couldn't bear the thought of the bastard getting his hands on her. Or that every time he thought of that kiss, his blood heated, and all he could think about was one more taste of her sweet mouth.

"I didn't like the idea of you spending the night in a shelter. Not after what happened with the SUV." It was a half-truth, but it would have to do for now.

Hannah worried her lower lip. "What do you make of all this?"

"I'm not sure yet."

"Do you think the SUV incident is related to…what happened to me up on the mountain? What happened back at Angela Pearl's?"

"I think that's something we've got to consider at this point." John watched her hand settle protectively over her abdomen and felt the need to protect flare within him. "I'm not going to let anything happen to you," he said.

He hadn't meant to say it; the last thing he wanted to do was take on the role of protector. He wasn't sure he was qualified. Not after Philly. Not after what had happened to Rhonda.

Her gaze met his, and in the depths of her eyes he recognized the first vestiges of a fragile trust he didn't deserve.

"Thank—" She jumped in midsentence when a scratch sounded at the back door.

John laughed outright. "Sorry, Red. That's Honeybear's way of letting us know he's ready to come it."

Rising, he strode to the door and flipped on the rear porch light. Honeybear sat on the step, wagging his tail, looking happy and impatient at once. Normally John would have opened the door and let the dog inside without so much as a second thought. Tonight he found his eyes scanning the shadows of the wooded area beyond. He'd never been uneasy living miles away from his nearest neighbor. But tonight the thought made the hair on the back of his neck prickle.

He hated to think of Hannah being in trouble. She was genuine and warm and more alive than any woman he'd ever known. She was brave in the face of danger. Hopeful in the face of crushing odds. Then there was the matter of her pretty eyes and all that red hair. The combination completely undid him.

Somehow she'd managed to tumble the wall he'd so carefully erected. She'd trespassed into territory he normally kept off-limits, managed to touch him despite his efforts to keep her at a distance. John figured the only question that remained was what the hell he was going to do about it.

As much as he didn't want it to happen, he'd stepped into the role of protector. The irony left a bitter taste at the back of his throat. He wondered how she would react if she knew about Philly. If she knew he was no better than the man who'd put those bruises on her.

Sighing, he opened the door. Honeybear bounded inside with a rush of cold air and a flurry of snow. John turned in time to see Hannah stoop and scratch Honeybear behind his floppy ear.

''I think he likes me,'' she said.

''He's just using you to get his ear scratched.''

She laughed, a musical sound that made his heart stutter in his chest. Even with the bruise on her cheek, dressed in an oversize sweatshirt and shapeless hospital scrubs, she was undoubtedly one of the most attractive women he'd ever laid eyes on. That she was standing in his kitchen, playing with his dog and laughing made John realize that for all his intentions, he wasn't doing a very good job at keeping this impersonal.

''Tonight,'' she began, ''when we were in Angela Pearl's kitchen, and that woman with the bruised face came down, you seemed…upset.''

An alarm trilled in the back of his head. That he was so transparent annoyed him. That she'd hit a sore spot dead on put his back up. ''What do you expect? The woman had just had her face pounded in by some scumbag. That ticks me off.''

''Oh, well, I just thought maybe you knew her or—''

''I don't.''

She cast him a startled look. ''I didn't mean to—''

''You didn't upset me.'' He stared at her, aware that his hackles were up, all too aware that she'd noticed. ''Look, I've got an early day tomorrow.''

''Oh. Of course.'' She straightened.

John hadn't meant for his words to come out so harshly. But he couldn't risk her getting the wrong idea about him. He wasn't a hero—not by a long shot. Hell, the way he saw it, he barely qualified as a nice guy. The sooner she got that through her head, the better. He figured he'd be saving them both a lot of grief in the long run if he put a stop to whatever was happening between them before it solidified into a problem he might actually have to deal with.

Chapter 9

The moon splashed silver light on the snow, showing her the way through the trees and boulders. Branches tugged at her clothes and slashed at her face like tiny knives. The ice and protruding rocks cut her feet with ruthless efficiency. Around her, the wind howled like a vengeful ghost.

Hannah ran as she had never run before. Arms outstretched, she covered the ground with reckless speed. Animal sounds tore from deep inside her. Panic and terror pooled at the back of her throat.

He was going to kill her.

She knew that as surely as she felt the life-sustaining heat draining from her body. As surely as she felt the life force of the tiny life growing inside her. As surely as the cold and exhaustion zapped the last of her strength.

Behind her, the glare of headlights sliced through the darkness. She looked over her shoulder, saw the vehicle less than a dozen feet away. Closing in on her, a relentless predator in the throes of a kill.

''No!'' she screamed into the darkness.

She turned to run, but a heavy hand bit into her shoulder. Her scream was cut short when his fingers closed around her throat. She lashed out with her hands and feet, but he didn't relinquish his death grip. The blow that followed stunned her, sent her sprawling into the snow like a rag doll. Pain and dread exploded inside her. She scrambled to her feet, heard the whoosh of air as he grabbed for her.

"No! I won't let you—"

"Hannah. Easy, honey. It's John. I'm here."

Strong hands pressed her down. She could still feel the crushing pain of his fingers on her throat. Terror raged inside her like an angry beast. She lashed out with her feet. Once. Twice. A fleeting sense of satisfaction flitted through her when her left heel connected with something solid.

"Ouch! Dammit. Cut it out."

"Let go of me!"

"It's me. Hannah! Stop struggling."

The familiarity of the voice stopped her. Gentle hands touched her, soothed away the terror. She opened her eyes. John leaned over her, his face suffused with sharp-edged concern. "It was only a dream," he said.

"Oh, God," she choked. "He was going to…"

"It's okay. You're all right. Take a deep breath for me, okay?"

She sucked in a shaky breath, felt the terror take a final jab at her. "I need to sit up."

Wordlessly he released her shoulders and moved to sit beside her on the bed. Never taking his eyes from hers, he scrubbed a hand over his face. "You scared the devil out of me."

"I'm sorry."

"No, it's okay." He studied her for a moment. "Are you all right?"

"No. I mean, yes. But—" Her voice broke. "I'm alive.

Sometimes after those dreams I just...can't believe I'm alive.''

"You're very much alive. And you're safe. Just give yourself a minute to calm down.''

A helpless laugh squeezed from her throat. ''I promised myself I wasn't going to let these flashbacks scare me so much. I was going to use them to remember. But this one... It was so real. I just couldn't...think. It's like I was there, and I knew I was going to die.''

"Where?''

"I don't know. I—'' Letting out a calming breath, she glanced around the room. The window was closed. Yellow light bled in from the hall. Nothing had changed. Nothing lurked in the shadows.

Still Hannah shivered. ''It was so real. I mean, he was here. I felt him...touching me. He...'' Remembering the feel of his hands around her throat, she touched her neck.

"Who?''

"I don't know.'' Frustration clawed at her when she couldn't give him an answer. ''The man who...hurt me. The man I know. He was here.''

"Stay put.''

Her heart scrambled wildly in her chest when John rose and stalked to the window. Parting the curtains, he checked the lock, then turned to her. ''There's no one here, Red. The doors downstairs are locked. Honeybear would have barked if he'd heard something. You had a nightmare. That's all.''

"I can still feel his hands around my throat, for God's sake.''

Something dark and ominous flashed in his eyes, and for a moment he looked...dangerous. ''No one's going to hurt you. I promise. You're safe.''

The first tinges of embarrassment washed over her. She felt the dampness of sweat on her forehead. Heard the rise of hysteria in her voice. She could only imagine what John must think of her. That she was a confused and helpless female. Or, worse, a total nutcase. "I'm sorry. I didn't mean to—"

"You're entitled." Letting out a breath, he scrubbed a hand over his face. "I heard you scream and got here as fast as I could."

Movement at the bedroom door snagged her attention. Honeybear watched them, his tail tucked between his legs, looking as if he was trying to decide whether to duck under the bed—or make a run for the other bedroom.

In spite of the fear and confusion clouding her brain, Hannah heard herself laugh. "Looks like you're not the only one I scared." Another breath, and she began to feel steadier. She looked at John. "I don't normally dream so vividly. I must sound like a raving lunatic. I can't imagine what you must think of me."

"I think you've been through some physical and emotional trauma." Reaching out, he set his hand gently on her shoulder. "It's nothing to be ashamed of or embarrassed by."

Her heart rate should have slowed, but it didn't. Hannah wasn't naive enough to believe the rise of her pulse rate was from the nightmare. She knew herself well enough to know it had more to do with his proximity and the way he was looking at her.

That was when she realized he was sitting on the bed next to her wearing nothing more than a pair of tapered boxer shorts. She knew she should look away, but her eyes refused to obey and skimmed over him in a single sweep. She'd figured he worked out. A man who made his living jumping out of helicopters had to be in top physical shape. But nothing had prepared her for the sight of six feet four inches of solid male. His shoulders were broad and corded with muscle. His chest was wide and covered with a thatch of black hair that ran unchecked down his washboard belly then tapered to a point that disappeared into the waistband of his boxers.

Disconcerted by the sight—and her reaction to him— Hannah quickly averted her eyes, wishing in vain she hadn't noticed. She had enough to worry about without realizing her protector had a to-die-for, gorgeous body.

His left arm was wrapped protectively around her shoulders. He was so close she could feel the heat of his body coming through the T-shirt she wore. She definitely liked his aftershave. Well, if it hadn't been so drugging. At some point, he'd threaded his fingers with hers. She tried not to think about the solid warmth of his thigh against hers. Or that for the first time in what seemed like forever, she felt totally safe.

"You okay now?" he asked quietly.

"Better." She smiled, but it felt forced. She was still shaking inside, though now she had to wonder how much of it was from the nightmare and how much was her reaction to the man sitting next to her.

"Do you want to talk about the dream?"

She didn't particularly, not when she was feeling so vulnerable and raw. But the logical side of her brain figured talking about it might help to dislodge the memories her mind had locked away.

Easing her hand from his, she shoved her hair from her face and took a deep breath. "It was the same as the flashbacks. I'm running. There's snow and it's cold, and I'm terrified. Only, this time, he was closer...."

"Who?"

"I don't know. A…man."

"How do you know this person is a man?"

"I saw his silhouette in the car."

"What kind of car?"

Her heart kicked when she realized she remembered more now than she had when she'd gone to sleep. Closing her eyes, she tried to envision it. "I don't know. Dark.

Blue or black, maybe. Large. I can't tell. I just see the headlights.''

"An SUV, maybe?"

"Maybe."

"What about the man?"

"I'm afraid of him. Not just a little. But a lot. I know what he's capable of.'' She could barely hear herself speak above the pounding of her heart. "I know him. I know him well.''

"What's his name?"

"I don't know.'' A nervous laugh broke from her throat. "That makes a lot of sense, doesn't it?''

"It doesn't matter if it makes sense. Just talk to me. Get this out while it's fresh in your mind. We'll figure out what it means later.''

Hannah closed her eyes and let her mind take her back to the dream. She could still feel the spike of terror. The pain of his fingers biting into her throat. The shock of the first blow.

"He struck me.''

John's face went dark, his jaws flexing like steel.

"It wasn't the first time.'' She felt herself recoil, like an insect that curled in on itself when prodded with a sharp stick by a cruel child. The shame inside her swelled like a fresh bruise. "I had a relationship with him. Not too long ago. But I walked away. It was…over.''

"I'm sorry you had to go through that.'' Setting his forefinger under her chin, he forced her gaze to his. "I'm sorry he hurt you.''

She wasn't sure why, but she had a difficult time meeting his gaze.

"Whatever happened, it's not your fault,'' he said.

"I know.''

He gripped her hand tighter. "What else do you remember?''

"That night in the woods. He was going to kill me. If

I hadn't gotten away, he would have...." She swallowed hard. "Not only would he have killed me...but my baby." Her own words shook her so thoroughly that for a moment, she couldn't speak.

John cursed beneath his breath. "Do you know why, Hannah?"

"No." She swallowed hard, felt the tempo of her heart increase, heard the rush of blood through her veins augment into a dull roar as fragments of the dream pummeled her.

"What else?"

"I ran until I couldn't go on. I was terrified. I didn't want my baby to die. When I reached the cliff..." Her mind rebelled against the knowledge of what she'd done next. The truth terrified her almost as much as not being able to remember. "Oh my God." She raised her eyes to his. "I didn't fall, John."

"He pushed you?"

The words chilled her, but not as much as the ones she was about to utter. "No."

Turning slightly on the bed, John touched her face gently. "Tell me what happened, Hannah."

"I...jumped."

His eyes narrowed. "To get away from him?"

She could barely bring herself to say the words. "I figured I had a better chance of surviving a fall."

"Good Lord." He scrubbed a hand over his face, then gazed at her over his fingertips. In the depths of his eyes, Hannah saw the slow boil of outrage. And for the first time, she also saw that he believed her. She wasn't sure why, but the fact that he did brought tears to her eyes.

"It's going to be all right," he said.

"I want to believe that. I'm not sure I do."

He thumbed a tear from her cheek. "Ah, you're not going to cry on me now, are you, Red?"

"Probably," she said. "If the situation is right, I can cry buckets, you know."

"You really know how to scare a guy."

A laugh squeezed from her tight throat. "I go right for the big guns."

"I don't have any tissues on me, but I've got a pretty solid shoulder." One side of his mouth curved. "Will that do?"

Pulling back slightly, she looked at him through her tears.

"Come here," he said.

"You sure about this?"

"I'm sure." He reached for her, tugged her closer.

Hannah closed her eyes and laid her head against the solid mass of his shoulder.

"I know this is hard for you, but you're doing fine," he said.

"I hate being afraid. I'm not a coward."

"I know you're not."

She sighed when his arms went around her. She snuggled closer, telling herself it was nothing more than a comforting hug between friends in the aftermath of a traumatic ordeal. If only she could make herself believe that.

"You remembered some important things tonight," he said. "If the dreams and the flashbacks you're having are memories trying to surface, I think that's good."

"I just wish they weren't so frightening. I wish I could remember without having to relive it."

"If it's any consolation, I'm here for you, okay?"

The sweetness of the words brought a fresh rush of tears to her eyes. "Now you're going to make me cry."

"You're welcome to stay for a few more days if you need to."

"I don't know, John. I've got a lot going on in my head." Not to mention the little problem of her insane attraction to him.

"If you're worried about that kiss…"

"Among other things." Pulling back slightly, she looked at him. "I didn't think of it earlier, but my being here…I could have put you in danger, too."

His smile warmed her despite the cold press of fear. "I'm flattered that you'd worry about me, Red, but I'm a big boy. I can take care of myself and you, too. No one's going to hurt either of us."

She nodded, but she wasn't sure she believed it.

"Are you feeling better?" he asked.

"Yes. Thank you."

His aftershave was getting to her again, making her feel pleasantly dizzy. She told herself the light-headedness was merely an aftereffect of the nightmare, but she knew it had more to do with the way her heart was zinging around in her chest.

When she raised her eyes to his, she knew neither of them was thinking about the nightmare any longer. In the span of an instant, something had shifted. A subtle transition that put them on equal ground, but with treacherous footing. One slip, and they would fall headlong into yet uncharted territory.

His face was only inches from hers, so close she could see the heavy stubble of his beard. She had the sudden urge to run her fingers over the black shadow, but she didn't. She knew if she touched his face, he would touch her back and things would get out of hand like they had back at Angela Pearl's.

Hannah knew the moment couldn't go on. It wouldn't take much for her to make another mistake with this man. They were playing a dangerous game by getting this close. He was kind and patient and just cocky enough to keep her on her toes. She was attracted to him beyond reason. Light-years beyond good sense. The combination was volatile at best. Downright explosive if she wanted to be truthful about it.

But temptation wreaked havoc on her willpower until it bowed beneath the power of his gaze. Forgetting good judgment and the hundred other reasons why she shouldn't kiss him, Hannah leaned forward and pressed her mouth against his.

The kiss should have been chaste, but it wasn't. John accepted her mouth, tasted heat and desire and the bitter taste of his own frustration. He endured the contact with stoic passivity. His arms remained at his sides. All the while his heart raged like a caged beast against his ribs.

It took every ounce of willpower he possessed to keep himself from deepening the kiss. His intellect waged a bloody battle with the side of him that didn't give a damn about right or wrong or any of those gray areas in between. But his blood was pounding. An alarm wailed in the back of his mind. The kind that usually went off an instant before he did something stupid. And he knew if she didn't pull back in about two seconds, his discipline was going to crumple and he was definitely going to do something stupid.

She didn't pull back.

John didn't remember reaching for her. She was incredibly small. Slender, but it wasn't for lack for curves. Hannah had plenty of curves. She wasn't wearing much beneath that T-shirt, either. His intellect might have known better than to notice, but his body had moved beyond good judgment and responded with an urgency that left him grappling for control—and in dire need of a cold shower.

Her lips were soft and enticing beneath his. Her scent wound around his brain like an entrancing mist, sinking into him, through him, until he was drunk on it. Her hair brushed across his cheek, making him wonder what it would be like to get lost in it. His fingers itched to ease her hair aside and bare her throat, so he could get a taste of the succulent flesh beneath. He wanted to wrap his arms around her and take her down on the mattress. He wanted her beneath him. He wanted to kiss her until neither of them could see straight. He wanted to get inside her, lose himself in her wet heat.

Need coiled low and hot in his belly, burning him. The blood built painfully in his groin. Urgency gripped him like a vise. The power of the sensations shocked him. Insanity beckoned like a siren to a sea-weary sailor.

Lust, he told himself in a moment of panic. He could deal with lust. He understood the dynamics of it, accepted it as part of being a man. It was all the other feelings roiling around in his head that worried the hell out of him.

His control shattered when she slipped her tongue between his lips. Raising his hands to her face, he tilted her head back and deepened the kiss. Using his tongue, he savored the sweetness of her mouth. Hannah gasped, but he swallowed the sound, went deeper, tasting, seeking, needing. Vaguely he was aware of her arms going around his neck. Her body coming against his. He moved over her. Never letting go of him, she eased onto her back beneath him. John came down on top of her. The earth moved when her legs opened to him. The need to get inside her blindsided him with such power that his head swam.

What the hell was he doing?

Sanity descended with a resonant thud. John broke the kiss, rolled off of her and got unsteadily to his feet. Hannah sat up quickly, her eyes startled and large. For a stunned moment they stared at each other, the only sound coming from their labored breathing.

"I didn't mean for that to happen," she said after a moment.

"That kiss wasn't such a good idea," he heard himself say.

"I was just..."

"Yeah, me, too." His voice sounded like two pieces of rusty steel grating together. "Nothing happened."

"We're still fully clothed."

Embarrassment sloshed over him when he realized he was standing there in his boxer shorts and in an obvious state he didn't even want to think about. Turning away, he started toward the door.

"John, I'm sorry I…woke you, but…thanks."

Guilt nudged at him for lusting after a pregnant woman who'd obviously been through so much. If his common sense hadn't intervened, he might have… Ruthlessly he cut the thought short. "I'll check the doors before I turn in."

"John—"

"Get some sleep, Red." He left the room without looking back.

Hannah woke to sunshine. It streamed through the window above her bed like yellow beams of spun gold. Outside, the spindly boughs of a conifer cradled handfuls of snow and scratched against the glass like a cold little bird. For a moment, she was disoriented. Moving tentatively, she felt her sore muscles protest, and abruptly remembered the circumstances that had brought her here—and the man who had welcomed her into his home.

Snuggling deeper into the covers, she took in the aspects of the bedroom. The beamed ceiling, paneled walls and glossy pine floor spoke of masculinity and an underlying solidity that made her feel…protected. A solitary dresser sat against the wall facing the bed. The headboard above her was brass and slightly tarnished. The sheets smelled of aftershave and man.

Hannah sighed as the memory of the kiss surfaced, sent a pleasant flutter to a place low in her belly. Not the baby, she realized, but something else that wasn't quite so benign. The response troubled her. She didn't have a clue how she was going to handle John or the way she was reacting to him. She wanted to believe she'd merely been shaken up by the nightmare last night. That John had lent a comforting shoulder. That the kiss had been chaste and comforting. But Hannah was honest enough with herself to admit the problem wasn't that simple. And that kiss had definitely not been chaste and comforting. How on earth could she be attracted to a man when she was carrying another man's child? A man to whom she could very well be happily married?

Or was she?

The question sent a shiver through her despite the fact that she was warm beneath the covers. Dreams had plagued her through the night. Dreams that ran the gambit from terrifying to senseless. Nightmares of running through darkness and snow, of being pursued by an unseen malefactor, of tumbling into a black abyss to escape an even darker fate.

But the nightmares had been tempered with softer dreams that had left her breathless and disturbed for a very different reason. Dreams of a raven-haired, blue-eyed stranger swooping down from the sky and taking her into his arms. A stranger with a gentle voice and trust-me smile. A man whose embrace shot sparks of electricity through every inch of her body.

Now was *not* the time for her to be thinking of electricity with regard to a man she would undoubtedly never see again after this was all over. John Maitland *was* attractive, she admitted. But Hannah couldn't let herself be taken in by his abundance of male charms.

Hearing movement on the other side of the room, she rolled over and found herself face-to-face with saggy brown eyes and a big black nose. "Honeybear," she said.

The big dog had nudged the bedroom door open and now stood next to the bed with his chin resting on the spread, wagging his tail. "Don't tell me you're a morning dog." He wagged his tail harder at the sound of her voice. Reaching out, she scratched behind a floppy ear. "You're pretty cute for a big lug."

Panting despite the chill in the cabin, the dog lumbered toward the door. "Okay, okay, I'm coming." Stepping into her scrub pants, Hannah finger combed her hair, realized her efforts were futile, then walked over to the door and peeked into the hall. The smell of coffee and bacon should have been mouthwatering—if her stomach hadn't been giving her not-so-subtle hints that food wasn't on the agenda this morning. Hopefully John would have some crackers in his pantry.

She was halfway down the hall when the bathroom door swung open. John stepped out wearing nothing but a towel and a grin. Hannah's heart fluttered once, then promptly dropped into her stomach. The sight of him damp from a shower and smelling of piney woods and soap shouldn't have left her head swimming, but it did.

"Morning." His biceps flexed as he scrubbed a navy blue towel over his hair. "How are you feeling?"

Hannah wasn't sure which of them was more surprised, but she definitely knew who was more uncomfortable— and it wasn't John. He seemed to be right in his element standing half-naked before her with damp flesh and that wide chest.

"Sorry 'bout the towel."

Heat rose in her cheeks when she noticed the way the towel in question rode low on his hips. Her first instinct was to look away, but she didn't want him to know she was rattled, so she kept her gaze steady on his. "No problem."

"Any luck with your memory?"

"No."

"I made coffee. Decaf for you."

"Great." The urge to let her gaze roam was strong, but she resisted. The last thing she needed to know was that

John Maitland had one of the most magnificent male bodies she'd ever laid eyes on.

"I fixed breakfast," he said.

"I...smell it." She didn't have the heart to tell him the smell of food held as much appeal as a pair of moldy socks.

"I figured you could use it." He gestured in the general direction of her abdomen. "Eating for two, and all."

If he hadn't looked so damn good standing there in that towel, she might have told him all she wanted were a few crackers. Her stomach was feeling temperamental at best this morning. But Hannah was too flustered to conjure up a response that was even remotely intelligent.

"I'll just get dressed," he said after a moment.

Her legs nearly went weak with relief. "Good idea. I'll just...be in the kitchen." Cautiously she eased around him and made a beeline for the kitchen.

John hadn't been exaggerating when he'd said he fixed breakfast. He'd cooked enough food to feed the entire Rocky Mountain Search and Rescue team. The man obviously knew his way around the kitchen. A plate heaped with pancakes warmed on the stove. Perfectly cooked bacon strips drained on a paper towel next to a bowl of fruit. The rinds of several oranges sat near an electric juicer, its pitcher full of fresh juice. The sight should have had her mouth watering. Unfortunately, her stomach had other ideas.

Searching through the cabinets, she found a glass, filled it with water and took a cautious sip. Not sure if her stomach was going to cooperate, she set the glass on the counter and started toward the pantry to search for crackers. A sheet of paper lying next to the juicer caught her attention. She read the heading. "Pregnancy: The First Trimester." She stared at the print, realizing from the date at the bottom of the page that John had already been on the computer that morning at a health site on the Internet.

"I didn't know if you wanted milk or juice, so I bought both."

She started at the sound of his voice and spun.

"There's a grocery just a few miles down the road," he said. "You were asleep. I picked up a few things."

He'd changed into a pair of faded jeans, a charcoal flannel shirt and hiking boots. The cap he wore was black with the RMSAR emblazoned at the crown. Eyeing her, he entered the kitchen and went directly to the refrigerator and withdrew a gallon of milk, took it to the small table and poured two glasses.

"Actually, I was hoping for some crackers or dry toast," she said.

"Got that, too. I hope whole wheat is okay."

"Fine."

He strode to the toaster and popped the button down. "I bought organic eggs. I thought maybe a cheese omelet would be a good source of protein and calcium."

The thought of eating eggs—organic or otherwise—made her stomach pitch. "John, I appreciate all this…" She tried not to look at the eggs he was breaking into a stainless bowl. "But I'm not really hungry this morning."

"You've got to keep up your strength, Red."

"No, really, I'm—"

He proceeded to break the yolks and whisk. "I could add some mushrooms or tomatoes if you like."

One look at the slimy concoction in the bowl, and Hannah lost the battle with her stomach. Dignity forgotten, she put her hand over her mouth and ran for the bathroom.

John stood at the counter with the whisk in his hand, staring after her for a full minute before realizing what had happened. Damn, he should have realized she was looking a little green around the gills. But he'd thought her paleness had more to do with lack of food than nausea. He hadn't even checked her pupils to see if maybe the nausea was from the concussion.

He shouldn't have overlooked something so obvious. Not John Maitland the medic. But he knew it wasn't the medic that had screwed up. John Maitland the man knew damn good and well why he hadn't gotten any closer to her this morning—because of that blasted kiss. Well, both kisses actually. Every time they got within shouting distance of each other, one of them ended up making a mistake and dragging the other one into it.

Chiding himself for not being more observant, he left the kitchen and headed for the bathroom down the hall. He stopped outside the door and knocked quietly. "Hannah? You okay?"

"Go away."

The toilet flushed. Compassion kicked through him at the sound of her being sick. He hated it that there was nothing he could do to help. "I'm sorry," he said. "I didn't know you were sick."

"Yeah, well, welcome to my pregnancy." The toilet flushed again.

"Is there anything I can do?"

"Get rid of those eggs."

As badly as he felt, he couldn't help but smile. "Right."

He heard the water in the sink run. An instant later, the door opened. Her face was damp with water, two shades too pale, and framed by strands of wet hair. She shouldn't have looked sexy, but she did.

"Don't say anything about food," she said.

"I won't."

"Especially eggs."

"No problem." He shoved his hands into his pockets. "Anything else?"

"Do you think you could come up with some dry crackers?"

Something went soft in John's chest at the sight of her

porcelain features framed by that tangle of red hair. It may have been uncombed, but he still wanted to run his fingers though it. "You're pale," he said.

"I'll be fine as long as you don't start talking about bacon and eggs, okay?"

He smiled. Damn, he was even starting to like her when she was grouchy. "How about a glass of ice water with those crackers?"

"Deal."

Forgetting about his self-imposed rule not to touch her, he took her face in his hands and leaned closer.

She stiffened. "Wh-what do you think you're doing?"

"Checking to see if your pupils are dilated. That okay with you?"

"Oh. Well…" He felt her relax. "Are they?"

"No." He released her and let his hands drop. "That's good."

"So, I feel like death warmed over because I'm pregnant not because I tumbled down the side of a mountain. Like that makes a lot of sense."

He grinned. "Sorry, Red, but that's about the size of it."

"How long does morning sickness last?"

"How would I know?"

"Well, you're a medic," she said. "And I saw your reading material on the kitchen counter."

Reading material? John winced inwardly. Shoot, he must have left the articles he'd downloaded and printed in the kitchen where he'd been reading as he cooked.

"You know, the article titled 'Pregnancy: The First Trimester.' It may have been presumptuous of me, but I figured it was about pregnancy."

"Oh, that one." Not sure why it embarrassed him having her know he'd been reading up on the subject of pregnancy, he gently took her hand and started toward the living room. "Have a seat, and I'll bring you the crackers."

A few minutes later, he joined her with a plate heaped with dry crackers and a few orange sections. He set the ice water on the table next to her. She was still too pale for his liking, but at least the sickly cast was gone.

"This might interest you." He set the article on the coffee table. "I don't know much about pregnancy, so I went out to a health site and downloaded and printed it."

"Thank you." She reached for the articles.

"Crackers first, Red." Taking a cracker from the plate, he handed it to her along with the glass of water. "You can read after you eat."

She rolled her eyes. "Oh, for Pete's sake."

"You didn't have dinner last night. You need to eat."

She took a bite of the cracker. "When I was sick this morning. The nausea…it was familiar to me."

"You've been sick before," he said.

Her eyes met his. In their brown depths, John saw a flicker of hope. "Yes, I remember being sick."

"That's great, Red. I mean, not about you being sick, but that you remember. That's terrific."

"I think it's happened to me a lot during this pregnancy."

He looked down at the half-eaten cracker in her hand. "Did you remember anything else?" he asked carefully.

"Not really. Just what I recalled in the dream last night."

John didn't miss the tremor that ran the length of her when she mentioned the dream. He'd heard people scream before. In the course of his career, he'd heard them scream in pain, in surprise, in fear and in anger. But he would never forget the sound of Hannah's scream or how it had sent him bolt upright from a deep sleep. She hadn't been simply afraid. She'd been terrified.

She finished the first cracker, and John handed her a section of orange.

"You know," she began, "I've been so caught up in

what's going on with me, I just realized I don't know anything about you.''

He couldn't tell her she didn't know anything about him by design. He didn't talk about his past. The John Maitland he'd been back in Philly no longer existed.

''What do you want to know?'' he asked.

''Where are you from?''

''Philadelphia.''

She smiled. ''I knew it was somewhere in the northeast.''

''How's that?''

''Your accent.''

''Accent?'' he scoffed. ''I don't have an accent.''

''You give words that end with the 'a' sound an 'er' sound. And you clip your words.''

''I do not clip my words.''

''Do, too. And you call me Hann-er.''

''Hannah,'' he said.

She laughed. ''You did it again.''

John feigned annoyance and rolled his eyes. ''Did not.''

''Okay John-from-Philadelphi-er.''

''You're giving me a hard time about my accent.'' He grinned. ''I can't believe it.''

''So, what brought you all the way from Philadelphia to Colorado?''

The question shouldn't have stopped him cold, but it did. John told himself it was a natural progression of curiosity. Innocent small talk. He'd heard the question a hundred times—and he'd answered with the same lie a hundred times. But no matter how many times he told it, the lie never got any easier.

''The job.'' He hated that he couldn't meet her gaze. Couldn't look into her guileless brown eyes and think of Philly. ''And the mountains,'' he added as a half-truth. ''I saw the Rockies when I was a kid, and they moved me. I knew I'd live here one day.''

He wondered how she would react if she knew the truth—if she knew about the darkness in his heart, if she knew whose blood ran thick in his veins. John assured himself the relationship would never go that far. After all, John Maitland the Untouchable didn't get close to people. He kept them on a need-to-know basis, and most people just simply didn't need to know.

The pager clipped to his belt chirped. He looked down, saw the number, felt the familiar rush of adrenaline.

"What is it?" Hannah asked.

"There's a call out—"

"Call out?"

John started toward his canvas bag of gear next to the door. "All the team members of RMSAR wear pagers. When a call comes through Dispatch, we get paged. I've got to go out for a few hours."

"Oh. Okay."

"It snowed in the higher elevations last night. There's probably been an accident." As much as he'd wanted to get out from under her line of questioning, only then did John realize he wasn't quite comfortable leaving her alone. Logic told him she would be all right here without him. But the part of him that was a man and feeling protective didn't like the idea that he could be wrong.

"You'll be safe here," he said, lifting his parka from the coat tree.

"Of course, I will." She nodded enthusiastically, but John didn't miss the quick flash of uncertainty in her eyes. He didn't blame her for being uneasy.

"No one followed us. No one knows you're here."

"Really, I'm okay. I mean, I've got Honeybear to protect me, right?"

John grinned. Oh, yeah, he was starting to like her just fine. "Hold that thought, Red. And make yourself at home. I've got to go. I'll be back in a few hours."

Chapter 10

The call turned out to be serious multivehicle accident with critical injuries that entailed two trips to Lake County Hospital and took more than four hours to clear. Even through the adrenaline and stress of two litter extractions and one resuscitation, John still hadn't been able to get Hannah off his mind. Worse, for the first time in his career, he hadn't been able to keep his focus. His timing had been off during the extraction. Luckily, he hadn't made a mistake, but several times he'd seen the cool looks he was getting from Buzz—and knew the older man knew why.

John knew stashing Hannah at his cabin for safekeeping wasn't the smartest thing he'd ever done. If he wanted to be truthful about it, keeping her there was probably downright stupid. So why had he offered? Why couldn't he stop thinking about her? And why in the hell couldn't he wait to get home?

The questions taunted him as he hauled his canvas equipment bag out of the Jeep and started toward the cabin. He still didn't have the slightest idea what he was going to do about her. He couldn't turn her out on the street. Not when she was pregnant and alone and obviously in trouble. His best option—the smart thing to do—would be to take her to another women's shelter. The problem was, John wasn't feeling particularly smart when it came to this woman.

Digging out his house key, he unlocked the door. The first thing he noticed was her scent. An intriguing mix of sweet and earthy with subtle undertones of woman. The next thing he noticed was the music. Classic rock and roll streamed into the living room from the kitchen and rattled all the windowpanes along the way. That she liked rock and roll made him smile.

Something had changed since he'd walked out that morning. He couldn't put his finger on it, but the cabin seemed…different. Alive with the essence of woman and all the subtle nuances that made a house a home. For the first time in a long time, John felt like he'd come home.

Shoving aside the wayward thought, he silently closed the door behind him. A fire blazed in the hearth. A little too much wood, not stacked just the way he liked, but the living room was toasty warm. The magazines he'd tossed haphazardly on the floor were neatly stacked next to the sofa. Normally, Honeybear would have come bounding out about now, and they'd have a friendly tussle on the rug. But the dog was nowhere in sight.

Where was his dog? Where in the world was Hannah?

Doing his best to ignore the rise of alarm, John set his bag next to the door and walked toward the kitchen. From the hall he could see that the light was on. The music grew louder as he neared the doorway, an old Eric Clapton number about a woman waiting for another love. Pausing in the hall, he peered into the kitchen, and felt his heart stumble in his chest.

Hannah stood in the center of the room locked in an awkward dance with Honeybear. With his oversize paws on her shoulders and his tail moving back and forth at a hundred miles an hour, the dog looked like he was having a pretty good time. Smiling, Hannah sang along with the lyrics, shuffling her feet in time with the beat.

John stared, mesmerized and unexpectedly charmed by the sight of her dancing with his dog. She was wearing one of his T-shirts over a faded pair of jeans. The T-shirt was three sizes too big, but the material flowed over her like fine silk. Her hair was pulled into a ponytail, but several unruly strands curled around her face. She looked lovely and happy and innocent—all the things he wasn't—and the spike of lust came so sharply, his mouth went dry.

An instant later Honeybear spotted him and barked, and the spell broke. Hannah's gaze snapped to John's, a small sound of surprise escaping her. Honeybear dropped to all fours. She stepped back from the dog. "I didn't hear you come in." Glancing self-consciously down at her T-shirt, she brushed off a clump of dog hair. "He jumped up on me, and the music was on, so I just..."

"Decided to dance with him?" John grinned.

"Well..." She smiled back.

He knew he shouldn't go to her, shouldn't touch her, shouldn't torture himself with that kind of temptation when he knew it would only lead to trouble. But the urge was too strong to fight. He'd been waiting for this moment all day, he realized. He tried not to think about what that meant in terms of how serious the situation had become.

He was across the room before he even realized he was going to move. "I was about to cut in. I hope you don't mind."

She broke into laughter. "You probably think I'm a loon."

"I think I'm jealous of my dog."

"He *is* a pretty good dancer."

"Let's see how I do." Taking her hands in his, he eased her closer and began to sway with the music. John wasn't sure why he did it; he knew better than to court trouble. But the instant her body came against his, the doubts no longer mattered.

"You're blushing," he said.

"I'm totally embarrassed. I don't normally dance with…you know…dogs."

"Honeybear's not just any dog, you know. He's an ex-search-and-rescue dog."

"Ah, a hero. Like you."

"I'm no hero, Red." She had the prettiest eyes he'd ever seen. The color of fine cognac through fluted crystal and so clear they took his breath. He liked the way the outer edges tilted up. The way her left cheek dimpled when she smiled.

"The cabin looks…nice." He breathed in her scent, fought a bout of dizziness. "So do you."

"Well, I…um, didn't have anything else to wear. I hope you don't mind my borrowing your T-shirt."

"It looks a lot better on you than it does me."

"I suppose that depends on the eye of the beholder."

He grinned at her. "You're flirting with me, aren't you?"

She grinned back. "My heart belongs to Honeybear."

Putting his hand over his heart, John feigned heartbreak. "And to think I called him my best friend."

He swept her into an overstated dip. Their gazes locked, and John felt the heat twist low in his belly. For an instant, his mouth was just an inch from hers. Her breath smelled like peppermint. Her lips looked soft and inviting. How he wanted to kiss her.

"I learned something about myself today," she said breathlessly.

He pulled her out of the dip. "That you like to dance with Newfoundlands?"

She smiled again. "You're not going to let me live that down, are you?"

Yeah, he definitely liked her smile. "Not a chance."

"I realized I like to stay busy," she said. "I hope you don't mind, but I straightened the cabin some."

"Thanks. It needed it." He smelled something delectable simmering on the stove. "What's on the stove?"

"Spaghetti." She shot him a tentative smile. "After those crackers this morning, I sort of worked up an appetite."

"Feeling better?"

"Lots." She stopped dancing. "Would you like to eat?"

"I want to dance."

The music changed to a slow song about a woman taking a man to heaven. John barely noticed the change in tempo. His senses were completely overwhelmed by the woman he held in his arms. A small voice of reason cried out for him to be cautious, to pull back and regroup and not react impulsively to the situation. He knew the dangers of getting too close. He'd once paid a lofty price for caring for the wrong woman. Combine that with his past, and he knew that to care for Hannah was a disaster waiting to happen. Not only for him, but for her.

But when he eased her closer, and she laid her head on his shoulder, he crushed the voice with a single blow.

"You're tense," he whispered.

"I just—I'm not used to dancing, I guess."

"You were doing fine until I walked in."

"Well, um, I was just goofing off."

"You look really good goofing off."

"Honeybear was stepping all over my toes."

"I'll have to talk to him about that." He grinned at her. She smiled back, and John felt an odd quiver in his chest. He wasn't sure what it meant, wasn't sure he wanted to know at this point. All he knew for certain was that she felt like heaven against him, and he would have sold his soul for a kiss.

"I want your hair down." Raising his hand, he tugged the band loose. Red hair cascaded down, flowing over his hand, brushing against his face. Setting his chin atop her head, he breathed in her scent, let it intoxicate him.

"My hair is a mess."

"I love your hair." His intellect ordered him to pull away and stop the situation before things got out of hand. He knew better than to give in to needs as simple and as dangerous as lust. A roll in the hay with a willing partner was one thing, but a woman who could turn his brain to mush—and his willpower to dust—by merely dancing with his dog was something else entirely.

He was about to pull away—he really was—when she sighed and relaxed against him. At the soft brush of her body against his, slow pleasure wound around him and squeezed like a snake, cutting off the flow of blood to the place in his brain where common sense resided. Her body conformed to his like gelatin to a mold. Even as an alarm clanged in the back of his mind, he knew he wasn't going to stop what he knew would happen next. He knew the mistake would cost him in the long run. But for the first time in a long time, John didn't let himself think about consequences.

Shoving the last vestiges of reason aside, he put his hand under her chin. Startled brown eyes met his. In their depths he saw the realization of what was about he was about to do. He gave her two seconds to stop him. When she didn't, he lowered his mouth to hers and stepped into heaven.

The power of the kiss made Hannah's legs go weak. Every nerve ending in her body stood up and took notice. By the time the message of what was happening reached her brain, it was too late. Her arms went around his neck and she kissed him back.

In the back of her mind, she knew she shouldn't have

let it go this far. She may not have her memory to draw upon, but she damn well knew better than to court disaster.

Kissing John Maitland was definitely a disaster.

Her brain told her to pull away and stop the madness, but her body scoffed at the command. His lips were firm and gently demanding against hers. His scent filled her nostrils, titillating her senses, teasing her body with dark promises she knew he could keep. When he probed with his tongue, the shock of pleasure made her gasp. She opened to him. Growling low in his throat, he moved closer and went in deep. A sharp pang of arousal coursed through her. Heat built low in her belly and spread like smoldering flames until she felt feverish. Her sound of surprise came out as a purr.

Her tongue tangled with his. Seeking. Tasting. Wanting. His breath caressed her cheek like the tip of a feather. His hands skimmed along her back, sending shivers all the way down to her toes. A little voice of reason reminded her this was a mistake. But the taste of his mouth, the feel of his hard shaft against the fire burning low and hot blinded her to the gravity of it. She told herself she merely needed to be held, needed the gentleness and warmth of his touch. But she knew they were nothing more than rationalizations.

His mouth worked dark magic on hers until she was dizzy with a thousand sensations that crumpled her logic, like a tattered scrap of paper. The onslaught of pleasure overwhelmed her intellect. Instinct usurped the bedraggled remnants of her good judgment, and she kissed him back with wanton abandon.

The music filled her ears and flowed through her like a drug. All the while, John filled her senses until she was mindless to everything but the feel of him against her.

He brushed a kiss next to her ear. ''I couldn't stop thinking about you today.''

She tilted her head, offering her throat. Goose bumps

raced down her body when he kissed the tender flesh there. "We shouldn't be doing this."

"I know. This is crazy."

"Totally insane."

"Not a good idea at all." She yelped when he grasped her hips and lifted her onto the counter. "I want you where I can get at you."

Before she could speak, he'd pulled her to the edge of the counter and moved between her legs. The music faded until all she could hear was a heartbeat. She wasn't sure if it was hers or his, but it was racing out of control, and pounded through every inch of her body. The heat in her belly augmented to a ball of fire. She felt herself go wet, but knew the dampness between her legs would do nothing to cool the fire burning there. The situation had become serious. A lapse in judgment on both their parts that would surely lead to a mistake they wouldn't be able to repair. As if the kiss wasn't enough of a mistake. But the feel of him against her fed something ravenous inside her. She gave the beast free rein, let it guide her.

A loud rap on the back door made her jump.

Tearing his mouth from hers, John shot a glare toward the door. "Oh, hell."

Hannah glanced up to see Buzz Malone standing outside, staring at them as if he'd walked up on Bonnie and Clyde.

John knew what this was going to look like to Buzz. Like he'd given in to a weak moment for a woman who could very well be taking advantage of an all-too-common male weakness.

Dammit, he did *not* want to be in this situation.

John figured he could handle Buzz. What he wasn't so sure about was how he was going to handle Hannah. Closer to the truth, he wasn't sure how he was going to handle his growing feelings for her. As impossible as it seemed, she'd gotten to him. She'd touched John the Untouchable. Not only physically, but she'd gotten under his skin—and inside his head.

Scrubbing a hand over his face, John looked at Hannah. "I'm sorry," he said.

"It's okay." She looked shaken and incredibly beautiful sitting on the counter with her cheeks flushed and desire sparking like gold dust in her eyes.

"Uh, I've got to get the door." Reaching for her, he eased her down off the counter. He tried sorely not to notice when a lock of red hair tumbled over his arm, but he reached out and tucked it behind her ear. When she looked up at him, the urge to kiss her was so strong, he had to turn away.

Lord have mercy, he was in deep.

Resisting the need to rearrange himself, clamping his jaw down in annoyance, John walked to the rear door and jerked it open. Buzz Malone wasn't smiling.

"Don't say it," John growled in a low voice.

Buzz gave him a narrow-eyed glare. "It's your ass."

"It's my ass, and it's my life. Stay out of it."

Frowning, he glanced past John toward Hannah. "She still claiming amnesia?" he asked in a low tone.

"She's not claiming anything. She's recovering from a concussion. Got it?"

"Yeah, I got it loud and clear the moment I saw you two—"

John cut him off with a curse.

"I thought you had more sense than this. I can't believe you're getting involved with—"

"What do you want, Buzz?"

Scowling, the older man lifted the battered case at his side. "I brought over a fingerprint kit. Since you didn't have time to drive to Denver today, I thought I'd lend a hand."

John sighed. "Come on in."

Buzz strode inside and set the case on the kitchen table. Hannah stood near the stove, looking like a woman who'd just been thoroughly kissed. Her hair tumbled wildly around her shoulders. Her mouth was kiss-bruised and wet. The tinge of pink in her cheeks told him she was just as uncomfortable with the situation as he was.

John sighed again. Oh, boy, this was going to be fun. "Hannah, you remember Buzz Malone?"

"Yes, of course." She strode forward and extended her bandaged hand to Buzz. "Nice to see you again, Mr. Malone."

Buzz was too much of a gentleman to refuse a woman's handshake—even if he didn't trust her—but it was evident he didn't approve of John's keeping house with her. He gently grasped her hand and shook it. "You seem to be feeling better."

She shot John an uncertain look. "Uh…yes, I am. Thank you."

He motioned toward the kit on the table. "I thought I'd get your prints and run them through the computer."

If Buzz had suspected she wouldn't be pleased by the prospect of finding her identity, her expression proved him wrong. Relief and hope and jumble of other emotions scrolled across her features. For a moment, John thought she would cry, but she didn't. Her eyes filled, but at the same time she dazzled both men with a hesitant smile. "Thank you," she said. "I can't tell you how much this means to me."

Surprise flickered in the older man's eyes, but he quickly resumed his scowl. Motioning toward the table, he said, "Sit down and we'll get this over with."

John pulled out a chair for her, and Hannah took it.

"Let's start with your right hand."

She lifted her hand to Buzz. With the smooth efficiency of a man who'd done the procedure a hundred times, Buzz removed the bandages. He stopped when her peeling fingertips came into view.

"Damn," he muttered.

"What is it?" Hannah asked.

Buzz grimaced. "I didn't realize how extensive your frostbite was. The tissue is too damaged for me to get a full set of prints."

She stared down at the hand Buzz held in his. "Are you sure? I mean, can you get a partial?" Helplessly, she looked at John. "Isn't there something else we can do?"

John didn't miss the quiver that ran the length of her. He looked at Buzz. "What do you think?"

The older man studied her fingertips. "I can probably get a pretty good thumb print. Maybe a palm." He pointed to the undamaged pad of her thumb. "We can run a partial, plug it in to the computer and see if anything comes back."

"How long before my fingers heal enough to get a good print?"

"The damaged tissue will slough off naturally," John said. "That might take a week or so."

"That's too long." She looked from man to man. "I need to know who I am. I can't just sit around and do nothing."

"I'll run it and see what comes up." Fishing the white fingerprint card from the case, Buzz took her hand, pressed her thumb into the ink, then rolled it side to side on the card. Gently, he did the same with her palm.

"That's all I can get for now." He shot John a hard look. "I'd like a word with you."

John met the other man's stare head-on. He admired and respected Buzz, but he was only going to let him push this so far. "Fine."

"Alone." Buzz looked over at Hannah. "You might want to go into the bathroom and wash off that ink. Use warm water. Don't scrub. You don't want to break the skin.''

Her eyes swept from John to Buzz. Squaring her shoulders, she rose, her eyes seeking Buzz's. For a moment, John thought she would say something, but she didn't. Without a word she turned and strode from the room.

''You've really got a way with subtle, Buzz. Maybe you should have just cuffed her and hauled her out to the car while you questioned me.''

For the first time Buzz looked chagrined. ''I'm not a cop anymore, but I know a con when I see one.''

''Someone hurt her, Buzz. Someone left her up on that mountain to die. Was that part of the con, too?''

''I'm not disputing that she's in trouble. What I'm concerned about is that she's involved you.''

''It's my choice.''

''You know what happened the last time you hooked up with a woman in trouble.''

''This is different.''

''You're not using your head, John. At least not the one stuck on the top of your neck.''

''This isn't how it looks. Even if it was, that's no reason for her to be at the top of your hit list.''

''I know what I saw when I knocked on the door. You're playing house with a woman who nearly shot you. Any woman who points a gun at one of my team members is automatically on my hit list. Not to mention when the media gets a whiff—''

''The media isn't going to find out.''

''People gossip in hospitals, John. This woman's story was a hot topic among the nurses and you know it. Eventually, some hotshot reporter is going to get a whiff of it and you're going to be right in the middle of it. That puts RMSAR in the center of it, and I damn well don't like it.''

''I'll handle it.''

''Don't let what happened in Philly make your decisions

for you. You don't need to make up for what's already been done.''

John winced at the mention of his past but recovered quickly. ''This isn't about Philly, and it isn't about me. It's about a woman who needs my help.''

''It's about your judgment and a woman who could cause you serious problems—''

''Don't let what Kelly did to you skew your thinking when it comes to women.''

It was Buzz's turn to wince, and John knew he'd hit a nerve dead center. Never taking his eyes from John's, Buzz closed the fingerprint case and rose. ''I'll run the prints.''

John rose, aware that his heart rate was up, that he was angry, not only with Buzz, but at himself, as well.

Buzz started toward the door, opened it, then turned back toward him. ''Watch your back,'' he said, and walked into the cold.

Chapter 11

It took Hannah all of two minutes to toss her meager belongings into the canvas bag. By the time she zipped the top and threw the strap over the shoulder, she was shaking. She told herself the shaking was the result of anger. Buzz Malone didn't know anything about her; he had no right to judge her. But she knew that wasn't the only reason she felt the sudden need to walk back to Denver.

Her attraction to John had become a serious problem that could no longer be ignored. Three earth-shattering, mind-blowing kisses in less than twenty-four hours promised to complicate a situation that was already infinitely complex. If she was married or otherwise involved in a serious relationship, how could she live with herself if she let this go any farther?

Worse, Hannah also knew her being here might have endangered John. She didn't know what kind of a person she'd been in the past; she hadn't a clue what she was involved in. All she knew for certain was that John was a decent man with a good heart, and she had absolutely no intention of involving him any more deeply.

Taking a breath, she started toward the bedroom door. The sight of John standing at threshold froze her in her tracks.

"I'm not letting you walk back to Denver if that's what you're thinking," he said evenly.

"I was hoping you'd offer to drive me."

"After what happened at Angela Pearl's, I don't think your staying there is a very good idea."

"Then take me to another shelter. Surely there's another shelter in Denver or Boulder."

"I'm sure there is," he said reasonably. "I was hoping you'd stay here."

"We both know that's a bad idea." The thought of venturing out into a world where maniacs in SUVs shot randomly at her was about as appetizing as another tumble down the mountain. But Hannah knew she didn't have a choice. "I don't want to come between you and your friend."

"Buzz and I have been friends for eight years. We might disagree about how I'm handling this, but it's not going to come between our friendship." His eyes narrowed. "That's not really what you're worried about, though, is it?"

Hefting the bag higher on her shoulder, she gathered the broken fragments of what was left of her courage and met his gaze head-on. "Look, this is getting really complicated—"

"Is it?"

She stared at him, incredulous. "In case you haven't been paying attention, I'm pregnant."

"I've noticed."

"Well, I didn't get that way by myself."

The muscles in his jaw flexed. "Spell it out for me."

"I'm carrying another man's child, John. Even if I'm

not married, I've got to be involved in a very serious relationship to have gotten this way. I may not have my memory, but I don't need it to know I wouldn't take something like that lightly.''

"You're not sure about any of that. You could be divorced for all you know. You're not wearing a ring.''

"Whatever the scenario, nothing good can come out of my staying here with you.''

"Unless your husband is the man who put those bruises on you.''

The words struck her like a boxer's punch, so solid and hard she was stunned for a moment. The strap slipped from her shoulder. The bag hit the floor with a thunk. "We don't know that, either.''

"I'm not going to rule it out.''

She'd considered the possibility. But to hear the words spoken aloud, to think that a man she loved would hurt her while she carried his child within her womb was too ugly to accept. "That doesn't explain the SUV. Or why someone tried to shoot me. That doesn't sound like something an abusive husband would do.''

"Maybe not. But the bottom line is, I don't want anything to happen to you, Hannah. I'm in a position to help you. Why won't you let me?''

She'd vowed not to let his words touch her—or affect her decision; Hannah knew what she had to do. But she could tell by the way her heart wrenched in her chest the words had already touched her deeply. "I can't stay.''

"If you're worried about what happened in the kitchen—''

"And at Angela Pearl's. And again last night. And every time we look at each other.''

He shoved his hands in the pockets of his jeans. "So we…acted irresponsibly. We're adults. We'll handle it.''

"I can't.'' Despite her best efforts, her voice quavered. "You're a decent man, John, and I thank you for everything you've done, but I can't stay here. If I'm married or otherwise involved with someone, I could never live with myself if…something…happened between us. I can't get…involved with you. I'm not that kind of person.''

"I know you're not. What happened was my fault.''

"I knew what I was doing.''

"You were vulnerable—''

"I won't change my mind, John. I'm sorry if you don't understand, but if you won't take me back into town, I'll find another way.''

The sudden chirp of his pager made her jump. John read the number and cursed. "It's a call out.'' He raked his hand through his hair. "I've got to respond.'' He looked at her. "Promise me you'll be here when I get back.''

Hannah knew it would be easier to call a taxi and make a clean break while he was gone. She knew John would give her the money if she asked. But she didn't want to ask. And she didn't want to walk away like that. Not after everything he'd done for her. "Will you drive me back to town later?'' she asked.

"I will, but I'm going to try to talk you out of it.'' When she started to protest, he raised his hand. "I'll take you wherever you want to go. Just promise me you won't do anything until I get back. Will you do that for me, Red?''

Hannah didn't have the heart to say no. "I'll wait, but I'm not going to change my mind.''

He lifted his hand as if to touch her, but dropped it to his side when she stepped back. "I'll be back as soon as I can,'' he said. "If you need me, call headquarters.'' Turning, he left without looking back.

He lurked in the shadows.

Even from where she stood, she sensed his anger. It was like a living thing inside him, a monster that appeared out of nowhere, as dark and unpredictable as a tornado, ripping through the countryside.

This wasn't the way she'd planned to tell him. Not in her worst dream. Tonight should have been one of the happiest days of their lives.

He'd turned it into a nightmare.

The first blow shocked her speechless. Pain zinged across her right cheekbone. Instant tears burned her eyes. But the physical pain was nothing compared to the outrage exploding in her heart...

Hannah jerked awake, shaken and disoriented, her heart racing. It took her a moment to realize where she was, and that she was alone. Raising her hand, she touched her cheek with her fingertips, almost expecting to feel pain. She told herself it was just a dream, but she knew it wasn't. Her memories were coming back, she realized, and none of them were good.

A glance at the clock on the mantle told her she'd been asleep for almost an hour. It seemed like only a minute or two had passed since she'd lain down on the sofa to wait for John.

Around her, the living room was dark. The embers of the fire glowed red and gold. Moonlight slashed through the front window and sprinkled silver drops over the braided rug, casting shadows that danced like dark figurines on the wall. Sitting up, Hannah gave her eyes a moment to adjust to the darkness. Her next thought hit her brain like a punch.

She'd left the lamp on, hadn't she? So then why was the house dark?

The burn of adrenaline cut through her belly like a saber. She sat up straighter and listened to the press of silence. The hiss of the fire. The buzz of the ceiling fan overhead. The tick-tock of the clock on the mantel. Across the room, Honeybear growled low in his throat.

"Honeybear?" she whispered. "Come here, boy."

For the first time, the dog didn't bound over and smother

her with messy kisses. The click of his toenails against the floor as he waddled into the kitchen was his only response.

A minute sound at the front window sent another zing of adrenaline through her. Rising, Hannah padded silently over to the window and peeked out. Silver moonlight sparked off the snow, illuminating the branches of the conifer that grew alongside the cabin. An ice-covered branch scratched against the glass like a spindly fingernail. No gun-toting maniac in an SUV anywhere in sight.

Letting out a sigh of relief, she flipped the light switch. The first vestiges of fear crawled over her when the room remained dark. "Okay," she said. "It's probably just a fuse."

Remembering John had given her his card with the number to RMSAR headquarters, she glanced around and found her canvas bag on the floor next to the coffee table. She pulled out the card, telling herself he would probably have to talk her through the dynamics of changing a fuse. She picked up the phone. Her plan died a quick death when she found the line dead.

Fear coiled like a snake in her gut. Hannah fought it, telling herself no one could possibly know she was here. Or could they?

The sound of breaking glass fractured her thin hold on control. She spun toward the kitchen. Over the wild drum of her heart, she heard Honeybear barking. And she knew.

Someone was coming in through the back door.

Forgetting the need for stealth, she sprinted to the front door, slammed the bolt lock aside and flung it open. Icy air greeted like a slap, but she didn't pause. She ran across the porch and down the steps, slipping on a patch of ice at the base of the stairs. Behind her, she heard the dog barking frantically. Concern for the animal halted her midstride.

"Honeybear!" she called out. "Come here, boy!"

But it wasn't the dog that appeared at the front door.

Less than a dozen feet away, a man stepped out on the porch. He was thickly built. Tall. With the unmistakable silhouette of a gun in his hand.

Hannah stared, terror singing through her veins. She couldn't see his face, but she knew he'd spotted her. Her brain screamed for her to run, but she couldn't tear her eyes away. The familiarity of his movements stunned her, tore at the barriers to her memory. She knew him, she realized. Knew she was in danger. Knew he would hurt her if she let him. Knew he would kill her and her unborn child if she gave him the chance.

Spinning, she sprinted across the yard toward the road. Her feet sank into the snow, her breaths puffing out in front of her. Cold seeped through her socks and bandages to numb her feet.

The first shot sounded ridiculously like a firecracker. But Hannah knew the sound, felt the kick of terror, looked frantically for a place to take cover. *Oh, God, please don't let him hurt my baby.* There were no neighbors in sight. No lights to guide her. Only trees and snow and her own terror.

Two more shots rang out. Arms outstretched, Hannah covered the ground with reckless speed. Across the road, into the drainage ditch. "Help me!" she screamed.

Hope exploded in her chest when headlights slashed through the darkness. "Help me! Please, help me!" Heedless to the dangers of the speeding vehicle, she sprinted toward the headlights. The Jeep skidded to a halt a dozen feet away. The driver's side door swung open. "What the hell?"

"John!" Surprise and relief and a hundred other emotions pummeled her. She scrambled toward him, slipped on the icy roadway and fell to her knees. "He's got a gun!"

"Whoa. Who's got a gun? What's going on?"

"He's here! In the cabin! He's got a gun!"

Strong hands grasped her shoulders as she struggled to her feet. "Slow down. Easy. Just calm down for me, okay?"

"He was in the cabin! He's armed. He'll kill us both!"

"Get in the Jeep." Yanking open the door, John practically shoved her inside. He snatched his cell phone off the console and thrust it into her hands. "Call Lake County Sheriff's Department. Speed dial two. I'm going to have a look."

She took the phone, punched the number. "He's armed, John. He'll kill you." With the phone to her ear, she started to get out of the Jeep, but John blocked her way.

"Stay put, dammit!"

For the first time it hit her that Honeybear hadn't come out of the cabin. "Honeybear's still inside," she said.

"I'll get him," he said. "You stay put. Get Lake County out here *now*." Without waiting for a reply, he started for the cabin at a dead run.

John's heart pounded pure adrenaline through his veins as he jogged across the porch and swung open the front door. He knew better than to walk into a situation like this without some kind of weapon to back him up. But the thought of an armed intruder breaking into his home, threatening Hannah or hurting a harmless animal like Honeybear made his temper boil.

The living room stood dark and ominously silent. Giving his eyes a moment to adjust to the darkness, he slipped into the room, listening, his every sense honed on his surroundings. The clock on the mantel ticked. The embers in the fireplace hissed like snakes. Moving silently across the living room, he peered into the hall to find it empty. On the kitchen floor, broken glass sparked like icy crystals. John's temper roiled at the sight of the broken pane; he felt the violation all the way down to his bones.

The son of a bitch had been in his home.

A sound from the hall spun him around. Ready to tear whomever had done this apart with his bare hands, John stepped into the hall. The bathroom door was closed. Something moved on the other side. Without giving himself time to debate safety, he kicked in the door.

Yelping once, Honeybear rushed out, his tail between his legs. Cursing the quick jab of fear—and an even sharper jab of sympathy for his dog—John followed the animal into the living room and knelt, aware of his heart beating hard and fast in his chest. "Let's have a look at you, big guy."

The animal licked John's hands. John winced at the sight of blood on the velveteen bridge of the wide nose. His temper stirred at the thought of some mindless goon hurting such a sweet-tempered dog.

"Is he all right?"

He jumped at the sound of Hannah's voice. "He's cut, but it's not too bad."

He told himself the urge to go to her, to wrap his arms around her trembling shoulders, was what she needed, not him. But John knew it was a lie. He knew the need to feel her softness and quiet strength against him was all his own, and he felt it raging inside him right alongside the anger and fear and the outrage at having his sanctuary invaded.

"Are you all right?" he asked.

"I need to sit down."

Shoving caution aside, he went to her. "What is it? Are you hurt?"

"Just a little nausea."

Putting his arm around her waist, he guided her to the sofa and settled her onto it. "Sit."

"Like I'm going to argue with you."

"Yeah, well, it wouldn't surprise me." He touched her shoulder. "Lean forward and put your head between your knees."

"John, I'm—"

"Humor me, Red, for God's sake."

She did as she was told.

John looked around the living room, taking a quick inventory in the semidarkness. Cold air poured through the open front door. Except for the broken pane in the kitchen, nothing appeared to be out of place. In the distance, the sound of a siren broke the stillness of the night.

"This is my fault."

John turned to see her sitting up, leaning against the sofa back. Her face was powder pale in the wash of moonlight. He shouldn't have noticed how beautiful she looked with her dark eyes and trembling mouth and her hair tumbling over her shoulders. But he did notice, and he felt the impact of her beauty like the blow of a sledgehammer.

"This isn't your fault," he growled.

"It's me he wants, not you."

"Who?"

She sighed. "I don't know."

"Like I'm going to hand you over." When she merely stared at him, he added, "For the next few days, it's a package deal, okay? If he wants you, I'm part of the package. He can damn well deal with me, too."

"Look, before you left tonight, you agreed to drive me—"

"I agreed to discuss it with you." He cut her a sharp look. "Here's a news flash. I've changed my mind."

"John, I'm the reason this happened."

"And I'm the reason he didn't get his hands on you," he snapped.

"He was armed. He could have—"

"He didn't."

She looked down at her hands twisting in her lap. "I've turned your life upside down. I didn't want that to happen."

"I'm not complaining, Red. Dammit, I'm involved because I want to be." John didn't mention the fact that he couldn't bear the thought of anything happening to her. Or that he could still feel the razor's edge of fear slashing his gut. He would never forget how she'd looked, running toward his Jeep in the darkness. Or the way his heart had frozen into a solid block at the thought of a bullet finding its mark.

Troubled by the thoughts, he glanced over at her. Even in the semidarkness he could see she was trembling. Her hands. Her shoulders. Her face was so pale that, in the moonlight coming through the window, she looked like a ghost. "Do you feel steady enough to tell me what happened?"

She nodded, her gaze meeting his. "I fell asleep on the sofa while I was waiting for you. When I woke up, the lights were out. I thought maybe it was a fuse or something, but when I tried the phone it was dead. Honeybear started growling, and the next thing I knew I heard the glass breaking."

The primal need to protect what was his—this woman, his dog, his home—made him grit his teeth in anger. "The son of a bitch."

"This isn't about you, John."

"He just made it about me."

"He won't let you stop him." She turned tear bright eyes on him. "He won't let you get in the way."

The fact that she knew those things stopped him cold. "How do you know that?"

Her eyes widened. "I'm—I'm not sure."

"Did what happened tonight somehow trigger your memory?"

"I know him," she whispered.

The hair on the back of his neck prickled. "Who is he?"

"I don't know his name, but he's familiar to me."

"How so?"

"I don't know…exactly."

"Do you know why he's trying to get to you?"

She shook her head. "No."

"What else do you remember?"

"He's the same man in the nightmare."

"Did you see his face?"

"I only saw him in silhouette." She rubbed her temples with her fingers. "The memory... It's so close. It's driving me crazy. I can't do this anymore. John, I need to know who I am." Tears shimmered like raindrops in her eyes when she looked up at him. "I want to see the psychiatrist Dr. Morgan recommended."

"We'll call him first thing in the morning, all right?"

She nodded. "I'm sorry I got you involved. I mean, you don't even know me. You don't know what kind of person I am—"

"I know exactly what kind of person you are." Easing down on the sofa beside her, he tried not to think about the irony of her words. John knew exactly what kind of person Hannah was. Because of that, he couldn't help but wonder how the kind and compassionate woman he'd come to care about so deeply would react when she found out the truth about him.

Chapter 12

Hannah didn't think the police were ever going to leave. For the two hours, she curled on the sofa fighting post adrenaline jitters and a bad case of morning sickness while a fresh-faced deputy fired off questions she hadn't the slightest clue how to answer. Another deputy took John's statement in the kitchen while John treated the cut on Honeybear's nose. By the time the last police officer walked out the door at midnight, Hannah was almost too tired to care.

Feeling the nausea roil in her stomach, the fatigue press into her with an almost physical force, she leaned against the sofa back and closed her eyes.

"If a picture speaks a thousand words, I'd say you were wiped out, Red."

She opened one eye to see John coming toward her, a box of crackers in his hand. "I'm totally annihilated."

Without asking, he opened the box and handed her two crackers on a napkin. "A couple of these might help."

"Ah, fuel for a pregnant woman's soul." Anxious for

the nausea to pass, she took a bite of cracker. "Do the police have any leads?"

"They dusted for prints, but it's doubtful they'll get anything." He grimaced. "The deputy told me you said the guy was wearing gloves."

She nodded, the image of the man's leather-clad fingers closing around the gun eliciting a shiver. "What else?"

"There was no blood from the broken back window, so they won't be able to type his blood. No tire tracks. They got a boot print, but identifying him that way is a long shot."

"He's not your run-of-the-mill burglar, is he?"

"We both know he didn't come in to steal."

"He came for me." She wrapped her arms around herself to ward off the chill that had crept over her. "He'll be back. I don't know how I know that, but I do. And it terrifies me."

"I'm not going to let anything happen to you." He scrubbed a hand over his jaw. "I told them what happened at Angela Pearl's. The sheriff's department agreed to put an extra patrol on duty tonight. A deputy is going to cruise by every couple of hours to keep an eye on things."

The words didn't make her feel any safer. At the moment, she didn't think anything could make her feel safe. Not when gunshots still echoed in her ears, and she could feel the sharp claws of terror piercing her as she'd run for her life.

"A patrol isn't going to be enough," she said.

His eyes were keen on hers. "What do you mean?"

"I mean, he's not going to stop."

"How do you know that?"

"I don't. But I feel it." She pressed her hand to her chest. "I *feel* it very strongly. I know he's dangerous and determined and he's not going to stop until—"

"That's not going to happen," he cut in.

"John, I can't stay here. I've got to go—"

"That's not going to happen, either."

She looked over at him and felt that familiar roll just below her ribs as he glared back at her. What was it about those vivid blue eyes that made her heart pitch like a tiny ship on a raging sea every time he looked at her?

"You agreed to take me to a shelter," she said.

"I'll take you to RMSAR headquarters."

His response should have annoyed her, but it didn't. She was scared; he was willing to help her. While that was an enormous comfort, all she could think of when she looked into his eyes was that she'd put him in danger, as well.

"What if he finds us there?" she asked.

Something dark jumped behind the calm blue of his eyes. "He won't."

Judging from his scowl, he wasn't going to back down, so Hannah let it go. She trusted John to keep her safe, trusted him with her life and her unborn child's life. But for all his courage and strength and determination, she wasn't convinced he realized fully what they were up against. She wasn't even sure herself.

"During avalanche season, some of us stay at headquarters so we're available in the event of a call out. There's a back room with cots and blankets as well as a vending machine." He held up the crackers, a smile softening his features. "We'll bring our own crackers."

"I can't hide out forever at RMSAR headquarters."

He silenced her with a don't-argue-with-me stare. "It'll keep you safe through the night. When morning comes, we'll get with Buzz and file a report with the Denver Police Department. Then we'll pay a visit to that shrink and see if he can help you remember."

The crackers had helped with the nausea, but the fear coiling in her gut was a hundred times worse. The logical side of her brain told her spending the night at RMSAR headquarters was the only smart thing to do. But the side of her that had grown to care about John knew that as long as she was with him, he was in danger, too.

John took the scenic route to RMSAR headquarters—Colorado-style. After strapping Hannah into the passenger seat and securing Honeybear in his extralarge pet carrier in the rear, he rammed the Jeep into four-wheel drive and did what he'd wanted to do since buying the thing—took to the back roads. Half an hour and twenty-two miles later, he slapped off the headlights and pulled stealthily into the rear lot. For the first time since leaving the hospital with Hannah the day before, he was utterly certain no one had followed them.

If only that were the sole danger they faced.

The sentiment rang like the echo of a rifle shot in his head. He knew better than to tempt fate or risk getting caught up in the very thing he spent so much time and energy fighting when it came to this woman. John could keep her safe; he could even afford to care about her a little. But he could never, ever let it go any deeper. That was John Maitland's number-one rule. A rule he never broke no matter how tempting the woman. Because as surely as his life had somehow become entangled with hers, he knew the time would come for him to walk away.

The thought sobered him as effectively as a glass of ice water thrown in his face. What was he thinking, letting himself feel something for a woman who'd already been through so much? A woman who didn't have a clue what kind of man he was, or understand the dangers a relationship with him would bring to her and her unborn child?

As he unlocked the door and ushered Hannah inside, he pondered his options, realized he didn't have a choice but to stay the night with her. As much as he didn't want to believe it, someone was trying to kill her. At this point, no matter how he felt about her, he was the only person who could keep her safe. He wouldn't shirk that responsibility. The trick, he supposed, was going to be getting through the night without doing something stupid.

"How did he know I was at your cabin?"

John took in the sight of her and felt that odd sensation of free-falling grip him just tight enough to make him woozy, like a glass of wine on an empty stomach. "Conceivably, he could have followed us from the hospital the day you were released."

"How did he know I was alone tonight?"

John had been hoping to delay discussing the matter for a while, at least long enough for her to get some sleep. He didn't like the pale cast to her face. Not when she was pregnant and still recovering from hypothermia and a serious fall.

Taking her hand, he guided her past the dispatch station to the sleeping quarters at the rear of the building. Reaching into a commercial-size storage unit, he pulled out two cot frames and began unfolding the first.

Walking around behind him, Hannah tugged down a rolled-up mattress. "We've moved around quite a bit, John. From the hospital to Angela Pearl's, to your cabin. Whoever is after me seems to be finding me quickly and with relative ease."

John took the mattress from her and unrolled it. "You're tired. Why don't we discuss this in the morning?"

"Why don't we discuss it now?"

Arching a brow at the challenge in her voice, he turned to her, felt that wave of dizziness engulf him when he saw the flash of temper in her eyes. Even angry and frightened, her beauty struck him hard enough to send him back a step.

"You're dead on your feet, Red." Taking her shoulders, he eased her to a sitting position on the cot. "You're not doing yourself or your baby any good driving yourself to exhaustion."

She stood back up. "Don't patronize me. I'll be dead *period* if I don't figure out what's going on and why."

"I'm not going to let anyone hurt you." Even as he made the promise, the thought of someone getting to her, hurting her, made him break a cold sweat. He knew self-recrimination was counterproductive, but he couldn't help but think he should have been there for her tonight.

"I can't sit around and wait for him to make a move," she said. "I need to do something."

"Like what?"

"Like…going through mug shots or hypnosis therapy."

"Tonight?"

She glared at him. "I hate this waiting."

"It's after midnight." He gentled his voice. "Sit down."

Sighing, she lowered herself to the cot.

"I called Buzz earlier and told him everything." Now it was John's turn to sigh. "He thinks our man is in law enforcement. Maybe a cop."

Her eyes widened. "What makes him think that?"

"Several reasons, but the kicker came earlier during the call out." John had debated on whether or not to tell her; he hadn't wanted to worry her. But he knew keeping information from her wouldn't help either of them. "The call out was a prank."

"You mean there was no accident?"

He nodded. "I've been on the team for six years, Hannah. In all those years, we've never had a false alarm. What's odd about this particular call is that it came in on a police emergency channel. From someone who knew exactly what to say to get us geared up and out the door quickly. He knew exactly where to take us on a wild-goose chase so you would be alone."

"That doesn't prove he's a cop."

"No, but when you consider the fact that he knew you'd been rescued by RMSAR when only one local newspaper carried the story. That he knew which hospital you'd been taken to. That he knew when you'd been released, and where you went from there.''

''He could have called the hospital—''

''The hospital doesn't give out information unless the person calling is family—or in law enforcement. I checked the newspapers. The only paper that has carried the story so far was the *Elk Grove Sentinel.* Unless our man lives in Elk Grove, it's unlikely he would have seen the story. The only way he could have known was if he had access to the police report Buzz filed.''

''That still doesn't—''

''Yesterday, when you had the flashback in Buzz's office, I was watching you, Hannah. You reacted to the photograph—''

''The police uniform.'' She raised stricken eyes to his. ''Oh my God.''

''Buzz thinks this guy put out a false alarm, knowing I would leave the cabin.'' His jaw flexed. ''So he could get to you.''

Leaning forward, she put her face in her hands. ''And my baby.''

The urge to go to her tested his control, but John held his ground. It wouldn't do him any good to touch her, not when she was vulnerable and the need was eating at him like a hungry rat. ''If this guy's a cop, then he'll know every move we make unless we keep it under wraps,'' he said.

She raised her gaze to his. ''Cops are supposed to be the good guys. Why on earth would a _____ officer want to hurt me? It doesn't make sense.''

''That's what we need to find _____''

''How?''

''You're remembering a littl_____ get in tomorrow to see the psych_____ ommended, or if you have another dream tonight...'' His words trailed when her eyes widened. ''What?''

''I *had* another dream,'' she said abruptly. ''In all the excitement, I'd forgotten about it until now. I didn't think it was important. I mean, the dreams are just blending together. They don't really make sense.''

Forgetting the rule about not touching her, he dropped onto the cot beside her. ''Tell me about the dream.''

''It was different than the others,'' she began. ''It was more like...déjà vu than a dream. Like I'd been there before.'' She looked at him, a line forming between her brows. ''I was standing in a kitchen. A typical kitchen with butcher-block countertops and yellow curtains. He was with me. It was our kitchen. We lived there...together.''

Jealousy stirred darkly in the pit of his stomach, but John curbed it with ruthless precision, determined not to react.

''It should have been a happy time,'' she continued. ''I felt that in my heart. I was going to tell him...something important.''

''Tell him what?''

''I'm not sure.'' Squeezing her eyes closed, she massaged both temples with her fingers. ''The memory is...close. I can feel it. I'm happy about the news. But I know he won't be. I know he's going to be angry when I tell him, but I don't understand why.'' Her head snapped up, her eyes filled with pain and seeking his. ''The baby.'' Her hand rested against her abdomen. ''I was going to tell him about the baby. His baby.''

John winced inwardly. He wondered what kind of a man wouldn't be happy about having a child. ''What happened?''

became...enraged after I told him I was pregnant. him like that before, but this rage was darker, He—'' A breath shuddered out of her, and she hand to her cheek. ''He struck me.''

For a moment, John couldn't see. The rage boiled black and violent and all too familiar in his chest. He'd had his suspicions all along about what had happened to her. He'd seen the marks on her body. Seen the fear in her eyes. He'd been there too many times himself not to see the truth. The reality of what she'd gone through infuriated him—and broke his heart.

"I'm sorry," he said after a moment.

She looked down at her white-knuckled hands, relaxed them.

"Who is he?" he asked.

"I'm not sure. The memory is…vague. But we were…together. My husband, maybe."

Feeling like his heart was about to explode, John rose and crossed the room, refusing to acknowledge that his hands were shaking. He couldn't look at her and want her and know she belonged to another man. He couldn't gaze into her pretty eyes and know the man who held her heart in his palm had hurt her so brutally.

But John had to know. "Do you love him?"

Her gaze met his levelly. "No."

"Are you still involved with him?"

"I left him after…he hit me. It was final. Official. Maybe even a divorce. I'm not sure, but I know it's over."

John told himself the words didn't matter. That he hadn't been secretly hoping to hear them. That his legs hadn't gone weak with relief the moment she'd uttered them. Knowing she was free wouldn't change his mind about getting involved.

"Do you remember his name?" he asked. "Or an address?"

"No."

"If Buzz were to show you some photos tomorrow, do you think you would recognize him?"

"I don't know. Maybe. I don't really remember his face. I just…have an impression of him in my mind." She let out a long sigh, regarding him thoughtfully. "You're…angry."

"The son of a bitch battered you. That pisses me off."

"I stopped it." A single tear broke over the barrier of her lashes, belying her strong words. She wiped it off with the back of her sleeve.

"Was it the first time?"

"I think so." Her gaze skittered away from his. "I'm not sure."

"Don't be ashamed." The words came out more harshly than he'd intended, but he didn't take them back. The thought of a man hurting her enraged him enough to make him shake inside and out, his chest ache with the need to protect her. But, dammit, he couldn't let her believe any of this was her fault.

John knew firsthand the ravages of that kind of shame. The burden of secrecy. Both of those things had cost him plenty growing up. As a boy, the weight had crushed him, stolen his childhood, his very innocence like a thief in the night. As a man, his father's legacy had left a cold place inside him—and a lonely future that didn't include the love of a woman.

For the first time, he realized just how far he'd ventured beyond his self-imposed boundaries. He cared about her, he realized, wanted her more than he could admit—even to himself. Worse, he saw both of those things reflected in her eyes every time she looked at him. The truth left him incredulous and deeply troubled. And he knew he was going to have to tell her the truth.

"Whatever happened, it wasn't your fault," he said.

"It was my mistake. I was in control of my life—"

"Batterers use violence as a means of control." He cut Hannah a hard look. "The women involved usually don't have a choice."

"I was with him by choice. I could have—"

"Could have what, Hannah? Controlled his temper for him? Left him? Stopped him?"

She looked down at her hands. "I could have used better judgment."

He wanted to go to her, to hold her and soothe away the shame and pain he saw in her eyes. Logic told him to walk away. To get the hell out of there before he made a mistake they would both end up regretting. But John wasn't thinking logically when he looked at her and felt the need burn him. Two swift strides took him to her. Her eyes widened, but he didn't stop. Leaning down, he took her hand and pulled her to her feet. He wanted her in his arms, and there was nothing on this sweet earth that could keep him from her.

"It's not your fault," he growled. "I want to hear you say it."

"Intellectually I know you're right. I ultimately did the right thing—I left him—but there's another side of me that wonders why I let it happen. Why did I put myself in that kind of situation? Why didn't I do something about it before it went that far? Why did I bring an innocent child into that kind of environment?"

"A woman doesn't plan for something like that to happen to her. It just happens. And, dammit, it happens a lot."

Her gaze sought his. Within its depths, he saw the questions, and he knew she deserved the truth about him before this went any further.

John took a deep, fortifying breath. "A woman is beaten every fifteen seconds in this country, Hannah. Domestic violence is the leading cause of injury to women between the ages of fifteen and forty-four in the United States—more than accidents, muggings and rapes combined. Think about that. Those women don't have a choice. Neither did you."

He didn't tell her that the women who leave their batterers were at much greater risk of being killed than the ones who stay.

"How do you know all that?" she asked guardedly.

The question sent a cold finger of dread down his spine. John had known this moment would come. It always did. This is what he wanted, he told himself. He wanted her to know the ugly truth about him. He should have been prepared for the pain, but he wasn't. He told himself things were better this way. That she had the right to know what kind of man she was dealing with. What he hadn't counted on was the confession being so damned difficult, or the cost so incredibly high.

"I know because I've been there." Gathering his courage, he turned to her and leveled her with a hard look. "I come from a long line of batterers. My father. My grandfather before him."

She blinked as if he'd posed her with a complex problem. "What are you saying?"

"I grew up watching my old man beat my mother. I've been around enough to know I've got the Maitland temper. I've got that same violence inside me."

"Just because your father battered your mother doesn't mean you're the same kind of man. A lot of people have tempers—"

"The stats see it differently." He clenched his jaw against the jab of shame. "Fifty percent of children who grow up in a violent home become batterers themselves."

"That means the other fifty percent grow up to become decent spouses and parents—"

"I've had relationships before, Hannah. And I've destroyed them. I've hurt the women who loved me." He felt his lips draw back in a snarl. "Dammit, I've looked down and seen my hands clenched into fists—"

"I don't believe you."

"I won't let that happen to us."

"You're not a violent man." She started toward him.

John didn't want her any closer. The urge to turn and walk away pounded him. He knew what would happen if she got too close. If she touched him. He might have the discipline to walk away to keep her safe, but he didn't have the willpower to walk away from her touch.

He jolted when her hand closed around his forearm. "You're decent and kind and courageous. I've felt the gentleness of your touch. I've experienced your kindness. I've seen the compassion in your eyes. And I've seen you risk your life for a person you didn't even know."

"If you're looking for a hero, you've got the wrong man."

"You're wrong—"

"You don't know about Philly. You don't know what happened the day I left."

"Then tell me. Let me decide for myself."

John stared at her, stunned by her faith in him. How could she believe in him without question when he didn't even believe in himself? Why couldn't she just make this easy on both of them and let him walk away?

"My old man was a cop," he began. "An alcoholic with a nasty temper and a mean streak that ran deep. It didn't happen often, but I saw him hit my mother enough times that by the time I was six years old I hated the son of a bitch."

Thirteen years had passed since he left Philadelphia, since he'd heard the sound of fists striking flesh. Since he'd heard his mother's cries. Since he'd had to hear her lie about the bruises. But even after all this time, John could still feel the helplessness and anger boiling in his chest because he couldn't do anything to stop it. Tonight, the memories pounded through him hard enough to make him sweat.

"He took a swing at me a couple of times and passed it off as discipline. By the time I was eight, I knew how to move fast enough to get out of his way. My mother wasn't that lucky.'' He laughed, but the sound that erupted from his throat tasted bitter. ''Sometimes I think she took the brunt of it to keep him off me.''

''Oh, John. I'm sorry.''

He risked a look at her, felt the need cut him hard and deep. Her eyes were soft and fierce at once as she gazed back at him. An intriguing mix of compassion and strength that completely undid him. No woman had ever looked at him like that. No woman had ever believed in him the way Hannah did. He wanted her, he realized, and hated himself for it. He might walk away later, but he knew if she touched him tonight, his discipline would crumble like ice beneath a pick.

''Why did she stay?'' she asked.

''The usual. Love. Denial. Some crazy notion of loyalty. She wanted to keep the family together, even though it was tearing all of us apart piece by piece.''

''What happened the day you left?'' she asked.

He wished like hell he didn't have to tell her. He didn't want to look into her clear, brown eyes and see condemnation—or God forbid, fear. But he knew the truth was the only honorable route to take. Just as he knew it was the only way to keep her from making a mistake that would end up costing them both.

''My old man and I got into it a couple of times over the years,'' he began. ''Most times I just took it. I was tough and fast and had a smart mouth that drove him nuts. By the time I was fifteen, I'd hit him back a few times. By the time I was sixteen, he'd stopped hitting her in front of me. He knew I'd stop him.'' He sighed. ''But one afternoon when I was seventeen, I came home from school early and found my old man there. He was drunk. Ticked off at my mother about something. They'd been arguing. I walked in the door just in time to see him throw the first punch.''

Across from him Hannah flinched. ''Oh, no...''

''I saw her fall. Heard her pleading for him to stop. Something snapped inside me when I saw her blood on his knuckles. I went after him with everything I had.''

''John, you can't blame yourself for that. You were seventeen years old—''

''I knew exactly what I was doing. I wanted to stop him. Dammit, Hannah, I wanted to hurt him. I wanted to hurt him so badly that he'd never raise a hand to her again.''

''You were protecting your mother.''

''I was enraged and out of control. Just like him.''

''He didn't leave you much choice.''

''I didn't just stop him, Hannah. I hurt him.'' John braced against the memory, but the shame sliced him like a blade. ''I don't remember most of it. Just that one minute his fist was drawn back to punch me, the next he was lying on the floor. Even after he was down and wallowing in his own blood, I didn't stop. I put my old man in the hospital that day. I nearly killed him.'' He raised his gaze to hers. ''That was the day I realized I'm an animal just like him. So, before you hang that hero tag on me, I think you'd better take a hard look at the man to see if he's really who you think he is.''

The words left Hannah reeling. With shock for what he'd gone through as a boy. With pain for the man he'd become. And with disbelief that he could think he was anything like his father. The sudden, wrenching need to make him believe that made her reach for him.

Clenching his jaw, John caught her wrist and lowered it to her side. He didn't speak, but she saw the war raging in his eyes. The war against desire and honor. If only she could make him believe the point of contention between the two was moot.

''I won't let you believe that about yourself.'' She didn't know everything he'd been through back in Philadelphia, but there was no way she would ever believe the man she'd known for the last two days was violent. She'd experienced his kindness and compassion firsthand. She'd watched him go pale, his eyes darken with fury when he'd seen the battered woman at Angela Pearl's. She may not know anything about herself, but she knew without a doubt John Maitland would always be a hero in her eyes. The realization that he believed otherwise broke her heart.

He jolted when she eased her wrist from his grasp and put her hand on his forearm. He shuddered at her touch, the muscles beneath her palm cording with tension. "Hannah...don't."

"Look at me, John."

He turned to her, his eyes dark and troubled, his face tight with an emotion she couldn't begin to name.

"You've proven to me in a hundred different ways in the last two days what kind of man you are. It's going to take a lot more than a mistake you made as a seventeen-year-old boy to make me believe you're a batterer."

"A child's exposure to violence is the strongest risk factor for transmitting that behavior from one generation to the next," he said.

"That doesn't mean you're a batterer."

"It means I'm at risk. It means any woman I care about is at risk. Dammit, I have a temper, Hannah. In my eyes that means you and your unborn child are at risk."

He started to turn away, but she didn't let go of his arm. "Don't turn away from me."

"I care about you too much to let this go any further."

"Maybe this has already gone a lot further than you realize."

A curse hissed through his teeth. "I don't get involved, Hannah. I don't do relationships. No matter what happens between us, there's going to come a day when I'll walk away from you. Because deep down inside, I know if I don't walk away, I'll end up hurting you. And that's the one thing I'll never do."

Chapter 13

Her faith devastated him and shook him all the way to his core. John wanted desperately to believe he didn't have the violence inside him. That his father's legacy hadn't affected his life or the decisions he'd made about getting involved.

Only, he knew better.

As Hannah stared up at him with eyes so clear he could look into them and almost see tomorrow, he felt the slow coil of hope burgeon in his chest. It was an unfamiliar emotion that made his throat tighten and threatened the walls surrounding his heart.

"You saved my life," she said simply. "You risked your own life to get me on board that helicopter. You've spent the last few days risking your safety to keep me out of harm's way. And now you expect me to believe you're a batterer?"

John felt those walls fracture with an almost audible crack. "I'd rather die than hurt you, Hannah. I could never live with myself if I..." He couldn't finish the sentence, found himself struggling just to get enough oxygen into his chest. "You deserve better."

"I deserve the truth."

"You deserve the opportunity to get the hell away from a man like me. I'm giving you that opportunity."

"What you're giving me is a cop-out."

This wasn't the reaction he'd expected. He stared at her, incredulous and a little angry, not sure what to say or do next.

"Your sense of honor is commendable, but misplaced," she said.

"Yeah, well, Red, my misplaced sense of honor, as you so aptly put it, is going to save both of us a hell of a lot of pain in the long run."

"The only thing that hurts at the moment is knowing you believe that about yourself." Raising up on her tiptoes, she brushed a kiss across his lips. "You're wrong."

Surprise and pleasure and a dozen other emotions he didn't want to name rippled the length of him. "Don't," he said.

"Stop me."

John endured the kiss, his heart pounding, his blood heating, his palms wet with sweat. The logical side of his brain told him to set her aside and get the hell out of there—pronto. But the moment their lips met, his intellect died a quick and painless death.

Sensation assaulted him, the warm pressure of her mouth against his, the scent of her hair, the sweetness of her breath, the heady rush of blood to his groin. Somewhere in the back of his mind, a tiny voice of reason told him it wasn't too late to walk away. He could drive her back to Denver. Drop her at a shelter or even the police department. Staying with her under the guise of keeping her safe was no longer a viable option. If he were any kind of man at all, he would get out before either of them did something irrevocable.

But the sweet urgency of her kiss cleared his mind of everything except the moment. The essence of her hovered like a sweet hologram, moving over him, through him. Softness and heat and unspoken promises breached the boundaries of his discipline. The walls he'd spent so many years erecting and fortifying shattered.

He kissed her back, tentatively at first, then hungrily. Her arms went around his neck. "How about if we just hold each other for a while?" she said.

Only then did he realize he hadn't put his arms around her. They hung at his sides. But the need to wrap them around her was so acute, he ached with it. "I don't deserve to hold you," he said. "I don't deserve to be with you like this."

Pulling away slightly, she took his hands in hers and met his gaze levelly. "I may not know my own name, but I know with all my heart you would never hurt me or any other woman."

Never taking his eyes from hers, he raised their clasped hands and kissed her knuckles. "If I were a better man, I'd walk away right now."

"If you were a better man, you wouldn't be human."

He thought about that a moment, then felt the grin emerge. "That's a scary—"

Before he could finish the sentence, she captured his mouth in a kiss that made his head reel. He heard a groan, realized it had come from him. Then passion overrode caution. Raising his hands to her hair, he cupped the back of her head and devoured her mouth. She opened to him, and he went in deep, tasting her, savoring her, putting every sensation to memory because deep down inside he knew this would be their one and only time together.

Fresh urgency plowed through him when she pressed her body against his. The last vestiges of his discipline crumbled. Need hammered at his common sense, scattering it like powdered snow in a gale. He wanted to feel her softness against him. Wanted the warmth of her flesh in his hands. He wanted to lose himself inside her.

He cupped her breasts, marveling at the weight of them in his hands. An involuntary moan rumbled up from his chest when he felt the hard peaks of her nipples through her bra. "I've got to touch you." With shaking fingers, he lifted the hem of her sweatshirt and dragged it over her head. "Now."

Her hair tumbled over her shoulders. Her sweet scent surrounded him, drugging him, driving him toward a cliff that promised a fatal fall. He deepened the kiss, fumbling with the clasp of her bra, desperate to touch her. The sound of his own heart raged in time with his labored breaths. The scrap of lace opened. Her breasts, swollen from her pregnancy spilled heavily into his palms. John groaned again, told himself it was lust that made his legs go weak, his head spin. But he'd had plenty of lustful encounters in his lifetime and none of them had ever come close to this. He didn't want to put a name to the magic exploding between them. If he did, it would be real, and he would have to deal with it. He had absolutely no idea how to deal with Hannah.

He cupped her, all the while gently caressing the sensitized tips with his thumbs. "You're incredibly beautiful," he whispered.

"You make me feel beautiful."

"You are. All of you. Right or wrong, I want you, Hannah. I've never wanted anyone so badly in my life." He barely heard his own voice over the thrum of blood through his veins. Wasn't even sure what he'd said, only that he felt the words all the way to his soul.

Breaking the kiss, he lowered his head and trailed kisses down her neck. He thought of the bruises on her throat and his mouth lingered there, seeking to heal the flesh, erase the hidden scars. She shuddered, but he didn't stop. Couldn't stop even if the building had been on fire and their lives in peril. John figured he could die right now and never be as happy as he was at this moment.

Her breasts were rounded, her nipples small, dark peaks. She gasped when he took her into his mouth. She arched, her breaths coming short and fast. He suckled and teased, barely hearing her cries of pleasure, barely aware of her trembling hands at the back of his head, pressing him into her.

Her stomach was soft and rounded. Closing his eyes, he skimmed his hands over her. Longing was an ache that thrummed throughout his body. He wanted her, wanted the child she carried within her to be his. Crazy thoughts, he knew, but John refused to consider logic when his entire world spun crazily out of control. Not when he was intoxicated on magic and prepared to make a fatal leap with this woman, knowing fully he wouldn't survive the fall.

Slipping his hands in the waistband of her scrub pants, he eased them down her hips. Her panties came next. She stepped out of them, then kicked them off. All the while, she kissed him. Driving him insane with her mouth. The feel of her body against his. The sighs emanating from deep inside her.

Breaking the kiss, he leaned forward and set his mouth against her ear. ''There's time to change your mind,'' he whispered.

''I'm not going to change my mind.''

He shouldn't have been relieved, but he was. Vastly. ''I've got a confession to make.''

Raising her gaze to his, she arched a brow.

''I've never made love to a pregnant woman before.''

A soft laugh broke from her lips. ''I think the generalities are the same. Think you can handle it?''

''Ah, watch the ego, Red, will you?'' He smiled, but it felt tight on his face. It stunned him to realize he was nervous. Very, very nervous. ''What about you?''

''I can definitely handle it.''

It took him a moment to find his voice. "I don't want to hurt you or...uh, the baby."

"Oh, you mean physically?"

"Well, yeah."

"I was reading from the medical Web site stuff you downloaded back at your cabin—"

"Did it mention mind-blowing sex?"

"Not in that exact context, but I gathered it's okay for a pregnant woman to have sex. It said some women's...uh, sex drive is exponentially heightened during pregnancy."

"Exponentially, huh?"

"I think that was the word."

"Ah, Red, we're in big trouble."

"That depends on your definition of trouble." Smiling, she raised up on her tiptoes and gave him an openmouthed kiss that left his head reeling.

John's vision blurred when she closed her hand around him. He jolted, felt his control teeter, his breath stall in his lungs. He hadn't been with a woman for several months and had to run his mind through a quick algebra equation to keep from losing it right then and there. He didn't want that to happen with Hannah. That kind of control was important to him. Giving her pleasure even more so.

Her skin was like velvet as he skimmed his hand down her side. Need drove into him as his hand moved over her slightly rounded belly, pausing at the triangle of curls. She opened to him when he reached the apex of her thighs. Parting her folds, he caressed her. Hot, wet silk met his fingertips. John closed his eyes as a hot burst of emotion shook him from the inside out. Her vulnerability touched him. Her beauty humbled him. Her trust shattered everything he'd ever known about himself.

He told himself this was only sex. Lust in its simplest form. Uncomplicated. Primal. A man and a woman reaching out for a moment of pleasure during a time of high stress.

He figured he'd become a pretty good liar in the last couple of days.

He stroked her, felt her body melt around him, the shudders begin. Her mouth sought his and he feasted on her, drinking in the essence of her like a thirst-crazed man at an oasis. Crying out, she arched, then shattered in his arms.

John held her while she trembled. He kissed her temple, her throat. He speared his fingers into her hair and lost himself in its heady essence. He couldn't get enough of her. A flash of insight told him he never would. This one and only time would have to be enough.

The kick of emotion came swift and brutal. This went deeper than the flesh, he realized with a start. Beyond anything he'd ever experienced. The realization sent a quick spike of panic through him. The world spun out from under his feet. When she opened her eyes and smiled at him, John realized the world as he knew it had been forever changed.

Hannah didn't need her memory to know she'd never experienced anything like that before. The man had taken her apart atom by atom, cell by cell, until she was nothing but a quivering mass of sensation tied together by emotions so complex she would never sort through them all. Lord. If she didn't know better, she might have believed she'd fallen for him.

The frightening thought was cut short when she suddenly found herself swept into his arms. "What are you doing?" she asked.

"I'm going to make love to a pregnant woman." Gently he lowered her onto the cot. Kneeling, he leaned toward her and kissed her mouth, her cheek, the sensitive spot just below her ear. The sensations coursing through her made her head swim. Hannah's heart beat wildly beneath her breast. Every nerve ending in her body hummed with anticipation when he stood and began unbuttoning his flannel shirt. Something niggled at the back of her mind, but her brain floundered helplessly as he finished with the shirt and his hands went to the buttons of his low-rise jeans.

She was still shaking from the sheer power of the climax he'd given her. Shaking inside and outside and every place in between. Never in a hundred years would she have even dreamed it could be like this between a man and a woman. Or that she had unwittingly ventured to a world where sensation and emotion collided and exploded and melded. A place where wounds were healed and hearts were mended. A virtual garden where faith and trust grew wildly and bloomed like sacred flowers.

"It's okay if you're having second thoughts."

His voice drew her from her reverie. "Not second thoughts," she said. "I'm just…"

"Nervous?"

She laughed to cover her discomfiture. "That, and about a million other things."

He sat down on the cot next to her and kissed her with devastating gentleness. "I'm nervous, too."

"Really?"

"I'll understand if you want to stop."

"I know you will. I don't want to stop."

His eyes searched hers. "So, then, what's bothering you?"

She hadn't wanted to think about what was weighing on her mind. For just a little while, she'd wanted to put the danger and ugliness aside. She wanted to feel alive and safe and loved—even if it was only an illusion. Still, until this moment, she hadn't realized just how important it was for her to talk about this first.

"I was married, John." She struggled with the words, not even understanding fully herself what she was trying to say. "I'm carrying another man's child."

She raised her gaze to his, and in a moment of blinding insight, she knew her heart wasn't merely at risk. She'd already handed it over to the man who sat beside her, about to make love to her.

The thought thoroughly undid her.

Heart pounding, body humming with arousal, she stared at him, felt the need and uncertainty flash like fire.

"We'll deal with it." He eased away from her, his jaw flexing. "I won't rush you. I won't press you. But I care about you too much to make a promise I can't keep."

"Then make me one you can."

"How about if I show you?" Holding her gaze, he kissed her fingertips, drew them into his mouth. Hannah watched, mesmerized and so moved she couldn't speak. She loved watching him, loved his voice, his northeastern accent, the way he mispronounced her name. She loved the way his hair spiked when it was mussed, loved the way he looked at her when she'd perplexed him—like she had just now. Dear God, was it possible she'd fallen in love with him? Was it possible she'd given her heart to this man when she had absolutely no idea what she would discover about herself when her memory returned?

"Make love to me," she said.

His eyes darkened, intensified, and it took every shred of composure she possessed to hold his gaze. "I'm not a strong enough man to turn you down," he said. "Even if it is the right thing to do."

"If this is a mistake, then it's one I need to make." Her breath caught when he brushed a strand of hair from her face. Closing her eyes, she pressed her cheek to his palm.

"Neither of us are going to be the same when this is all over and done," he said.

"I know." She didn't want to think about what would happen when this was over and done. She had no idea what state she'd left her life in, whether or not they would even survive the next twenty-four hours.

John kicked off his jeans, then stepped out of his boxers.

Hannah swallowed at the sight of him, felt the slow burn of lust creep into her center.

Her mind blanked when he leaned forward and kissed her. Before he'd been gentle, even tentative. This time, his mouth swooped down on hers, taking her breath and devouring her like a hungry predator. The kiss held dark promises of all the things to come. Promises she knew he would make good on. Heat swirled low in her belly, and wet heat pulsed between her legs. Her breasts grew heavy and ached for his touch.

She kissed him back, matching every dark promise with one of her own. He moved over her. Sensation pummeled her until she was mindless with need. All the while he kissed her mouth, her throat. His hands caressed her, wreaking havoc on what little control she had left. She groaned involuntarily when his mouth met her breast. She felt her body writhing beneath his, but she couldn't stop. It was as if someone had doused her with flammable liquid and set her aflame.

He kissed her breasts, her belly, his five o'clock shadow driving her to sweet insanity as he worked his way lower. She knew better than to let herself be swept away like this, but Hannah was helpless to stop the tide.

"Open to me," he said. "I want to taste you."

She couldn't speak, couldn't think. While her intellectual side knew opening herself up to this kind of intimacy would only hurt them both in the long run, her body obeyed. Her legs opened, and he lowered his mouth to her most intimate area.

A thousand lights exploded behind her lids when his mouth found her center. She heard his name, realized she'd cried out. Once. Twice. Oh, sweet heaven, she hadn't expected this. The pleasure built until she thought she couldn't bear it. Sweat broke out on her brow. All the while, his mouth gave her mind-bending pleasure with such intensity that she thought she would scream.

The first wave crashed over her with stunning force. Hannah felt her body clench. Reaching. Wanting. Needing. John. She cried out as the release poured over her, through her, tumbling her until she didn't know up from down, right from wrong.

She reached for him, desperate to join their bodies. Touch his heart. Reach into his soul and make him believe all the things she already knew.

His eyes were dark and intense as he moved over her. She opened to him. Felt his touch like a jolt of electricity, charging through every cell in her body.

"However this turns out, whatever happens between us tonight, I want you to know I care about you, Hannah. I care about you so much I ache."

She told herself she wasn't disappointed. That she hadn't expected him to proclaim his love for her. Not when he had some very serious issues to deal with and she hadn't the slightest idea where she stood as far as her own life. But his words sliced her just the same, like a blade across her chest, leaving her open and bleeding.

He entered her with devastating slowness that took her breath, wrenching every last shred of caution from her. "I love you," she whispered.

She felt him go rigid for an instant. Heard her name on his lips. Then sensation assaulted her when he began to move within her. Long, powerful strokes that took her breath and stole every last ounce of rational thought. Her senses faltered until all she was aware of was John and the magic between them. Words no longer mattered as their bodies became one and their hearts joined in a chorus as ancient and beautiful as the mountains.

He took her to the precipice of her pleasure and a mind-numbing free fall. Then her bones melted, and she knew their fates had been sealed forever.

Chapter 14

I love you.

The words rang in John's ears as he lay sleepless on the cot and stared at the ceiling. For a man who'd just had the best sex of his life, he figured he ought to be feeling a hell of a lot better than he was. Maybe he would if he could get out from under the guilt. If he could keep the emotions from creeping into his brain and wrapping their stealthy fingers around his heart. If he could maintain his vise grip on control long enough to get her safely away from him.

None of those things was happening.

He had his reasons for leaving her words unanswered. Even so, it didn't make hurting her any easier. It didn't make his own hurt any less acute.

John had made the ultimate mistake. For the first time in his life, he'd fallen hard and fast and irrevocably in love. The knowledge thoroughly terrified him. It should have terrified her, too, considering what he was, but he knew it didn't. Hannah didn't understand what love could do to a man like him. What it did to his emotions, his control. She had no idea what a man like him could do to a relationship. Growing up in that Philadelphia tenement, he'd seen love as an ugly beast with a black heart and devastating bite. He'd seen passion as a trap and promised himself he'd chew his own leg off before he let himself get snared. He'd been on the receiving end of violence too many times as a boy not to fear it. As a man, he vowed never to hurt anyone the way he'd seen his old man hurt his mother.

He lived by the rule of distance. Physical distance. Emotional distance. Too bad he hadn't had the discipline to follow those rules when it came to Hannah. The thought made him feel sick. John figured he knew what it was like to be standing on the gallows and feel the noose slip around his neck.

Rising from the cot, careful not to wake Hannah, he stepped into his boxers and walked barefoot down the hall toward the kitchen. The building was cold, but he didn't care. He needed the diversion to start working on getting her out of his system. Judging from the tightness in his chest, he knew he'd be working on that for a long, long time to come.

In the kitchen, he started a pot of coffee. Honeybear rose from his place near the door and padded over to him. Smiling, John reached down and scratched behind the dog's ear, comforted by the animal's presence. "Well, I've blown it this time, haven't I, big guy?"

Honeybear looked at him with those wise brown eyes and grunted as if in agreement. "Yeah, I thought so." The dog ambled back to his bed. John looked out the window. Dawn would break in another hour. Dispatch would arrive shortly thereafter. He figured the smartest thing to do at this point would be to hook up with Buzz and take Hannah to the police station in Denver. There, the older man would find a shelter for her while the police solved the mystery of her identity and what had happened to her up on the mountain. John simply wasn't up to it. Not after touching her. Not after looking into her eyes and wanting a future he knew they could never have.

A scream from the back room stopped his heart dead in his chest. A hundred scenarios jumped through his mind. Whirling, he sprinted down the hall. "Hannah!"

"No! Please, *no!*"

Terror resonated in her voice, hung in the air like gun smoke after a shot. At the door, John saw her sit bolt upright, legs thrashing, her eyes wild. "Richard, no!"

John rushed to her, dropped to his knees beside the cot, wrapped his arms around her. "Hannah. Easy. It's me. John."

She fought him, lashing out with her fists. He sensed her panic, gently restrained her. "Hannah! It's John. Take it easy, honey."

An instant later she relaxed against him, as if all her energy had been sucked out of her. "Oh, God. Oh, John. He was here."

"Who?"

"Richard," she choked. "He tried to—"

"No one's here. You're safe."

"He had a gun. He was going to—"

"Shhh. It was just a dream." But even as he said the words, the hairs at his nape stood on end, and he looked uneasily over his shoulder. "Take a deep breath for me, okay?"

She drew a shaky breath, then pulled away from him and sat up straighter. "It wasn't just a dream." Looking dazed, she glanced around the room. "I—I have to go back."

"Back where?"

"To the mountain."

"Wait a minute—"

"No." Her gaze locked with his. "I have to go back. To the place where you found me."

John had never seen her like this. Terrified and emotionally wrought, but with a steel determination in her eyes that dared him to argue. He couldn't think when she looked at him like that. "Are you all right?" he asked after a moment.

"I'm okay."

"You're shaking."

"So are you."

"Yeah, well, blood-curdling screams at six o'clock in the morning tend to do that to a guy."

She blew out a sigh, then hit him with that power-punch gaze again. The same gaze that turned him inside out every time he saw it. "I'm glad you're here."

"So am I."

The blanket had fallen off her shoulder. He glimpsed the swell of her breast before she tugged it over her. Her beauty humbled him, made him think of crazy possibilities, that anything was possible when deep down inside he knew it was not. Damn, he was in deep. He wanted her again, he realized. Wanted her beneath him, crying out his name as he filled her with his seed, marking her as his, branding her heart to his.

Shocked by the power of his reaction to her, John eased away and sat back on his haunches. Now was not the time for him to be thinking of her in terms of sex. Not when her scent was playing games with his self-control and she was close enough for him to reach out and touch.

But the image of her lying vulnerable and open beneath him as he'd stroked her to climax flashed in his mind's eye. His body responded with a vehemence that left him incredulous and disturbed. He'd had plenty of lovers in his lifetime. Quick, emotionless relationships that had been based on physical need and doomed from the start. But John had never been moved like this. He'd never had his world rocked. Hannah was sweet and genuine, and the most responsive lover he'd ever taken. The power of their lovemaking had left him stunned and more than a little

overwhelmed. He'd never imagined making love to a pregnant woman would be the most erotic experience of his
life.

No, this wasn't working out the way he'd planned.

"Why do you need to go back to the mountain?" he
asked, hoping she didn't hear the grate of frustration in his
voice. "It's January. There's two feet of snow at that elevation."

"I remember more every time I have the nightmare,
John. This time, I remembered...I left...something up on
the ridge. I don't know what it was. A book, maybe..."

She was talking too fast, her words tumbling out bro-
kenly. "Take it slow, Red," he said gently. "What did
you leave behind?"

Brows drawn together in fierce concentration, she
pressed her fingertips to her temples. "I'm...not sure. A
clue maybe. I remember thinking that I wasn't going to let
him get away with...killing me or my child." Her voice
broke with the last word. John watched her fight the tears,
watched her win. "I thought I was going to die that night,"
she said. "I was terrified, but I was also angry. I wanted
to leave something behind that would...incriminate him.
Not so much for me, but my baby. I couldn't bear the
thought of... I didn't want him to get away with killing
my unborn child."

The thought of such a horrendous act sickened him. "So
you left behind some kind of clue?"

"I think so. The memory is foggy. A book maybe. A
box. A wallet. Something small and dark. I don't know.
It's driving me crazy." Closing her eyes, she massaged
her temples. "It's not making any sense."

"If you thought you were going to die, and you left
something behind to incriminate him, that makes perfect
sense."

Her troubled gaze met his.

"What kind of book?" he pressed.

"I don't know. A small book. Dark. Black. Or blue, maybe. With compartments."

"A phone book? Organizer?"

"Dammit, I don't know." Frustration echoed in her voice. "I have to go back."

Glancing over his shoulder, he looked down the hall, saw that the windows beyond were gray with the light of dawn. "Don't ask me to—"

"How far are we from the place where you rescued me that day?" she cut in.

John didn't like the way she was looking at him. Not with that light in her eyes that told him she was determined to do something he didn't necessarily agree was a smart thing to do. "I'm not taking you to Elk Ridge."

"I'll do it without you."

"I won't let you, Hannah."

"This isn't your decision. It's mine. Dammit, I deserve to know who I am. I deserve—"

"You're recovering from hypothermia, not to mention a serious fall."

"I feel fine."

"You're three months pregnant, for God's sake. You're not going to risk the—"

"Don't you dare pull that on me. I'm pregnant, John, not sick. Don't get the two confused. Pregnant women run in marathons, for Pete's sake."

Her tone should have angered him, but it didn't. It scared him. "Come here," he growled.

When she didn't acquiesce, he reached for her. The world shifted beneath his feet when she fell against him. His brain faltered when her scent enveloped him. Feeling his control leaching away, he closed his eyes. "I need to hold you for a moment, okay?"

She felt small and vulnerable and soft in his arms. He wondered how such a small person could wield so much strength. How this one woman could make him feel so out of control.

"I need to do this." Pulling back slightly, she looked at him. "But I need your help."

"I'm not going to help you."

"Yes, you are."

He didn't intend to kiss her. But one moment, he was gazing into her eyes, stroking the back of her head, trying not to identify exactly what it was that scared him so damn much. The next instant, his mouth was on hers, devouring, seeking something elusive, something so vital he felt he might die if he didn't attain it.

A sigh escaped her when he slipped his tongue between her teeth. For a moment, he thought she would resist, but she didn't. She opened to him, and he went in deep. When her body arched and she moved against him, John saw stars. Flashes of light alternating white and black and exploding like fireworks. Vaguely he was aware of the blanket slipping from her shoulders, his hands moving to her breasts. He cupped her, marveled at her softness, swallowed the sound that escaped her when he brushed his fingers over the hard peaks of her swollen nipples.

He wanted to make love to her. Wanted to be inside her. He wanted to hold her just one more time, because he knew the time to walk away was near. But he kissed her again and his resistance was lost. And at that moment John knew he'd lost not merely the battle, but the war. As he jumped into the free fall and tumbled toward oblivion, he tried not to think of what it was going to cost them both.

Dawn broke with a cold north wind and the threat of snow in the higher elevations. With the whine of the snowmobile's engine filling the hangar, Hannah huddled in her coat and tried not to feel guilty for demanding John take her up to Elk Ridge on such a cold day. She knew it wasn't a good idea in terms of safety—not when there was a madman on the loose and a snowstorm building in the west—but she also knew it was the only way to find out who she was and what had happened up on the mountain.

Casting her a dark look that told her in no uncertain terms that he wasn't happy about the trek, John pulled the remainder of their gear from the locker and turned to her. "This is the smallest snowsuit I've got. Put it on, along with the boots and gloves."

She reached for the suit and stepped into it, zipping it all the way up to her chin. "How long will it take us to get there?"

"About an hour."

"What about the ravine where—"

"No dice." He cut her a sharp look that dared her to argue.

He started to turn away, but she stopped him. "I know you don't think this is a good idea—"

"For the record, I think this is an insane idea."

"I can't do it on my own. You have the gear. You know these mountains. You know how to reach the area."

"I also have the good sense to know a crazy idea when I hear one."

She caught his gaze, held it. "John, I left something up on that ridge. Maybe it's not in the ravine. Maybe we can just walk the area and find it."

"And maybe I need my head examined for listening to you." When she only continued to look at him, he cursed. "The damn thing's probably under two feet of snow."

"I need to do this—"

"And I need to keep you safe!"

She stared at him, taken aback by his quick anger, shaken by the realization that she was nearly in tears. His eyes bored into her for an instant, making her feel too many emotions at once until they all tangled up inside her.

"I don't like the idea of being so isolated when someone has been taking potshots at you," he said more gently.

"You called Buzz. He knows where we are."

"Buzz isn't going to do us any good if we're an hour away from RMSAR and some madman decides he wants use you for target practice."

A shiver rippled through her hard enough to start her teeth chattering. She tried to hide it, but she could tell by the way his jaw flexed that he saw it. "Dammit, Hannah—"

"I don't have a choice," she whispered. "I need to know who I am. Please help me."

"It would have been smarter to go to the shrink Dr. Morgan recommended."

"If we don't find anything on the ridge, I'll call the doctor and make an appointment. But I know with everything in my heart that when I find what I left behind, I'll get my memory back." Feeling the burn of tears behind her eyes, determined not to break down now, not in front of him, she bit her lip.

Cursing softly, he reached for her. "You're stubborn as hell," he said.

"Thanks. I think." Hannah's legs went weak when he pulled her against him. The instant his arms went around her, the rest of the world melted away, and she knew that no matter what she found up on the mountain that everything would be all right. It had to be.

"I'll take you up, but we're not going to stay," he said. "It's twenty degrees colder at that elevation. It's isolated. I don't want anything to happen to you."

"Nothing's going to happen."

Gazing down at her, one side of his mouth hiked into what amounted to a very worried smile. "That's what people say right before something happens."

She wanted to say something flippant. Something that would tell him she wasn't afraid. But the way he was looking at her wreaked havoc on her motor skills. For a moment, as she gazed into his eyes, she couldn't speak. All she could do was listen to her heart weep with love for a man who'd sworn he could never love her back.

The snowmobile whined like a banshee through the forest, tearing up the snow and grating over ice-crusted granite. John maneuvered the machine down a mild slope to an open meadow, then picked up speed as they skimmed across a small frozen lake. He should have been ecstatic racing through the breathtaking scenery as the sun broke over Elk Ridge to the east. Instead, he felt like he'd been gutted, then turned inside out to dry.

I love you.

Hannah's words haunted him. He would give up his own soul for the chance to say those three small words in return. But no matter how much he wanted her and the child she carried, he could never put her in the kind of peril a relationship with him would bring.

He wasn't sure when or how it had happened, but at some point he'd fallen in love with her. A frantic little voice tried to deny it, but John was honest enough with himself to see the truth. Just as he was honest enough with himself to know that walking away was the only honorable thing to do. He tried not to think about how badly it was going to hurt to look at her for the last time and end it.

Hannah sat behind him, her arms wrapped around his waist, her legs bracketing his hips. Even troubled as he was, knowing the tentative relationship they'd formed was doomed, he couldn't help but marvel at the feel of her against him. They'd made love twice the night before and then again after the nightmare—a mistake he would carry with him the rest of his days. But he would never forget those precious hours. Already he wanted her again. Wanted her so badly he ached with the need to hold her tight. He told himself things were better this way. She was better off without him. His life was simpler solitary-style.

Too bad his heart wasn't getting the message.

An hour out, John slowed the snowmobile atop a rise where the trees parted and the snow was thin on the wind-blown granite. Dodging rocks the size of Volkswagens, he eased the vehicle over to an outcropping of rock and shut down the engine. Unbuckling his helmet strap, he stood and faced Hannah. "The terrain gets steep and rocky from here," he said. "We'll have to hike it."

Sliding off the snowmobile, she lifted her helmet and shook her head. A tangle of red hair spilled over her shoulders. John stared, felt the need grip him. He loved her hair. Loved the way it felt between his fingers. Loved the smell of it. Loved the way it tickled his face when she was over him, his body buried deep inside hers.

He was going to miss her.

Before he even realized he was going to move, he reached out and touched her cheek. Her startled gaze locked with his. In the depths of her eyes, he saw the questions, the hurt. She knew he was going to end it, he realized, and the pain twisted his heart savagely. The trickle of need augmented to a flash flood, sweeping through him, its power shaking him. Without preamble, he reached for her, pulled her to him and kissed her hard on the mouth. She gasped, but he swallowed the sound, absorbed the emotion behind it. Their tongues tangled. He growled low in his throat. She purred. Spearing his hands through her hair, he angled her head toward him, and kissed her deeply, all the while desperation coiled like a tightly wound spring.

An instant later, he released her. She stumbled back, her cheeks flushed, her eyes wary and surprised. "I don't understand you. You won't tell me how you feel, yet you kiss me like that."

He couldn't tell her that physical love was the only way he could show his love for her. He could never say the words. Physical love was safe. Emotional love carried a price he wasn't willing to pay. "I'm better at destroying relationships than I am at being in them," he said.

"I don't believe that."

Around them the wind rattled the branches of the aspen and whispered through the pines. In the distance, a bald eagle called to its mate.

"We need to talk," he said.

Her expression turned wary. "About us."

He nodded. "Things have gotten…complicated."

"That's not necessarily a bad thing."

"It is because I haven't exactly been honest with you."

The wariness in her eyes sharpened. "What do you mean?"

He knew this wasn't the time to discuss this. Not out in the middle of nowhere with heavy weather moving in. Not when they were both exhausted and scared. But John needed to tell her the truth—all of it—even though he knew it would hurt her. He figured they'd both be better for it in the long run. "There are some things in my past I haven't told you. Things you need to know."

"I know everything I need—"

"You don't know why I didn't make the cut as a cop. You don't know why the academy rejected me." He clenched his jaw against the quick slice of shame. "You don't know why I can't legally carry a firearm in the state of Colorado. You don't know about Rhonda."

He wanted to reach for her, but he didn't. He wouldn't now. To confuse the matter by touching her would make it worse for both of them. John Maitland might have inherited his father's temper, but he wasn't cruel.

"I don't understand," she said.

"The police academy rejected me because I have a record, Hannah. Not just a record, but a domestic violence conviction."

"You told me about what happened in Philly," she said.

"You were seventeen years old and trying to protect your mother from—"

"This has nothing to do with Philly," he cut in. "This happened five years ago, with a woman, right here in Colorado."

The wariness in her eyes turned to shock. "But—"

"I was arrested after a fight with my live-in girlfriend. She pressed charges. It went to court—"

"I don't believe—" She started toward him, but he shook his head, stopping her.

"This isn't easy, Hannah. In fact, it's pretty damn tough. Don't make it harder by trying to rationalize what I did."

"I don't know what you did. I sure as hell don't believe you're a violent man."

A humorless laugh squeezed from his throat. "The prosecutor thought differently. So did the jury."

"I want to hear it from you."

He hadn't wanted to get into the ugly details, but now that he'd cracked open the Pandora's box of his past, he knew he didn't have a choice but swing it wide and tell her everything.

"I met Rhonda at an art festival on Pearl Street in Boulder about five years ago. She was an interior designer. Talented. Temperamental." Remembering her and his own naiveté, he sighed. "Troubled. But she was fun and basically a good person. We dated for a few weeks." He looked at Hannah. "Slept together from the start. I didn't intend to let it get serious. I didn't even realize she was getting serious. But slowly her things started showing up at my apartment until one day we were living together.

"Even five years ago I knew what I was capable of. I have a temper. I'm not easy to live with. At first things were good between us. But she wasn't the independent type. She was needy, hung on a little too tight. I overlooked it, maybe because I didn't want to deal with it. Maybe because I didn't care enough. I don't know. But by the time I realized she was in love with me, it was too late.

"I couldn't let it go on. Not knowing what I did about my temper and relationships. The night I told her I was moving out, she went ballistic. She had a way of pushing my buttons, so I left the apartment to have a drink and cool off. When I came home a few hours later, she was even angrier. We argued. When I started packing, she lost it." The memory made him break a sweat, brought back the darker memories of Philly, all the fears of the boy who'd grown up in a violent home. "She was…irrational, screaming at me, throwing things, making crazy threats. She locked herself in the bathroom. I was going to let it go and just get out of there, but I heard glass break. I thought she was going to hurt herself. When I walked in, there was blood all over. She'd put her hand through the mirror. She was hysterical, unreasonable, angry. I did my best to reason with her, but she was out of control. I knew better than to touch her when I was just as angry, but she tried to throw herself through the glass shower door." He grimaced at the bitter taste creeping up the back of his throat. Damn, he hated the taste of shame.

"I stopped her from going through the glass, but she fought me, biting and kicking." Shame washed over him, thick and stinking, smothering him. "I left bruises on her arms." He would never forget the way she'd looked at him after seeing the bruises. The sense of betrayal in her eyes. The shock and disgust that had crashed down on him like an avalanche.

"The neighbors called the cops. They came out, saw the blood and bruises and arrested me. Rhonda pressed charges. A couple of months later, it went to court. The prosecutor had photos of the bruises. That's all it took for the jury to convict me." It had been a long time since John had relived that night and the nightmare of the trial. Even now, five years later, the shame and guilt pounded

him ruthlessly. "I paid a fine, spent thirty days in jail."
He looked at Hannah. "And I learned a valuable lesson
about myself."

Hannah stared at him, her face stricken and pale. "You
didn't hit her."

"No, I didn't. But I wanted to."

"You tried to keep her from hurting herself, John. You
controlled yourself. That's what separates us from ani-
mals."

"I didn't control myself back in Philly." Fighting off
an uncomfortable wave of emotion, he rubbed his hand
over his face. "I put those bruises on her. I looked down
and saw my hands clenched into fists, Hannah. If I had
lost control…"

"You didn't. That's what counts."

Her trust devastated him, especially when he didn't deserve it. "I lost control in Philly, Hannah. I care about you
too much to let you get tangled up with me."

"I'm already tangled up with you."

For a moment, he couldn't speak. His brain couldn't
even form a rational thought. And despite his resistance,
he felt himself slip a little more deeply in love with her.
"Dammit, that isn't what you're supposed to say."

"Do you expect me to forget everything I know about
you and turn tail and run just because some prosecutor got
a jury to believe something when you didn't bother to
defend yourself?" Her voice shook with the words, but
her eyes remained fierce. "You let yourself get convicted
of a crime you didn't commit, because you felt guilty
about your father."

"You deserve a man you don't have to be afraid of."
He didn't like the kick of jealousy that jumped through his
veins at the thought of another man in her life, but he
ruthlessly shoved it aside. This wasn't about him. It was
about her and her right to be loved by someone who would
never hurt her.

"I'm not afraid of you."

John sighed. "When we're finished here, I'm taking you to Buzz."

"I don't want to see Buzz."

"He's going to take you to the police station, then drop you at another shelter—"

"I don't want to go to another shelter."

"You don't have a choice. If we stay together, I'll only end up hurting you. Dammit, Hannah, I'd rather die than hurt you."

Surprising him, she stepped forward and poked her finger into his chest hard enough to send him back a step. "Listen to yourself. How can you possibly believe you're capable of laying a hand on me?"

"I've been convicted, Hannah. I put my old man in the hospital. I nearly killed—"

She poked him in the chest again. John stepped back. "You were a seventeen-year-old kid," she snapped. "You stopped your father the best way you knew how."

"What about Rhonda? If the cops hadn't arrived when—"

"You didn't hit her, John. For whatever reason, she freaked out. You took responsibility because you felt guilty. That's the bottom line. That's what kind of man you are."

John stared at her, aware that his palms were icy and wet inside his gloves, his heart beating like a drum. He didn't like the way this was working out. Didn't like Hannah poking holes in the logic behind the reason for his solitary existence. Couldn't she see he wasn't the right man for her? Couldn't she see this was hurting him as much as it was her?

She stared back at him, her mouth set, her eyes alight with anger. John thought he'd never seen a woman look as beautiful as Hannah did at that moment. The lust spiked through him with such force that he felt dizzy. His hands began to shake. His knees followed suit. If his discipline hadn't been made of steel, he might have reached out and pulled her into his arms.

His discipline held.

"We can talk about this later." He said the words, but he had no intention of discussing any of this with her again. When he took her back to RMSAR, John was going to turn her over to Buzz and walk away from her once and for all.

Knowing his resistance would fail if she didn't stop looking at him with those liquid brown eyes, he turned away and pointed toward the barely visible snow-covered path that ran up the side of the rise. "There's a road just over the ridge. A one-lane gravel road full of switchbacks. Washouts where the beavers have built dams. Once we reach the road, we're on Elk Ridge. The road isn't passable during most of the winter months, but snow has been light this year. Someone with an SUV could probably get through. If someone drove you up here that night, that's the road they would have taken."

"How far are we from the point where you rescued me?"

"The road is a hundred yards on the other side of this ridge. We've got about fifteen minutes of moderate climbing. Once we reach the road, the gorge where you fell is a ten-minute walk through relatively level terrain." He frowned. "Think you can make it?"

"Of course I can."

He knew better than to touch her, so instead he reached out and zipped her snowsuit up to her chin. "Cold?"

"No."

"Don't be too proud to tell me if you're in trouble." He let his gaze slip to her abdomen. "You're pregnant. Pregnancy can cause fatigue, especially at this altitude."

"I feel fine." Her eyes searched his. "You can ignore this all you want, but I'm not going to let it go."

John prayed he had the strength to do the right thing when the time came. "Let's go," he said, and started for the path.

Chapter 15

The climb was more difficult than she'd thought, but Hannah didn't complain. She barely felt the fatigue sinking into her bones, the threat of morning sickness seesawing in her gut, or the cold numbing her fingers and toes. The only sensations reaching her brain at the moment were pain and grief and a stark sense of loss.

Damn John Maitland and his twisted sense of honor, anyway.

She knew exactly what kind of man he was. Courageous. Heroic. Too damn honorable for his own good. He'd proven it to her a hundred different ways in the last few days. And because she knew him so well, she knew he would keep his word and walk away from her when all was said and done.

The thought broke her heart.

But Hannah knew there was nothing she could do. She might know what kind of man he is, but John didn't. Until he realized that the mistakes of the seventeen-year-old boy he'd been didn't define the man he'd become, until he came to terms with his past—including the conviction for domestic violence—there was nothing she could do to change his mind. It might not have hurt so much if she hadn't fallen crazy in love with him.

After ten minutes of climbing, they reached the ridge. Neither of them spoke as they took a few minutes to catch their breath. The terrain was rugged and steep. The pines scattered about were sparse and gnarled from mountain extremes. She'd expected the landscape to be familiar, but it wasn't.

John raised his hand and pointed. "The ravine where you were rescued is about twenty yards that way."

The scene flashed in Hannah's mind. John swooping down from the helicopter. Wind and snow flying. His hands gentle and reassuring. His voice smoothing away her terror. "Even if I live to be a hundred, I'll never forget that moment." She risked a look at him. "I'll never forget that you saved my life."

He gazed back at her, his jaw set, his eyes as blue as the alpine sky. "I was doing my job, Red."

She couldn't help but wonder how he could look at her like that and know in the back of his mind he was going to walk away. The sense of loss staggered her. She wasn't going to be able to reach him, she realized. And though he stood less than a foot away from her, she sensed him slipping from her grasp.

Unable to speak for the emotions spiraling through her, she walked to the edge of the road and stopped. Beyond, she could hear the rush of wind through the trees, the crackle of aspen leaves, the call of a bird from the top of an ancient pine.

"That was a tough climb," he said after a moment. "Are you feeling all right?"

"I'm okay."

"You're pale. Why don't you sit down and rest for a few minutes while I have a look around?"

She was about to decline when a glint of silver in the snow twenty feet away snagged her attention. A swirl of remembrance danced in a corner of her brain. A silver buckle. Soft leather. The flash of memory made her heart pound. Without speaking, she started toward it, first at a walk, then she was running. Something dark lay just beneath the snow. Dropping to her knees, she brushed away the snow and reached for a leather strap.

"Hannah, wait."

Ignoring John's voice, she tugged on the strap. A small leather handbag materialized. Navy, not black. Inexpensive. The familiarity of it jolted her. "Oh my God."

Hannah started when John laid a gentle hand on her shoulder. "Yours?" he asked.

"Yes."

Plucking off his gloves, he eased the purse from her grasp. "Easy, Red. Let me."

"I need to see what's inside."

"Okay." He unzipped the closure with trembling fingers and dumped the contents into the snow.

The memories tangled inside her like barbed wire, cutting her. Even before he reached for the wallet, she knew. "My name is Beth Montgomery," she said.

John went perfectly still. His gaze met hers. "Beth," he repeated.

"Hannah is a client. The note you found was for her." She pressed the bag to her chest, let the memories wash over her. "I own an antique shop in Boulder. Hannah was trying to match some china her grandmother had given her. I was going to meet her at the shop." She looked down at the bag. "This is my purse. I dropped it the night my ex-husband tried to kill me."

"Do you remember his name?"

"Richard Montgomery. He's a Boulder police officer. A detective. Vice."

"That explains a lot. The son of a bitch."

Beth stared at him, her heart beating out a maniacal rhythm in her chest. Tears stung her eyes, clogged the back of her throat. She looked down at the contents of her purse spread out on the snow. "He tried to kill me that night," she said. "I ran, but I knew he was going to catch me. All I could think about was the baby—" Her voice broke. Pressing her hand to her abdomen, she struggled on. "I threw my purse down in the snow, hoping someone would find it. He wasn't armed. I'd...taken his gun. But I knew he would use his bare hands..."

"Easy, honey." Grimacing, he touched her shoulder. "Why was he trying to kill you?"

"I saw..." A violent shudder wracked her. "I saw him murder a man in cold blood."

John swore, scrubbed his hand over his face. "Tell me."

"Richard was under investigation by Internal Affairs. It had been going on for a while. He'd been involved in a high-profile arrest several months back. The case was about to go to trial, but some evidence had disappeared from police evidence—a briefcase full of cash and a couple of kilos of cocaine. The defendant—Joseph Peretti—was going to walk. IA claimed Peretti paid Richard to steal the evidence."

"Did he?"

"Richard never talked to me about it. I always believed he was innocent. A few weeks after the divorce, I went to the storage warehouse where he kept some of his things. I was looking for some photographs of my parents that had gotten mixed in with his things when we split. The next thing I knew Richard walked into the warehouse with Peretti. There was a third man with them. He'd been beaten. He was gagged. His hands were bound behind his back." The vividness of the memory made her shudder. "I'm not sure how I had the presence of mind to hide, but I did. Behind some old furniture about ten feet away from them." The images rushed at her with frightening clarity.

The shuffle of shoes on concrete. The terror in the man's eyes. The pitiful sound of his voice as he cried out behind the gag.

"There was a roll of plastic against the wall. Richard spread it on the ground. Peretti forced the man to lie down on the plastic." Her stomach roiled when she remembered what happened next. It was an image she would never forget. One she would take with her to the grave. "The bound man was screaming into his gag. I covered my ears, but I couldn't shut out the sound. I'll never forget the sound of his screams. I closed my eyes, but I couldn't block out what happened next." She looked up at John. "Peretti shot that man in cold blood."

The muscles in John's jaws flexed. Simultaneously something dark and unpredictable flashed in his eyes. "You witnessed a murder."

Because she was unable to speak, she just nodded.

"Aw, honey…"

"I remember everything," she choked.

"Come here." He reached for her and Beth stepped into his embrace and let herself be held.

"Did the men find you?" he asked after a moment.

"I was so shaken, I knocked over a box. Peretti went crazy. He wanted to…" She could barely bring herself to say the words. "He wanted to kill me right there. Richard talked him out of it. Said he'd…take care of me." Pulling back slightly, she looked up at John. "I thought Richard was going to let me go. I thought maybe he was working undercover or something. I didn't want to believe he could do something like that. But after he got me in the car, he started screaming at me, telling me it was my fault. That I'd been in the wrong place at the wrong time. That Peretti would kill him if he didn't shut me up.

"Richard had hit me in the past—that was what ended our marriage—but I didn't think he'd kill me. By the time we reached the mountain road, he was sobbing." She pressed her hand to her abdomen. "I tried to talk to him, but he was hysterical. We struggled. I don't know how I managed, but I got his gun. Then I threw open the door. He grabbed my coat, so I slipped out of it and ran. Somehow I lost my shoes. He came after me. I could hear him running, shouting. I knew he was going to kill me. When I reached the ravine, I jumped."

John cursed and an uncomfortable silence ensued.

"It's going to be okay." Holding her with one arm, he worked the cell phone from his coat.

"Who are you calling?"

"Buzz."

Closing her eyes, she pressed her face against his snow-suit, let his essence surround her. A moment later, John snapped the phone closed and cursed. She looked up at him. "What is it?"

"We're out of range. I can't get through." His jaw flexed. "We're going to have to hike it back down to the snowmobile. You up to it?"

"Of course, I am."

He grinned at her, but she knew the grin was only a facade to put her at ease. She wasn't the only one who was scared.

"You'd say that even if you were in labor." Taking her hand, he started toward the path from whence they'd come. "We're going to have to hurry—"

John's body jolted, faltered in midstride. "What the…" Cursing, he reached down and clutched his right thigh. An instant later, a rifle retort shattered the silence. Beth saw blood come through his fingers on his thigh. Terror zinged through her.

"John! Oh my God. *John!*"

She watched him fall as if in slow motion. He went down on his knees then rolled onto his side. For a horrible instant, she thought he was dead.

"Get down!" he said.

Beth dropped to her hands and knees, crawled over to him. "You've been shot!"

"Dammit." Pain contorted his face. She saw fear in his eyes as he quickly scanned the surrounding woods, the high ridge overhead and to the north. "Crawl over to those rocks," he said between clenched teeth. "We're sitting ducks here."

"Not without you."

"Do it, dammit!" Clutching his leg, he rolled onto his stomach. "I'm right behind you. Go!"

Another bullet zinged off a rock less than two feet away from his head. Adrenaline sent her scrambling toward the rocks. Looking over her shoulder, she saw John a few feet behind her. His face had gone pale. She tried not to notice the bloody trail he left in the snow. She didn't want to think about who was shooting at them. She didn't want to think about why. But she knew. And she knew if they didn't come up with a plan quickly, Richard Montgomery would kill them both.

John reached the outcropping of rock an instant after Beth. Pain blazed like fire in his thigh, alternating hot and cold, numbing his leg all the way to his toes. Nauseous, sweating beneath his snowsuit, he rolled onto his back and closed his eyes.

"God, John, you're bleeding," Beth said. "Tell me what to do."

Gritting his teeth, he risked a look at the hole in his snowsuit, felt a rise of bile in his throat. The wound was bleeding profusely, but not enough so that he feared a blood vessel had been torn. Still, if they didn't get it stopped soon, he risked going into shock. He wouldn't do either of them any good if that happened.

He struggled out of the snowsuit. "Tear the jeans," he said. "I need to see the wound."

Never taking her eyes from his, Beth gently put her

fingers into the hole and ripped the material. Even through the pain, John saw that her hands were shaking, her face had gone as white as the snow. "Easy. It's just a flesh wound. Don't panic on me. I'm going to be okay, all right?"

She choked out a laugh. "I think those are supposed to be my lines, aren't they?"

Despite the pain and the rise of fear, a wave of affection rolled through him. She was so kind. So brave. Raising his hand, he touched her cheek. "You're doing fine," he said.

"It looks bad, John."

"Hey, I'm a medic, remember? Piece of cake." Even so, his stomach clenched when he looked down and saw the blood. John wasn't squeamish. He'd seen all kinds of injuries in his time as a medic—compound fractures, head injuries, motor-vehicle trauma—but to look down and see his own blood pooling in the snow sent a cold wave of fear rolling through him.

The flesh was bruised and already swollen. There was no exit wound, so he assumed the bullet was lodged somewhere near the bone. "Whoever said bullet wounds don't hurt was really full of it. Damn thing hurts like hell."

She shot him a worried look. "Can you walk?"

"We need to stop the bleeding first," he said through gritted teeth. "Need to apply direct pressure."

She looked at him helplessly. "Tell me what to do."

"Your scarf. Wad it up and press it hard against the wound. Use both hands. Don't be afraid to hurt me. You won't."

Never taking her eyes from his, she unwound the scarf from around her neck, folded it and pressed it against the wound.

"Harder," he said.

She swallowed, increased the pressure by putting her body weight into it.

John closed his eyes against the pain, rode the wave of

dizziness. "Good girl," he said between gritted teeth. "You're doing great, Red. Just keep up the pressure."

"Don't you pass out on me, John Maitland."

"Just resting my eyes."

"Open them, damn you. We've got some unfinished business."

"I'm not going to touch that one."

He sensed her nearness an instant before he felt the gentle warmth of her mouth against his. Even through the pain, his body responded. He marveled at the sensation and kissed her back. He wanted more, opened his mouth to taste her more fully, but she pulled away.

He opened his eyes, would have smiled if he could have managed it. "Ah, Red, that was cruel."

"It got your eyes open, didn't it?"

"I'm not sure if I've told you this, but I really, really like you."

"In between all the nonsense about you being a violent man, I sort of gathered that."

Grimacing, he looked around the small clearing where they were pinned. "I wish I hadn't let you talk me in to bringing you up here. I shouldn't have done it. I'm sorry—"

"It was my idea. Don't try to take responsibility for something I did, okay?" She tossed a worried look over her shoulder. "How did he know where to find us?"

"I called Buzz before we left. If Montgomery is in vice, he could have an illegal tap on the phone at RMSAR headquarters."

She continued pressing the scarf against his thigh. "What are we going to do?"

John didn't like the dizziness swooping down on him every few seconds. He didn't think he'd lost that much blood, but his head felt fuzzy, his thoughts disoriented. He was having a difficult time concentrating. "He's going to try to take out me first, because I'm a bigger threat." He looked at her, felt a wave of longing and regret tangle in his gut. "We need to split up," he said.

"No—"

"You make a run for the snowmobile. I'll keep him off you—"

"John, I'm not leaving you. Even if it's the smart thing to do I can't leave you in this condition, for God's sake."

"Beth, this isn't the time for you to play hero. Think about your baby."

She flinched, set her hand against her abdomen in an unconscious gesture that told him she knew he was right. The pain etched into her face nearly undid him, but John resisted the urge to reach for her. He would say or do whatever it took to get her to safety—even if he had to manipulate her. "If we split up, and you make it to the snowmobile, there's a chance we can get out of this."

"All right," she said, but she didn't look happy about it.

"Good girl." He reached for the cell phone, groaning when an ice-pick stab of pain shot from his thigh all the way down to his toes. "Take this." He handed her the phone.

"I don't want to leave you without communication—"

"I'm going to run for the ravine. Chances are, he'll come after me first. If you stick to the line of trees along the trail, he won't be able to sight you on the riflescope. Once you reach the snowmobile, get moving and don't stop."

"John, you're in pain. You're bleeding. How can you—"

"Hey, I jump out of helicopters for a living, remember?"

She made a sound that was half laugh, half sob. "You'll say or do anything to keep me safe." Her gazed locked with his. "That's what kind of man you are."

Shoving back emotions that would do nothing but distract him, he pressed the phone into her hand. "When you get a safe distance away, try the speed dial again. Call the sheriff's office. Then call RMSAR. Tell them we're on Elk Ridge."

Tears welled in her eyes as she shoved the phone into her pocket. "I don't want to leave you like this."

"It's the only way, Red. Come on. I'm counting on you—"

His words were cut short when she leaned forward and kissed him hard on the mouth. Despite the pain in his thigh and the blood loss playing with his concentration, John kissed her back, responding not only physically, but emotionally. For an instant the pain and fear melted away, and it was just the two of them, mouth to mouth, heart to heart, soul to soul.

Beth pulled away first, her eyes fierce and wet. "I love you," she said. "I don't care if you want to hear it or not."

John stared at her, wanting to say the words so badly his chest hurt. But he couldn't do it. The ensuing burst of emotion jolted him all the way to his soul. He'd wanted to send her off by saying something cocky. Wish her luck. Tell her to be careful. But for the first time since the day he'd left Philly, tears burned behind his eyes. He blinked rapidly to clear them, and an instant later, she was gone.

Too late, hotshot.

He sat there for several agonizing seconds, watched her disappear down the trail, the ache in his chest so powerful he couldn't move.

I love you.

Ruthlessly he forced her words from his mind. He couldn't think of her in those terms now. Couldn't bear the thought of something happening to her. Losing her. God, this was making him crazy.

Getting to his feet, he looked up at the ridge overhead, the line of trees, the jagged rocks. Hell or high water, he had to find a way to distract Montgomery, keep him off Beth long enough for her to reach the snowmobile.

He looked down at the crimson snow, felt the warmth of fresh blood run down his calf. Damn, he was in a bad way. The pain was yielding to numbness. That was good. The bleeding had slowed, but it hadn't stopped. He figured he had another twenty minutes or so before he passed out.

Tying the scarf tightly around his thigh, he leaned against the cold rock and waited for his head to clear. Once he started for the ravine, he would be in plain sight if Montgomery wanted to take a shot at him. He had to be ready. He had to move fast.

He figured he was as ready as he would ever be.

Stepping out from behind the rock, he raised his arms and waved. "Come on, Montgomery! Here I am! Come get me, you cowardly son of a bitch!"

The retort of a rifle answered. Gritting his teeth against the pain, John broke into a lumbering run toward the ravine where he'd found Beth. Montgomery had taken the bait. John had bought Beth a few extra minutes to get away. Now all he had to do was come up with a plan to stay alive.

Beth ran as she had never run before. Arms outstretched, animal sounds tearing from her throat, terror egging her on. She tried not to think about John up on the ridge, alone, bleeding and in pain. She tried not to think about his crazy plan, or that he just might be heroic enough to pull it off.

But she'd seen the amount of blood he'd lost and the glassy look in his eyes. She'd seen the way he'd had to grit his teeth against the pain just to get the phone out of his pocket. How was he going to sprint twenty-five yards, dodging bullets the entire way, when he barely had the strength to stand?

The only consolation was that he would have cover in the ravine. It was the very same ravine where she'd taken cover the night Richard had tried to kill her. If John made it into the ravine safely, there was no way Richard could get to him. What worried her was the twenty-five yards of open ground he had to cover to get there. He would be a sitting duck for a crazy man with a rifle.

She was midway down the path when the scream of an engine shattered the silence. Out of the corner of her eye, she saw movement, a flash of color. An instant later, a man on a snowmobile broke from the tree line and headed directly for her.

Richard.

Heart hammering, she picked up speed and changed direction. The engine behind her whined. So close she could smell the exhaust, hear the track shoes scrape against exposed rock. An instant later, the solid weight of a body crashed into her. She saw the dark silhouette of his rifle. A glimpse of sandy hair. Then strong arms wrapped around her, knocking her off balance. Beth screamed, felt her legs tangle as he took her down in a full body tackle. She rolled with the momentum, but he rolled with her, overwhelming her, smothering her. And she knew with a dreadful sense of inevitability that he was going to kill her if she didn't think of something quick.

John dangled from the end of the rope, listening to the sudden, stark silence all around, a fresh sense of horror raging through him. Montgomery had done the unthinkable. When he'd realized he wasn't going to be able to get at John, he'd turned the snowmobile around and gone after Beth.

John sweated profusely beneath his snowsuit. Once he'd reached the ravine, he uncoiled the length of safety rope at his waist and used it to rappel down. The rope had saved his life, but it wasn't long enough, and now he was stuck halfway down. He needed to reach the gun Beth had dropped, then somehow get back up and reach her before Montgomery did.

Pain from the bullet wound echoed through his body with every beat of his heart. But the pain in his body was nothing compared to the fear exploding in his heart.

Beth was too kind, her heart too generous for her life to be wiped out at the hands of a violent man like Montgomery. The world was a better place with her in it. She filled his life with goodness. His heart with love. His soul with hope for tomorrow. All John could think of as he dangled from the rope was that he hadn't had the guts to tell her he loved her. Lord knew he did. He loved her with all his heart and soul. Had since the moment he'd laid eyes on her at this very spot. But he'd been so caught up in his past, so determined to do the right thing, he'd let something precious slip away.

And now a madman was going to kill her.

He couldn't let that happen. Not to the woman he loved more than life itself. "Hang on, Red," he said. "Hang on sweetheart. I'm coming for you."

Gazing down at the rock and scrub twenty feet below, he studied the terrain. It was a long drop, but the scrub would break the fall for the most part. Hopefully he wouldn't come out of this with a broken leg, to boot. Hopefully he'd be able to reach the ravine floor, get the gun and get back up before Montgomery hurt her.

Saying a silent prayer, he let go of the rope.

Beth fought him with every ounce of strength she possessed. She fought for the child growing inside her, for the kind and gentle man who'd risked his life to keep her safe. She fought because she didn't want Richard Montgomery to win. Not this time.

But her strength was no match for his, and in seconds, he had her trapped beneath him, her arms pinned above her head. For several terrible moments, they stared at each other, their labored breaths spewing a white cloud of vapor into the frigid air between them.

"Don't fight me, Beth. You can't win," he said.

"Let go of me!" When she looked into his cruel eyes, the full force of her terror ripped through her. She saw death in his eyes, knew his heart was cold and black enough to wipe out her life along with the life of his own unborn child.

Beth did the only thing she could and screamed.

"No one's going to hear you up here," he said when she finished. "Just like the last time. You remember, don't you?"

"I don't remember anything," she lied. "I don't know who you are."

He clucked his tongue. "You've never been a very good liar, Beth. You're still not." Removing his glove, he touched her face gently with the backs of his fingers. "I can feel you trembling beneath me. I see the truth in your eyes. I can see how terrified you are. You know exactly who I am, don't you?"

She turned her head, but he set his weight more squarely on top of her and continued caressing her cheek. "I didn't want it to come to this."

"Don't take this any further," she said.

"I know you'll have a hard time believing this, but I really didn't want to have to hurt you."

"Then don't. Let me go."

"I can't. Not after what you saw." He swore viciously. "If only you hadn't been in the warehouse that day. Looking for photographs of all the stupid things. But you always did have a penchant for being in the wrong place at the wrong time."

"I don't remember what I saw."

"Angel, it's not what you saw. It's the person I was with who saw *you*." Something cruel and unnerving glinted in his eyes. "Joseph Peretti isn't the kind of man to tolerate a witness to a murder. Especially if the witness is a cop's ex-wife.''

Joseph Peretti. The name terrified her. She'd seen it in the newspaper too many times to discount what he was capable of. Organized crime. Extortion. Murder for hire. ''I didn't see his face,'' she whispered.

''I wish that mattered.'' For a moment he looked regretful. ''I really do.''

Beth's heart pumped pure terror though her veins. The fear was so intense, she was dizzy with it. Oh Lord, where was John? What could she do now? She knew she had to fight, had to win this time. But how was she going to best a man who outweighed her by a hundred pounds?

''Peretti wanted to kill you himself that day in the warehouse,'' he continued, ''but I talked him out of it. I'm not sure why I brought you up here that night. I knew what I had to do. But I've always liked you, Beth. Even if I didn't love you, I knew killing you wasn't going to be easy.'' He sighed heavily. ''I didn't want it to work out this way, but Peretti said he'd kill me if I didn't get rid of you. I don't want to die simply because you were in the wrong place at the wrong time.''

Easing off of her, he rose, then, holding the rifle aside, offered his hand to help her up. For an instant she considered running, but knew he would catch her. Time was what she needed. Time to come up with a plan.

Struggling to stay calm, she took his hand and let him pull her to her feet. ''You can tell him I'm dead. I'll disappear—''

''I considered that. Until I saw you with that young stud of yours.'' Something cold and dark played behind his eyes. ''Seeing you with him…well, that changed everything.''

Jealousy, she thought, and dread billowed like a roiling thunderhead inside her. *John.* Her legs went weak. Oh,

God, he was going to kill John, too. She couldn't let that happen. Not John.

"I'll bet you think you got yourself a real hero, don't you? A man who makes his living saving Boy Scouts and little speckled pups. I'll bet you think he's the next best thing to a superhero, don't you, angel?"

"I barely know him. We—"

"Don't bother denying it. I saw you together. I saw him touch you. I saw the way you look at him. The way he looks at you." The muscles in his jaw bunched. "You know what that does to a man, angel? To see another man put his hands all over his wife? That's my child you're carrying inside you. My seed that put it there. That doesn't make any difference to you, does it?"

Nausea rose in her throat as the meaning of his words registered. "Let me go, Richard."

His lips pulled back in a snarl. "A lowly cop isn't good enough for you, is that it? I was never good enough, was I?"

"Stop it—"

"Let me tell you a secret about lover boy, angel. Your hero has a record. Assault. He couldn't even make the police academy." A cruel smile twisted his mouth. "You've got a habit of falling in love with losers, don't you?"

"He's nothing like you," she said.

She knew an instant before he moved that he was going to strike her. The old fear coiled, but she didn't shrink away. Instead she sidestepped, heard the whoosh of air as his fist missed her temple by less than an inch.

"Bitch." Montgomery's eyes went flat and dark as he started toward her. "I'm going to make you sorry you ever set eyes on him. Then I'm going to make him pay for touching you."

Beth raised her hands, backed up in an effort to keep distance between them. "Stop it."

"The divorce has only been final a few weeks. You couldn't even wait for the ink to dry on the decree before you jumped in bed with another man, could you?" Lips curling, he drew back to strike her.

A gunshot shattered air.

"What the—" Montgomery spun.

Beth jolted, and looked up to see John level a pistol at Montgomery's chest. "If you touch her, I'll drop you," he said.

Her heart staggered in her chest. Relief and joy and sudden fear for him rioted inside her. "John."

"Are you all right?" he asked, never taking his eyes from Montgomery.

Unable to speak for the emotions coursing through her, she nodded.

"Step away from—"

Montgomery grabbed her so violently, she was nearly knocked off balance. She choked out a single cry as his viselike hand went around her arm and pulled her against him like a shield.

"What are you going to do now, lover boy?" Montgomery taunted. "I got what you want, don't I?"

Beth knew immediately John was in no condition for a confrontation. He was still bleeding badly. Blood had soaked the denim all the way down to his boot. His face was nearly as pale as the snow. The gun trembled in his hand. But his eyes were as cold and dangerous as the pistol he clenched in his hand. "Let her go," he said.

Beth knew that if they were going to get out of this mess alive, she was going to have to act quickly and decisively.

Out of the corner of her eye, she saw Montgomery's grip tighten on the rifle. Her heart did a sickening roll when she saw the muzzle jerk, rising. John's gaze zeroed in on the other man. "Don't do anything stupid, Montgomery. I'll put you down."

"And risk hitting her?" He laughed. "I don't think so."

Beth's heart pounded like a drum against her ribs. Her hands were free. The rifle barrel was less than a foot away. She could picture herself reaching for it, wresting it from him, swinging it like a bat...

"Drop it, Montgomery, or I'll tattoo your shins and you'll never walk upright again," John warned.

"That's my revolver." Montgomery's mouth opened, fluttered. "How the hell—"

"She took your gun the night you tried to kill her."

"I came back for it," the other man said. "I searched—"

"You didn't look in the ravine." John's jaw flexed. "The ravine she jumped into to get away from you." He pulled back the hammer with his thumb. "Toss the rifle over here."

"Screw you. You slept with my wife, you bastard."

"Ex-wife," John corrected. "And no other woman is ever going to have to worry about that temper of yours again. Now toss the rifle, or I'll make sure you walk with a limp the rest of your lousy life." Grimacing, favoring his leg, John moved forward but he stumbled and went down on one knee.

Beth knew that was her only chance. Pushing away from Montgomery with all her might, she grabbed for the rifle. Vaguely, she felt the cold steel of the muzzle against her palms. He yelled something obscene, and she saw the murderous light in his eyes when he turned to her.

But Beth had taken him by surprise. Yanking the rifle from his grasp, she staggered backward, then swung it like a bat as hard as she could. She heard the whoosh of air. Saw shock on Montgomery's face. Then the sickening crack of the solid wood stock against his knee.

Montgomery fell forward, howling in pain. His murderous gaze landed on Beth. "You're going to pay for that!"

Knowing he would make good on the threat, but unwilling to let him hurt her or her unborn child ever again, Beth stepped back, aimed the rifle at the ground next to his foot and pulled the trigger.

The force knocked her back a step. Montgomery scrambled to his feet, dancing away from where the bullet had hit the ground.

"Don't test me!" she cried. "I'll kill you."

Fear permeated his eyes as he stumbled toward the snowmobile and slipped onto the seat. "I won't let you get away with that," he snarled as he started the engine. "I'll get you. If it's the last thing I do, I'll make you pay."

Angry now, Beth jerked the rifle toward the snowmobile engine cover and fired twice in quick succession. The engine sputtered and died, two dime-size holes in the cover smoking like the muzzle of a recently fired gun.

Montgomery gaped for a moment, then slammed his fist against the snowmobile's steering wheel. "You bitch!"

A fresh wave of anger swept through her. Choking back a cry, she pointed the rifle at him. "I'll kill you if you ever touch me again," she said.

Raising his hands, fear showing plainly on his face, Montgomery slipped off the seat. "I'll be back for you. That's a promise." Favoring his injured knee, he took off at a lumbering run down the trail.

Beth kept the rifle leveled on his retreating form. Her finger curled on the trigger. The rifle trembled in her hands. She blinked back tears.

"Let him run."

John's voice washed over her like cleansing rain, smoothed out her anger, and the residual fear.

"He's getting away," she whispered.

"He won't get far. In five minutes this place is going to be swarming with ticked off search-and-rescue guys." Strong hands went to her shoulders, and squeezed reassuringly. "Easy, honey. It's over."

"You can't be certain..." Beth's heart stopped dead in

her chest when John's knees buckled and he crumpled to the snow. "John!" Forgetting everything except the man she loved, she dropped the rifle into the snow and fell to her knees beside him. With trembling hands, she eased him onto his back.

He looked at Beth, one side of his mouth hiking into a half smile. "Now might be a good time to call the cops," he said.

Working the phone from her coat, she hit the speed dial button with shaking fingers. Relief trembled through her when the sheriff's office dispatch answered. "This is an emergency," she said. "I'm with John Maitland of Rocky Mountain Search and Rescue. He's been shot. We're up on Elk Ridge. We need a medic and the sheriff's department right away. Buzz Malone knows the location."

When she looked down at John, his eyes had closed. "John?" Fear coiled and sprang free inside her. "Stay with me, Maitland. Don't you pass out on me."

"Just…tired."

"Tell me what to do to help you."

"Just don't stop touching me." A wan smile touched the corners of his mouth. "I love it when you touch me. I love it when you worry about me. When you kiss me."

Beth choked out a laugh. "How can you joke around at a time like this?"

"Who's joking?"

"You're seriously hurt."

"I'm not worried. The men of Rocky Mountain Search and Rescue are the best of the best, Beth. They won't let a scumbag like Montgomery get away. And they're sure as hell not going to let one of their own die up here."

A noise off to her right made her jump. Just when she was certain Montgomery had returned for the rifle she'd usurped, a man on horseback took his mount up a small incline and halted twenty feet away. Beth recognized him as Jake Madigan, the man she'd met at headquarters the night John had taken her there.

Raising his hand, Jake waved at John. "Maitland," he said. "How bad are you hurt?"

John raised his head and squinted. "Jake?"

"You okay, partner?"

"Thigh wound. In and out. No arterial bleeding, but I've lost a good bit."

"He's lost a lot of blood," Beth added. "Please send someone to help us."

Without preamble, the man jerked a radio out of his saddlebag. "This is Coyote zero five three. I've got a code red. Team member down. I repeat, team member down. Code red."

Another voice crackled over the radio. Jake was too far away for Beth to hear the details, but he spoke into the radio again. "Elk Ridge. Rough terrain. You're going to need to swoop and scoop. Female companion uninjured. Do you roger that, Eagle two niner?"

A second later, the man on horseback sheathed the radio. Pulling a flare from his saddlebag, he popped the cap, struck the flare against it and tossed it on the ground. Red smoke billowed into the still air. "Chopper will be here in about two minutes. You two just hang tight." The horse wheeled, but he looked over his shoulder. "Which way did the perp go?"

John struggled to a sitting position. "He's on foot, Jake. Headed south down the path toward our snowmobile."

Jake grinned. "I reckon I ought to go round him up." The horse tossed its head impatiently, the bridle jingling. Jake touched the brim of his black Stetson. "Ma'am." Then he left the same way Montgomery had.

Beth looked questioningly at John. "He got here fast."

"Well, we're fast, but not that fast. Buzz probably called him and asked him to ride up here. Jake was probably already in the area."

"I remember meeting him."

"He's a good cop."

She looked down at his leg, felt a trickle of worry. "How are you feeling?"

"Faint. I think I need a little mouth-to-mouth. Think you can handle that?"

Beth rolled her eyes. How was it that he could make her smile even when she was scared out of her wits? "You're impossible."

"I'm just crazy about you."

Snuggling closer, she leaned forward and pressed her mouth against his. "Better?"

"Mmmm. I'll let you know. A little more pressure would be good."

In the distance, the rat-tat-tat of a helicopter broke the silence. As it drew nearer, the treetops shivered in the gale. Leaning back slightly, John glanced down at his watch. "Six minutes," he said. "They're slipping."

"I'm sure it's because you weren't there to keep them on their toes."

"Probably." He grinned. "I'm not sure if I've told you this, but I'm damn good at what I do."

"You have. More than once, actually. But you're right. You are damn good at what you do. Not to mention pretty good at kissing, too."

"Honey, I'm just getting warmed up."

"Not too warm, I hope. In case you've forgotten, you've been shot."

"Minor inconvenience." He looked down at his leg. "The bleeding stopped. Thanks to you." His hand covered hers, tightened. "You saved my life."

She choked out a laugh. "I figured it was the least I could do."

"Things might have worked out differently if you hadn't..." His voice trailed off.

The intensity of his gaze told her he understood fully

how close they'd come to dying today. Her chest constricted with emotion. Tears stung her eyes, but she didn't care. "John, I thought—"

Her words were cut short when he pressed a kiss to her mouth. Closing her eyes against the burst of joy that came with knowing he was safe and alive and so close she could feel the steady drum of his heart against hers, she melted against him. "I couldn't shoot him," she said. "Even after what he did to us."

"It's okay, honey. You're not a killer. But you're very, very brave."

"I wasn't sure if I'd ever see you again."

"I couldn't let that happen." Raising his hand, he laid it gently against her cheek. "Not without telling you how much I love you."

The words fell upon her like laughter on sorrow, rain upon a place of draught, sunlight upon frozen tundra. Joy, as golden and bright as daybreak speared through the darkness, lighting her soul. "I didn't think I'd ever hear you say that."

"I'm saying it now, and I mean it." He blinked to clear his vision. "I love you, and I love that child growing inside you."

She stared at him, her pulse quivering like a butterfly. "I love you, too."

"I've never loved anyone before," he said.

"I'll make sure you get plenty of practice."

Overhead, the chopper hovered, kicking up snow and small debris. John looked up, saw Buzz about to disembark the cage. He figured he had about a minute left before it got crowded. He had a few things to get off his chest.

"You showed me how to trust my heart, Beth. You taught me to trust myself." Reaching out, he thumbed a tear from her cheek. "I was wondering if you might want to take a chance on me."

Tears streamed down her cheeks, but she managed to smile. "Do you think you could be a little more specific?"

"Will you marry me?" He pressed his hand flat against her abdomen. "Will you let me be the father of your child?"

He hadn't expected his voice to break, but it did. He felt tears on his cheeks, but he didn't care. "I want to spend the rest of my life loving you. Both of you."

"Yes." She kissed him gently on the cheek. "My hero."

Happiness washed over him, as soft and warm as morning on the mountain. In that moment, John knew he'd found something precious and rare that came once in a lifetime. As the chopper hovered overhead, he lowered his mouth to hers and sealed the promise of forever between them with a kiss.

* * * * *

Feel like a star with Silhouette.

We will fly you and a guest to New York City for an exciting weekend stay at a glamorous 5-star hotel. Experience a refreshing day at one of New York's trendiest spas and have your photo taken by a professional. Plus, receive $1,000 U.S. spending money!

Flowers...long walks...dinner for two... how does Silhouette Books make romance come alive for you?

Send us a script, with 500 words or less, along with visuals (only drawings, magazine cutouts or photographs or combination thereof). Show us how Silhouette Makes Your Love Come Alive. Be creative and have fun. No purchase necessary. All entries must be clearly marked with your name, address and telephone number. All entries will become property of Silhouette and are not returnable. **Contest closes September 28, 2001.**

Please send your entry to: **Silhouette Makes You a Star!**

In U.S.A.	In Canada
P.O. Box 9069	P.O. Box 637
Buffalo, NY, 14269-9069	Fort Erie, ON, L2A 5X3

Look for contest details on the next page, by visiting www.eHarlequin.com or request a copy by sending a self-addressed envelope to the applicable address above. Contest open to Canadian and U.S. residents who are 18 or over. Void where prohibited.

Silhouette®
TM *Where love comes alive™*

Our lucky winner's photo will appear in a Silhouette ad. Join the fun!

SRMYAS1

HARLEQUIN "SILHOUETTE MAKES YOU A STAR!" CONTEST 1308
OFFICIAL RULES
NO PURCHASE NECESSARY TO ENTER

1. To enter, follow directions published in the offer to which you are responding. Contest begins June 1, 2001, and ends on September 28, 2001. Entries must be postmarked by September 28, 2001, and received by October 5, 2001. Enter by hand-printing (or typing) on an 8 ½" x 11" piece of paper your name, address (including zip code), contest number/name and attaching a script containing 500 words or less, along with drawings, photographs or magazine cutouts, or combinations thereof (i.e., collage) on no larger than 9" x 12" piece of paper, describing how the Silhouette books make romance come alive for you. Mail via first-class mail to: Harlequin "Silhouette Makes You a Star!" Contest 1308, (in the U.S.) P.O. Box 9069, Buffalo, NY 14269-9069, (in Canada) P.O. Box 637, Fort Erie, Ontario, Canada L2A 5X3. Limit one entry per person, household or organization.

2. Contests will be judged by a panel of members of the Harlequin editorial, marketing and public relations staff. Fifty percent of criteria will be judged against script and fifty percent will be judged against drawing, photographs and/or magazine cutouts. Judging criteria will be based on the following:

   - Sincerity—25%
   - Originality and Creativity—50%
   - Emotionally Compelling—25%

   In the event of a tie, duplicate prizes will be awarded. Decisions of the judges are final.

3. All entries become the property of Torstar Corp. and may be used for future promotional purposes. Entries will not be returned. No responsibility is assumed for lost, late, illegible, incomplete, inaccurate, nondelivered or misdirected mail.

4. Contest open only to residents of the U.S. (except Puerto Rico) and Canada who are 18 years of age or older, and is void wherever prohibited by law; all applicable laws and regulations apply. Any litigation within the Province of Quebec respecting the conduct or organization of a publicity contest may be submitted to the Régie des alcools, des courses et des jeux for a ruling. Any litigation respecting the awarding of a prize may be submitted to the Régie des alcools, des courses et des jeux only for the purpose of helping the parties reach a settlement. Employees and immediate family members of Torstar Corp. and D. L. Blair, Inc., their affiliates, subsidiaries and all other agencies, entities and persons connected with the use, marketing or conduct of this contest are not eligible to enter. Taxes on prizes are the sole responsibility of the winner. Acceptance of any prize offered constitutes permission to use winner's name, photograph or other likeness for the purposes of advertising, trade and promotion on behalf of Torstar Corp., its affiliates and subsidiaries without further compensation to the winner, unless prohibited by law.

5. Winner will be determined no later than November 30, 2001, and will be notified by mail. Winner will be required to sign and return an Affidavit of Eligibility/Release of Liability/Publicity Release form within 15 days after winner notification. Noncompliance within that time period may result in disqualification and an alternative winner may be selected. All travelers must execute a Release of Liability prior to ticketing and must possess required travel documents (e.g., passport, photo ID) where applicable. Trip must be booked by December 31, 2001, and completed within one year of notification. No substitution of prize permitted by winner. Torstar Corp. and D. L. Blair, Inc., their parents, affiliates and subsidiaries are not responsible for errors in printing of contest, entries and/or game pieces. In the event of printing or other errors that may result in unintended prize values or duplication of prizes, all affected game pieces or entries shall be null and void. **Purchase or acceptance of a product offer does not improve your chances of winning.**

6. Prizes: (1) Grand Prize—A 2-night/3-day trip for two (2) to New York City, including round-trip coach air transportation nearest winner's home and hotel accommodations (double occupancy) at The Plaza Hotel, a glamorous afternoon makeover at a trendy New York spa, $1,000 in U.S. spending money and an opportunity to have a professional photo taken and appear in a Silhouette advertisement (approximate retail value: $7,000). (10) Ten Runner-Up Prizes of gift packages (retail value $50 ea.). Prizes consist of only those items listed as part of the prize. Limit one prize per person. Prize is valued in U.S. currency.

7. For the name of the winner (available after December 31, 2001) send a self-addressed, stamped envelope to: Harlequin "Silhouette Makes You a Star!" Contest 1197 Winners, P.O. Box 4200 Blair, NE 68009-4200 or you may access the www.eHarlequin.com Web site through February 28, 2002.

Contest sponsored by Torstar Corp., P.O Box 9042, Buffalo, NY 14269-9042.

If you enjoyed what you just read,
then we've got an offer you can't resist!

Take 2 bestselling love stories FREE!

Plus get a FREE surprise gift!

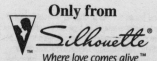